KU-155-947

TAKE MY CHILD

TAKE MY CHILD

Gwen Madoc

NEATH PORT TALBOT LIBRARIES

Severn House

This first world edition published in Great Britain 2006 by
SEVERN HOUSE PUBLISHERS LTD of
9–15 High Street, Sutton, Surrey SM1 1DF.
This first world edition published in the USA 2006 by
SEVERN HOUSE PUBLISHERS INC of
595 Madison Avenue, New York, N.Y. 10022.

Copyright © 2006 by Gwen Madoc.

All rights reserved.
The moral right of the author has been asserted.

British Library Cataloguing in Publication Data

Madoc, Gwen
    Take my child
    1.   Wales - Social life and customs - 20th century - Fiction
    2.   Domestic fiction
    I.   Title
    823.9'14 [F]

    ISBN-13: 978-0-7278-6391-1 (cased)
    ISBN-10: 0-7278-6391-6   (cased)
    ISBN-13: 978-0-7278-9183-9 (paper)
    ISBN-10: 0-7278-9183-9   (paper)

Except where actual historical events and characters are being
described for the storyline of this novel, all situations in this
publication are fictitious and any resemblance to living persons
is purely coincidental.

All Severn House titles are printed on acid-free paper.

Typeset by Palimpsest Book Production Ltd.,
Grangemouth, Stirlingshire, Scotland.
Printed and bound in Great Britain by
MPG Books Ltd., Bodmin, Cornwall.

NEATH PORT TALBOT
LIBRARIES

CL.	FAM	
DATE 17. 7. 06	PR. £18·99	
LOC	CS	
NO	2000 474839	

One

It was dark and cold in the old cowshed, but the heat of David's body pressed against hers, his arms tightly embracing her, and the warmth of her own feelings for him kept the chill away.

'Please, Ruth, please. You don't know how much I love you.' His voice was husky with desire as he pleaded. 'I'll be gentle, I promise. Please, darling.'

He trailed hot kisses across her cheek and nuzzled the curve of her neck giving a low groan and she shuddered with ecstasy at his touch.

'I love you desperately, Ruth,' he whispered. 'You're in my thoughts night and day.'

Her body ached to give in to him, to know the wonder of his lovemaking, but her fear was stronger than her desire.

'No, David, we mustn't,' she murmured weakly, stirring in his arms. 'Someone might find out. I'd be shunned.'

'No one will find out,' he said persuasively.

She put a restraining hand against his chest. 'Suppose there are . . . consequences?' she said, her voice quivering at the thought. 'Suppose I fall for a baby . . .'

She suffered enough already from her parents' rigid piety. If she ended up disgraced by getting herself in the family way she could never face Jacob Williams' terrible wrath and the contempt he would heap on her.

'It won't happen, Ruth, darling. I'll be careful.'

'My father would throw me out without a second thought,' she said.

'I can't believe your mother would let him do that.'

'Oh, David, you don't know what they're like. My mother is as stiff-necked as he is. They criticize and judge me continually. They'd both disown me. What would I do then?'

'There's nothing to be afraid of, I swear it, darling.' His arms tightened about her even more. 'I'm begging you. Let me love you.'

'No, David.' She struggled in his arms, pushing at him and sat up. 'If you love me like you say you do,' she panted desperately. 'You'll wait until we're married.'

'When will that be?' He sounded hurt. 'You're only sixteen. Your father won't let you marry for a while. I can't wait, Ruth. I want you now. I love you so much it is driving me crazy.' He reached for her and tried to press her down on to the hay-strewn floor. 'Don't torture me like this.'

'No, David, I can't.' She pushed his arms away and struggled to her feet. 'I must go home.'

'But it's early yet.'

'What time is it?'

He stood up, a darker shadow in the gloom. She heard a box of matches rattle and then he lit one. In the flickering light he looked at his pocket watch.

'Quarter to eight.'

'What?' She was appalled. 'I must go.'

Jacob Williams had set a curfew of half past seven, summer and winter, and she had never before broken that strict rule. He might even be out looking for her.

At the thought, she hurried from the cowshed and on to the rough track that let up to Prosser's farm.

'Ruth!' David followed her. 'Wait! I'll walk you home.'

'No, just as far as the post office,' she said. 'Someone might see us.'

They started along the track towards the village, a high moon lending some light. The November cold cut into her through her coat and also seemed to make sounds sharper.

All at once she thought she heard a boot strike a stone behind them and she turned fearfully to stare back the way they had come.

'Someone's there, David. Spying on us.'

'It's your imagination, Ruth.' He sounded dejected and

she guessed he was disappointed at her earlier stubbornness, but she forgave him because she loved him so.

When they reached the post office, the first cottage on the road through the village, Ruth stopped.

'Goodnight, David, my love,' she said in a low voice. 'I'm sorry if I've hurt you.'

Pushing her close to a hedge nearby, he took her in his arms and kissed her. She clung to him, eagerly taking his kiss.

'I'll speak to your father tomorrow, Ruth,' he said finally in a determined tone.

'What?'

'I'll ask him to let me marry you. It's the only way. I can't go on like this, wanting you.'

'Oh, David! That's wonderful. Come around after tea-time. I'll prepare the way.' She struggled from his grasp. 'I must go now. I've never been out this late before. Goodnight, David darling.'

The sensation of David's fervent kiss was still warm on her lips as, with trembling nervousness, Ruth opened the back door of the cottage and walked into the kitchen where the gas light was turned down low as it usually was at night.

She was relieved and astonished that her parents were not waiting there for her, grim expressions on their faces. She had expected to meet her father's fury immediately, but the cottage seemed silent. Had they gone to bed? She could hardly believe it.

She took off her tam and slipped out of her coat, hanging it behind the back door. Could she get to her bedroom un-noticed, she wondered hopefully. If so she might postpone facing his anger and inevitable sermonizing until the morning. All she wanted was to slip between the sheets and dream about David; imagine what it would be like to be his wife, to know his love-making without dread and guilt.

She tip-toed to the door to the passage and opened it quietly only to jump back in guilty surprise. Her mother, Olive, stood there in a nightgown, a shawl around her shoulders, her long hair in a braid.

'Mam!'

3

'Don't you Mam me, you wayward girl,' Olive Williams chided harshly, her lips a thin line. 'What time do you call this?'

Ruth swallowed. 'It's not that late, Mam.' She swallowed again before telling the practised lie. 'I spent the evening with my friend Louisa. The Morrisons don't go to bed until half past nine most nights.'

'I'm not interested in the errant ways of those Morrisons,' Olive snapped. 'You know your father's rules in this house. Indoors by half past seven. In bed by half past eight. That's the Christian way. Follow those rules and you'll come to no sin.'

Ruth glanced back at the clock. 'But it isn't half past eight yet, and I was just going to bed.'

'Don't back chat me!' Olive exclaimed angrily. 'Your father is waiting for you in the parlour.' She shook her head disapprovingly. 'He's very angry, I can tell you, and I don't blame him. You've got some explaining to do, my girl.'

'But . . .'

'Don't argue!'

Olive hustled Ruth along the passage to the parlour. The door stood open and Ruth went in reluctantly.

Jacob Williams sat on a bentwood chair, his bulky torso as upright as a ramrod. His hands resting on his knees were trembling a little. She looked into his bewhiskered face, and flinched, her heart sinking seeing the fanatical glint in his pale eyes. This would be a haranguing to outdo all others.

'Father, I can explain . . .'

'Silence!' Jacob thundered. 'You speak when spoken to. Have you no respect for the head of this house?'

Ruth bent her head. 'Yes, Father.'

'You disappeared very quickly after Bible class this evening,' Jacob continued sternly. 'Where have you been until this ungodly hour?'

Hesitating, Ruth ventured to look up at him, conscious of her mother standing close by listening intently. Would they believe her usual story? She took a deep breath to steady her voice before she answered.

'Like I told Mam, Louisa invited me around to her house

4

after Bible class. I didn't notice the time going by. It's never happened before, Father, and it won't happen again.'

He stared at her for a moment. 'I tremble,' he said censoriously at last, 'for fear the good Lord will strike you down where you stand, your mouth soiled with lies.'

'It's true, Father . . .'

'You lie!' he stormed. 'When you didn't return home at half past seven I walked around to the Morrisons' house. You weren't there, and Louisa hadn't seen you. What've you to say to that?'

Ruth felt her throat close and she was silent.

'Well?'

She had to say something. 'I went for a walk on my own up along by Prosser's farm.'

'What? Alone in the pitch darkness? I think not.' Jacob stared at her accusingly. 'Lies drip from your lips like fouled water,' he exclaimed contemptuously. 'My guess is you were with that scoundrel, David Beale, weren't you?'

'David isn't a scoundrel,' Ruth protested angrily. David was loving and warm and not dried up with piety.

'I've warned you about him,' Jacob went on. 'You loiter in the bakery when he's serving there. I've seen you.'

'He's a heathen!' Olive put in forcefully. 'Never shows his face in chapel. His mother can hardly hold her head up with the shame of it. He's wickedness incarnate.'

'You don't know anything about him.' Ruth raised her voice, a thing she would never dare do as a rule.

'I know he's a coward,' Olive insisted. 'Otherwise he'd have enlisted to fight for his country like any decent young man does these days.' She gave a grunt of disdain. 'But where was he when better men were dying at Ypres back in the spring? Hiding his face in his father's bakery, that's what.'

'You don't know what you're talking about,' Ruth exclaimed hotly. 'David's too young to die in battle.'

'He's twenty-one!' Olive shook her head. 'He's an insult to King and country, and you should be ashamed, too, for standing up for him.'

'David is a wonderful man,' Ruth retorted heatedly. 'We love each other, and he wants to marry me.'

5

There was a deep silence. Ruth glanced at both her parents to see their reaction, but their features were stony.

'He's coming here to see Father tomorrow,' she went on staunchly in the face of their hostility. 'He intends to ask for my hand in marriage. And I want to marry him.'

'He'll be sent packing before he sets one foot over my threshold,' Jacob said, getting to his feet. He towered above her like an avenging angel. 'You're not to see him again. Understand? Now, go to your room.'

Ruth turned and left, feeling rebellion rise in her breast as she climbed the stairs. David and she loved each other and nothing would stop them being together.

The following morning breakfast was eaten in silence, her father totally ignoring her presence at the table. Olive had little to say either, other than to give her instructions regarding her chores for the day; a thorough cleaning of the two bedrooms followed by a good scrub of the kitchen flagstones. Cleanliness was next to godliness. It was the same old routine every week.

Directly after breakfast Jacob went off on foot to tend his ironmongers' shop on the main road that ran though the village of Gowerton, a quarter of a mile away. The Beales' bakery was right next door. She should have known her father would be watching her every time she went in there.

Ruth got on with her chores, putting her back into the work, wanting to finish as soon as possible. David had promised to call after tea-time. She wanted to pretty herself up before then. Despite what her father had said last night, she prayed he would relent when David made his offer. Her father would see just how sincere he was.

Promptly at noon Jacob returned home for his midday meal, a nourishing vegetable stew, with chunks of fresh crusty bread. Ruth smiled secretly to see her father tuck in, knowing the bread had been prepared and baked by David himself, as his father was training him to take over the business.

They were halfway through their meal when a knock sounded at the front door. Jacob spoke to her for the first time that day.

'Ruth, go and see who that is, and ask them what they

6

mean by disturbing a god-fearing man at his meal.'

Her father was never pleased to have his mealtimes inter-rupted by uninvited visitors.

She opened the door to find the tall figure of David standing there in his best suit; his cheeks pink as though scrubbed, his hair smoothed flat with water.

'David!' Ruth's hand flew to her head, conscious that wayward strands of her hair were hanging from beneath her limp mop-cap and her apron was none too clean after kneeling on the kitchen floor.

'I've come to see your father, Ruth,' he said, determination in his voice. 'I've come to ask for your hand, as I said I would.'

'It's dinner time, David!' Ruth exclaimed, glancing appre-hensively along the passage behind her. It was the worst possible moment to choose. 'I thought you'd call after tea.'

'I can't wait until then, Ruth, love,' he said. 'We've waited long enough.'

Ruth bit her lip anxiously. David's jaw was set firm and his lower lip protruded a little, as it usually did when stub-bornness was setting in. The light in his blue eyes told her it was no use arguing with him.

'Come in,' she invited. 'Go into the parlour. I'll tell Father you're here, but, David . . .' She hesitated. 'He's not in the best of moods. I was caught coming in late last night. Don't let on we were together.'

She left him standing beside the aspidistra while she went back to the kitchen. Her father was just wiping his mouth with a napkin. He glanced at her, his expression impatient.

'You took long enough,' he said. 'Who was it?'

'David Beale. He's in the parlour,' she answered, a knot forming in her chest. 'He's come to speak to you, Father.'

Jacob Williams swiftly rose to his feet, his expression darkening. 'How dare he show his face here? And at this time of day, too.'

'Bad manners are to be expected of a man of his sort,' Olive put in decisively. 'Ungodly and uncouth.'

Ruth ignored her mother's unfair remark. 'Surely you'll have the courtesy to speak with him, Father?' she said, trying

7

to hide a chiding tone in her voice. 'It would be ill-mannered not to.'

Jacob gave a grunt of impatience but put down his napkin and strode out into the passage and then into the parlour. Ruth was hot on his heels, along with her mother.

'Mr Williams, sir,' David began and then hesitated.

Ruth detected a quiver in his voice and she smiled encouragingly at him. 'I'm sure my father would like you to sit down, David,' she said.

'Mr Beale will not be here long enough to sit,' Jacob snapped.

'Hear him out, Father, please,' Ruth cut in.

'Be quiet, girl,' Jacob instructed harshly. 'And leave us.'

'But, Father . . .'

'Be gone!'

Ruth retreated to the open doorway and passed through it but stood in the passage outside holding the door partially open.

'Mr Williams, sir,' Ruth heard David begin again. 'I'm here on an important matter.' His voice sounded stronger now and Ruth was cheered by it. 'I've come to ask you officially for Ruth's hand in marriage. I love her and she loves me and we hope to marry soon.'

Ruth heard Olive's tongue click with disapproval, while Jacob gave a disdainful grunt.

'Impertinence!' he said severely. 'In any case, Ruth is just turned sixteen, too young to experience the more odious duties of a wife. She'll not wed until she is gone eighteen.'

'I'm willing to wait, Mr Williams,' David answered eagerly.

'Then you'll wait in vain,' Jacob said abrasively. 'I'd no sooner give my daughter to you than to the next vagabond that passes through the village.'

'I don't understand. Why are you against me?' David's voice had an edge to it now and Ruth realized he was getting angry. 'I come from a respectable family,' he continued. 'My prospects are good. I'll inherit my father's business, and I intend to open shops in other villages round about, too. Ruth would never want for anything as my wife.'

'Money isn't everything,' Jacob said. 'You're a backslider

as far as chapel is concerned. A man who is careless of his own soul is careless of everything else in life including a wife.'

'That's absurd! I've never heard such senseless piffle!'

Ruth winced at David's words and tone and bit her lower lip in apprehension.

'How dare you insult me, sir, in my own house,' Jacob stormed.

'I don't mean to do that,' David said hastily. 'My intentions towards Ruth are honourable and sincere. I'd be a true and loving husband all her life.'

'That's as may be,' Jacob retorted. 'But I'll never give my approval for her to marry such an ungodly man as you.' He cleared his throat importantly. 'And the matter of Ruth's future husband is settled anyway. I have already given her hand in marriage to Pastor Edwin Allerton.'

There was silence except for a gasp of surprise from Olive. Ruth was rooted to the spot for a moment, stunned at the unexpected pronouncement, unable to take in her father's words.

Pastor Allerton? Her future husband? How could that be? She hardly knew the pastor of Soar Chapel where they attended worship regularly. He was less than an acquaintance to her, and he was old, at least thirty. This was a bolt out of the blue, and Ruth felt as though she really had been struck by lightening.

'What?' She heard David's voice quiver with uncertainty as he finally spoke.

'It's all settled,' Jacob said firmly. 'There's no need for you to remain here another minute. My daughter is spoken for.'

'Ruth has agreed to marry him?' There was incredulity in David's voice.

'I have agreed,' Jacob said. 'And I speak for my daughter.'

Ruth could bear it no longer. Despite the probability of incurring her father's wrath, she charged into the room.

'No, David, I've not agreed!' She rushed towards him, clutching at his arm. 'I know nothing of this arrangement with Pastor Allerton. He hasn't even spoken to me of it himself.' She tossed her head defiantly. 'I'll refuse him anyway.' She looked up earnestly into his face. 'I love you,

David, and want us to marry. You must believe me.'

'I . . . I don't know what to believe. I know your father's reputation well enough to know he would not lie about such a serious matter.'

Jacob gave a snort of annoyance at the words. 'I lie? How dare you. I insist you leave my house now, Beale.'

David looked down at her. She saw suspicion in his eyes and her heart was sore that he would doubt her. 'David, please!'

'How can you be betrothed to a man and not know of it, Ruth? I'm shocked, and hurt, too. You've misled me.'

'No, David!' She clutched his arm more tightly. 'This is none of my doing, I swear it. And I'll not go through with it, I promise you.'

David was silent as he stared at her one last time and then strode purposefully towards the door.

'Yes, go and good riddance,' Olive put in spitefully. 'You should be ashamed of yourself, still hanging around your mother's apron strings while brave men are risking life and limb, fighting for their country.'

'David, don't go,' Ruth appealed, hurrying after him. 'This is all a mistake. I'll put it right.'

But he was gone down the passage and through the front door. Ruth went to chase after him but her mother quickly caught at her arm, preventing her.

'You stay indoors, my girl,' she said angrily. 'Would you make a spectacle of yourself and us by dashing into the street without a hat or coat on? Have you no common sense?'

Aghast, Ruth turned to her parents. 'What have you done? You've sent away the man I love.'

'I've done what's best for you,' Jacob said firmly.

'Best for me?' Ruth shrugged out of her mother's grasp. 'Promising me in marriage to a stranger? Pastor Allerton is old enough to be my father.'

'Nonsense!' Jacob exclaimed. 'He is merely twelve years your senior. A perfect age gap between husband and wife. He'll be a steadying influence on you.'

'There's only two years between you and Mam.'

'Ruth, I forbid you to argue with me,' Jacob said sternly.

'Honour your father and your mother. Have you forgotten that commandment?'

'Listen to your father,' Olive chimed in. 'As a dutiful, Christian daughter should.'

'Is it right and Christian to force me to marry a man I don't love?' Ruth said desperately. 'Pastor Allerton hasn't even had the nerve to ask me to my face. Talk about cowardly!'

'He did the right thing,' Jacob declared. 'He spoke to me first. And I have agreed. It will be a much better match for you than to throw yourself away on that backslider, Beale.'

'Backslider and a coward,' Olive said waspishly.

'David is a decent man,' Ruth cried out. 'And he truly loves me. How can Pastor Allerton love me? He doesn't even know me.'

'He told me he has been watching you for some time, and believes you will make an appropriate wife.'

'Appropriate!' Ruth exclaimed loudly. How cold that sounded. 'What about love?'

Jacob looked stern. 'The love of God is all you should be concerning yourself with, my girl.'

'Why wasn't I told of this arrangement sooner?'

'I intended to tell you last evening,' Jacob said. 'But you failed to return at the appointed time. This is one reason why I went in search of you. It's a good thing I did. Your foolish behaviour with David Beale has been nipped in the bud, before Pastor Allerton got wind of it.' Jacob gave a cough. 'Otherwise he might have thought he was getting damaged goods.'

'Father!' Ruth was shocked. 'Have you no faith in my morality? How could you think such a thing of your own daughter?'

'It's Beale's morality I doubt,' Jacob snapped. 'I believe the man to be unprincipled. He is certainly ungodly.'

'Judge ye not lest ye be judged!' Ruth burst out.

Jacob looked furious. 'How dare you quote the scriptures at me? Go to your room and stay there until I say you may leave it.'

'I will not, and I won't marry Pastor Allerton either. You can't make me.'

11

Jacob's neck seemed to swell and his bewhiskered face grew red.

'You will do as I command, my girl, or you're no daughter of mine. I'll wash my hands of you, and cast you out as unworthy. You'll not be welcome in this house.'

'What?' Ruth said, aghast. 'You can't mean that, Father.'

'I do. Pastor Allerton is a pious and godly man. He has honoured our family by asking for your hand and you will accept him.'

'But it's not what I want!'

'What you want is neither here nor there,' Jacob said angrily. 'I demand you obey me.'

'You should be thankful to make a good marriage,' Olive said.

'You'll have plenty of time to get to know Edwin Allerton before the marriage,' Jacob said. 'I'll not have you wed any man until you are gone eighteen.'

'As the pastor's wife you will be looked up to by the community,' Olive continued. She shook her head wonderingly. 'I can't understand your reluctance.'

Ruth gave her mother a withering glance. 'Perhaps you've never been in love.'

'The love you mean is sinful,' Olive said severely. 'Women must suffer men's appetites to beget children. But to encourage and enjoy such attentions is wicked.'

Ruth's shoulders drooped. She felt she had no strength left to fight them, but that did not mean she was prepared to give up. Her eighteenth birthday was not for two years yet; plenty of time to find a way out. In a day or two she would go to David, talk to him. Their love would stand against all odds, and prove indomitable. She was sure of it.

Ruth was summoned from her chores the following morning when Olive came to tell her that Pastor Allerton was downstairs in the parlour awaiting her.

'Quickly, slip into your best Sunday frock,' Olive urged.

'I will not!' Ruth declared. 'He'll see me in my mop-cap and apron or not at all.'

'You'll shame us!'

'I won't be put on display like a prize pig,' Ruth said firmly.

Ruth ignored her mother's angry tutting, and went downstairs, although her innards churned with nervousness. Swallowing down her anxiety with difficulty, she entered the parlour, her mother following behind fussily.

'Good morning, Pastor Allerton,' Olive began. Her voice had an obsequious tone which set Ruth's teeth on edge.

'Good morning, Mrs Williams.' Pastor Allerton was sitting on the horse-hair sofa but rose quickly at their entrance. Her father, sitting in his bentwood chair, made no move to get up.

Ruth gave Edwin Allerton a quick overall glance before lowering her gaze to the lacquered floorboards. He was as tall as her father but nowhere near as well built. His thick mane of dark hair that reached his collar gave the impression of a head too large and heavy for his narrow shoulders; his frame, clothed entirely in black, reminded her of a pillar draped in mourning.

She had never looked closely at his face before, but she saw now that his smooth features were commonplace, yet remarkable for lack of any signs of aging.

'Good morning, Ruth.' Edwin Allerton's voice was deep. She had often heard his sonorous tones ringing through the chapel as he gave his sermons. 'I trust you are well.'

Ruth lifted her head to look at him. There was no smile on his face, and it occurred to her that she had never seen him smile, certainly not when shaking hands with members of his congregation as they left the chapel after services. She had always regarded him as a sombre, serious man of little interest.

'I'm well, thank you,' she answered quietly. She was reluctant to be rude to a minister of the chapel.

'I believe your father has told you of our decision for your future.'

'Decision?' Ruth frowned, feeling pique. 'That's a cold way to speak of marriage, Mr Allerton,' she said sharply.

'Ruth!' Jacob rose to his feet abruptly, his tone admonishing. 'I do beg your pardon, Mr Allerton,' he said. 'Young

13

people today have no sense of decorum. Ruth needs guidance and teaching.'

Edwin Allerton tilted his large head. 'I'm sure, when she is my wife, I shall find much pleasure and satisfaction in teaching her better ways.'

Jacob gave a cough. 'Yes, quite so.' He indicated the sofa. 'Do resume your seat, Mr Allerton.' Jacob sat down on the bentwood chair again.

Edwin Allerton also sat. 'Sit next to me here, Ruth,' he said patting the sofa. 'We must get to know each other now that everything is settled.'

Ruth lifted her chin stubbornly, making no move to join him.

'But everything is not settled, Mr Allerton,' she said. 'You have yet to ask me and I have yet to refuse your offer.'

He stared at her in some surprise.

Jacob jumped to his feet again, his face changing colour to a dark red. 'Ruth, you go too far! You're underage. It's not your place to accept or refuse. I do that for you.'

'Jacob is right,' Edwin Allerton said. 'You're far too young to understand such matters or even to know your own mind.'

'I'm not a child.'

'Of course not,' he said evenly. 'Nevertheless, you must believe that your father and I have your best interests at heart. You will come to accept this as time goes on.'

Ruth gave a hard swallow. 'You're not my choice for husband, Mr Allerton,' she said. 'I love another.'

'What?'

Edwin Allerton turned his head to stare at Jacob, and for the first time in her life Ruth saw a look of fluster on her father's face.

'Childish fancies, Mr Allerton, I assure you,' Jacob said hurriedly. 'Ruth is chaste and protected. There is no other man in her life. How could there be? She is but a child yet.'

'I love David,' Ruth burst out. 'He has asked me to marry him. He has even spoken to my father.'

Jacob looked furious although he tried to hide it from the other man. 'David Beale did approach me,' he admitted. 'But this was after we had made our agreement. I assure you, Mr Allerton, Mr Beale's offer was totally unexpected and unwelcome, and he was sent packing.'

'I know the Beale family,' Edwin Allerton said. 'But I have not met their son, David.'

'A backslider, Pastor,' Olive exclaimed. 'And a scoundrel, I've no doubt.'

'How did you meet David Beale, Ruth?' Edwin Allerton asked.

'At his father's bakery,' she admitted. 'My mother always sends me for the daily bread.'

'I see,' he said mildly. 'Yes, I understand now. A childish passing fancy.'

'Sinful!' Olive proclaimed.

'Not sinful,' Edwin Allerton said, shaking his head. 'But foolish perhaps. I've noted that very young people take themselves far too seriously.' He lifted a hand and waved it airily. 'It's of no importance.'

Jacob looked relieved. 'No importance at all,' he agreed.

'Yet, Ruth will see no more of this young man, I think,' Edwin Allerton said. There was an edge to his tone.

'You have my solemn assurance.'

'Good, now let us set the date for the nuptials.'

Jacob squared his shoulders. 'My daughter shall not know the married state until she is eighteen in two years time, Pastor. I am adamant on this point.'

Edwin Allerton's lips moved as though he were attempting a smile. 'I would prefer not to wait so long, but I understand your concern as her father,' he said. 'Ruth and I will get to know each other in the interim. I'm sure under my influence she will forget all her girlish fancies.'

'I've not yet agreed to marry you,' Ruth burst out. 'And I'll never agree not to see David again.'

'Ruth!' Jacob exclaimed. 'You will remember our previous conversation, and the consequences of disobeying me.'

'There's no need for rebuke, Jacob.' Edwin Allerton looked at her calmly, which confused her. She expected him to be angry. 'We are betrothed to marry, Ruth,' he went on. 'And we will marry. This is as much a certainty as is the Kingdom of Heaven.'

Two

R uth felt like a prisoner over the next week. Her father questioned her each evening about her movements during the day, although Olive watched her like a hawk, refusing to let her even step outside the front door alone. She accompanied her parents to chapel as regularly as ever, but was not allowed to attend Bible class if Olive was not free to go with her. Seeing her friend Louisa was also out of the question it seemed.

'I don't want you mixing with those Morrisons,' Olive said when Ruth begged to see her friend. 'I suspect the whole family of irreligious behavior.'

'They go to chapel regularly,' Ruth reminded her.

'It's all show. They have backsliding ways,' Olive insisted. 'Louisa is a bad influence on you.'

Raw cold though the days were in late November, Ruth longed to breathe some fresh air to clear her head. And she ached to see David. What must he be thinking and feeling? She had to talk to him; explain that no matter what her father decreed, no matter what Edwin Allerton wanted, she would marry no one but David.

At the start of the first week in December Olive rushed to visit a friend, Mrs Cooper, another staunch member of the chapel, who had just received news that her soldier son had been killed in action.

Olive left strict instructions. 'You remain indoors, mind,' she commanded severely. 'Mr Allerton will be coming to tea today. It's time your courtship began.'

As soon as her mother's back was turned, Ruth put on her woollen tam, pushing a hatpin through it and swung her woollen cloak over her shoulders. She wrapped a warm muffler around her neck, and set off for David's home, being careful to keep to the back lanes.

She was just emerging from the lane that ran behind the Beales' cottage when she saw Louisa. Ruth hesitated, not wanting to attract her attention. Louisa was such a chatterbox and was bound to give her away at some time. But her friend turned her head at that moment and, spotting her, stopped and stared keenly at her.

'Hello, Ruth. You're a stranger these days,' Louisa began, swinging her blonde pigtail behind her. 'I was beginning to think you were too good for us now you're engaged to be married to Pastor Allerton.'

Ruth was startled. So the news was all over the village already.

'You're a dark horse, I must say!' There was a touch of envy in Louisa's voice. This so-called engagement had obviously given her a new status in the community.

Ruth bit her lip in consternation. 'I'm just sixteen,' she reminded her friend defensively. 'Engaged is too strong a word. It's more like an understanding between Mr Allerton and my father, and none of my doing. It'll all be forgotten by my eighteenth birthday, you just wait and see.'

'That's not what I heard.' Louisa pouted. 'You might've told me, Ruth. After all I am your best friend.'

'There's nothing to tell,' Ruth insisted sharply. 'And I doubt that I'll really marry Mr Allerton.'

She had decided a long time ago that it was unwise to tell her friend about her feelings for David and how he reciprocated them. Her love for him was too deep and too tender to be talked about, especially now when there was acrimony between them.

Louisa sniffed and tossed her head. 'Are you walking into the village?' she asked, obviously wishing to change the subject.

Relieved, Ruth shook her head. 'I'm on a message from my mother to the Beales' house.'

'Oh!' Louisa looked disappointed. 'I was hoping you'd help me choose a Christmas present for *my* mother.'

'Another day,' Ruth said quickly. She was even more

anxious now to straighten matters out with David. 'I'm expected back right away.'

'It's terrible news about Peter Cooper, isn't it?' Louisa said mournfully. 'That's the fourth young man the village has lost this year. Oh, this awful war!'

'Yes,' Ruth said simply.

Even in her own tribulation over David, Ruth's heart went out to Mrs Cooper. Losing a child must cause unbearable pain. She hoped she would never know the misery of such a loss.

'My father says there are still German spies in hiding round about us,' Louisa continued with a quiver in her voice. 'He says they'll rise up and burn our homes to the ground when the zeppelins finally fly over Gowerton to drop bombs.'

Ruth was skeptical. 'They won't come here, surely.'

'They've dropped bombs on London.'

'That's a city. Gowerton is no more than a village; mostly farming land.'

Ruth shook her head. 'My father says the beastly Hun intend to starve us to death by destroying the crops.'

Ruth felt fear then. 'How does he know that?'

'A stall-holder in Swansea Market told him when he was down there buying up provisions last week. My father says things are not going well for us at the front line. There'll be even worse food shortages if the war goes on much longer.'

Ruth knew that the newspapers were full of war news, but her parents would never let her read them for fear she might be corrupted, whatever that meant. Consequently, the war had seemed a distant thing, but it appeared to be creeping closer.

'I'm calling in to that new haberdasher's on the main road,' Louisa told her with a crooked smile, her mood changing like the wind. 'There's a young shop assistant there, and he's so handsome.' She waved a hand. 'See you soon, Ruth.'

Ruth watched her friend walk away and then turned into the gate of the Beales' cottage. She had been to David's home only once before and by invitation. His mother's greeting had been a little stilted on that occasion, and she wondered what her reception would be today.

It was Mrs Beale who answered the door. Her eyes and nose were reddened and Ruth realized she had been crying.

'Is David here, Mrs Beale?'

'What do you want with him?' Mrs Beale asked sharply. 'Haven't you done enough damage?'

'I must speak with him,' Ruth rushed on. 'I want to explain.'

'Explain?' Mrs Beale sniffed. 'You've led him on in a shameless way, and you call yourself Christian.'

'Please, Mrs Beale, let me see him.'

The older woman shook her head. 'He won't see you. My boy is going to the war. Yes!' She nodded her head. 'He's going to enlist and it's all because of you.'

'What?'

'Oh, you can look shocked.' Mrs Beale burst into fresh tears. 'I'm going to lose my son,' she wailed. 'He never thought of enlisting until you jilted him.'

Ruth stepped forward to put her arm around Mrs Beale's shoulders to comfort her. 'But I haven't jilted him,' she exclaimed earnestly. 'He mustn't enlist. Let me speak to him.'

Mrs Beale shrugged away Ruth's comforting arm. 'Of course you've jilted him, and cruelly, too,' she said through sobs. 'It's all around the village about your betrothal to Pastor Allerton. So it's too late for you to explain.'

At that moment footsteps were heard on the staircase and then David appeared. His face was white and drawn so unlike his usual self and Ruth was shaken to realize it might be her fault.

'David!'

He stared at her stonily. He had never looked at her that way before. She had only ever seen love in his eyes.

'What're you doing here, Ruth?' he asked dully. 'Come to gloat have you?'

'David, please don't say such things to me.' Ruth rushed towards him as he stood on the bottom stair. 'I love you, and I want to marry you. Mr Allerton and my father took things into their own hands. They didn't even consult me.'

'I can't believe you really had no idea of it beforehand,' David said accusingly. 'But you said nothing to me. You let me believe . . .' He turned his head away. 'I'm not good enough, perhaps? Edwin Allerton has standing in the village. He's looked up to. I'm just the baker's son.'

'You know that isn't true!' Ruth exclaimed. 'I thought you knew me better than that.' She was disappointed in his attitude. 'You give up very quickly, David,' she said reproachfully. 'I could think by the way you're talking that you're glad to be free of me.'

'You want to quarrel with me,' he accused her harshly. 'That would make it easier for you, wouldn't it?'

'No, I don't want to quarrel. I want to marry you. I've always wanted that.'

'I think you should go, Ruth,' Mrs Beale cut in. 'You're upsetting my son more.'

Ruth ignored her. 'David, please don't enlist. It's madness. You don't need to.'

'Don't I?' he asked harshly. 'Your mother is always making pointed remarks about my lack of courage. But I'm not afraid to go to war. Anyway, I can't stay around Gowerton when you're married to Allerton. I couldn't stand it.'

'Won't you stay and fight for me?' Ruth asked desperately. 'The proposed marriage is two years away. Together we could find a way out. If we show my father how much we love each other he might relent and let us wed.'

He stared at her. 'I'm not a fool, Ruth,' he said. 'Your father will never accept me. He's made that abundantly clear. And you're deceiving yourself if you believe otherwise.'

Ruth stared at him beseechingly. What he said was probably true, but at least he could try, make a fight for her.

'David, whatever your opinion of me, please don't enlist,' she pleaded earnestly. 'Think of your mother, think of me.'

'You! I'm enlisting to forget you.'

'Oh, David!' Ruth felt cut to the quick.

'See what mischief you've done?' Mrs Beale asked. 'So will you go now?'

Ruth stared at David, her eyes welling up with tears. 'When you come back I'll still be here, David, waiting for you. I'm not married to Pastor Allerton yet, and hope never to be. I love you.'

David stood a moment and then he turned on the stair and retreated upstairs without another word.

Mrs Beale held the door open wide. 'Go and don't come back,' she said. 'You're not welcome here.'

Ruth stepped outside and the front door was immediately closed on her. She returned home the way she had come, through the back lanes, ashamed for anyone to see the tears she shed.

But she was determined to fight against this idea of marriage to Edwin Allerton. She would do all she could to resist.

When she was twenty-one she could marry whoever she pleased, and no one could stop her. Meanwhile, she would wait for David. Let heaven be kind and bring him home safe and sound.

Ruth had to endure several visits from Edwin Allerton over the Christmas season. She was merely polite to him, and tried to stay aloof, refusing to be amicable as her father demanded.

'I won't pretend what I don't feel,' she told her father when he challenged her on her stand-offishness. 'That is hardly a Christian virtue, Father.'

Jacob blustered and blared, but Ruth tried to ignore him. Her father had the upper hand ultimately, of course; she still remembered his threat of disowning her, but she was careful not to treat Edwin Allerton with anything other than respect for his calling. She would give her father no cause to take action.

Meanwhile, Edwin Allerton might yet be put off her by her lack of enthusiasm for him. Time alone would tell.

Mid January her parents relaxed their vigilance and told her she was free to come and go as she pleased, albeit within their set rules.

On her way to the post office to send 'thank you' notes to relatives for their Christmas gifts, she met Louisa and discovered the reason for her parents' change of heart.

'Have you heard about David Beale?' Louisa asked straight away.

Ruth glanced at her friend suspiciously. She had been careful not to reveal her feelings for David, but how much did Louisa know?

'No. What?' she asked at last.

'He went to the enlistment office in Swansea before Christmas. He'll be staying at his uncle's house there until it's time for him to join a regiment,' Louisa said lightly. 'My father says it won't be too long before he finishes what little training the army gives and will be on his way to France.'

Ruth was silent, struggling not to show how upsetting the news was for her, and gave a little prayer for him.

'He's the last one I'd have thought would enlist,' Louisa went on. 'Too full of himself, and in line for his father's business as well.'

Ruth was incensed. 'You know nothing about David. He's a wonderful young man.'

Louisa raised her eyebrows and smiled crookedly. 'Better not let Pastor Allerton hear you talk about another man like that. He might think there's something going on.'

Ruth grated her teeth. 'Sometimes, Louisa,' she said angrily, 'you can be very stupid. Now, good day to you.'

She felt crushed by Louisa's news, and over the next few days thought deeply about it. Worried for him away fighting though she was, she could not help feeling let down as though he had deserted her to her fate. It chaffed her that he had given up so easily and her heart ached at the thought that he might not have loved her as much as she loved him. Now she might never know.

In late February her mother let her resume the chore of fetching the daily bread from the Beale's bakery. She was hopeful that David's father, George Beale, might have news of David. In the past Mr Beale had always given her a cheery smile, but today his glance at her was cold as she placed her mother's order.

'Any news of David, Mr Beale?' she asked hopefully.

'He's been shipped out with hundreds of other men as far as we know.' He shook his head. 'His mother is very worried, as am I.'

'I'll pray for him,' Ruth said simply. It was all she could do.

George Beale grunted and turned away.

'Can I call and see Mrs Beale?' she said to his turned back.

'I think not, Ruth,' George Beale answered in a hard voice. 'Your face is the last one she wants to see.'

'But how else will I get news of David?' Ruth exclaimed. 'I'm as worried as you are, Mr Beale.'

'Huh! You best concern yourself with your intended husband,' he said. 'Leave us alone, Ruth. We have enough to bear.'

She came away from the bakery feeling very chastened. The Beales blamed her for their misfortune, and her heart was sore at the thought for she did not deserve it. She had done nothing wrong.

Ruth could hardly endure to look at Edwin Allerton the following Sunday afternoon, when she and her parents were invited to the Manse for tea before going in the pastor's gig to the chapel for the evening service. Here was Edwin, safe and complacent in the fine stone house the chapel authorities had provided for their pastor, while David . . . heaven only knew what David was going though at this very moment.

At that thought the piece of cherry cake handed to her by Edwin tasted like sawdust and the tea like brine, although Olive seemed to be enjoying it and complimented the pastor's housekeeper, Mrs Cardew, on her skills as cook.

'I've been thinking, Jacob,' Edwin began, delicately touching his wide mouth with a napkin. 'I see no real reason why Ruth and I should not wed next month, after her seventeenth birthday. It's a respectable age for a girl to enter into the matrimonial state.'

Ruth was dismayed and stared at her father. It was too soon. She needed more time to find a way out of the arrangement, but would he go against the pastor's wishes?

Jacob gave an apologetic cough before answering. 'I disagree, Pastor,' he said to her relief. 'I have always had it in mind that Ruth should wait until she is twenty-one as I told you before, but I am willing to concede to eighteen. I will not change my mind, I think.'

There was a fleeting expression of anger on Edwin Allerton's face, and Ruth was surprised. It was unusual to see any expression of emotion on his face at all. She thought him a cold fish. It struck her then that he was also a man used to getting his own way, very much like her father, and would not tolerate his wishes or demands defied. One more reason to dislike him.

'I see,' he said shortly and hesitated.

Ruth held her breath. Would he back out? She prayed that he would.

'Then we must wait,' he went on tightly. 'Although, I would like to hear Ruth's view.' He turned his glance on her. 'Most young girls aspire to be married, and have the respect of their peers for their raised status. What are your feelings, Ruth?'

She swallowed hard. Dare she repeat her true feelings now? She could feel her father's intent gaze on her.

'I agree with my father,' she said carefully. 'It's too soon, and besides . . .' She wetted her lips before going on. 'I'm of the same mind as I was when you told me of your decision, as you called it. My heart belongs to another.'

'Ruth!' Jacob was angry. 'We'll hear no more of that.'

'David Beale is at war,' Edwin Allerton said complacently. 'It seems he thinks more of fighting for his country than for your affections.' He tilted his head. 'As it should be, of course.'

'David believes I jilted him,' Ruth said sharply. She was taken aback that he spoke so calmly after her outburst. 'I can't speak for his feelings, but I'm sure of my own, Mr Allerton.'

'You may call me Edwin, under the circumstances. We are to be man and wife, my dear,' he said. 'David Beale may be away for years or he may not return at all. I suggest you forget him and any foolish notions you hold.'

'Oh!' Ruth was shocked by his callous dismissal of another man's life.

She was glad when it was time to leave for chapel. Her parents went to the front entrance where the gig was waiting. Ruth was about to follow them, when Edwin grasped her arm and held her back.

'Ruth, make no mistake about it,' he said tensely. There was an underlying warning in his tone. 'I am adamant.' He raised a hand and touched her cheek with his forefinger, his eyes glinting in a way that made her breath catch in her throat in fear. 'I've watched you for some time, my dear Ruth, and I tell you now that I want you and no other. You will be my wife.'

Three

T he chapel hall seemed overpoweringly hot and noisy, with the chattering voices of women and the clicking of many knitting needles. There was a drive on in the village to knit more socks, mufflers and mittens for the soldiers in France than the surrounding communities could produce. Most of the women and girls in Gowerton had been roped in.

Ruth, sitting at a table with Louisa, put down the sock she was knitting to wipe her damp forehead with a handkerchief.

'I've often been tempted to put a note inside a sock,' Louisa confided, clicking away. 'You know, a cheering message to some poor soldier in the trenches. Who knows, it might be a man from our village, like David Beale for instance.'

'Don't be absurd, Louisa.' Ruth could not keep the sharpness from her tone.

She had received not one word of news about him since he had gone away last Christmas, but she thought of him every day, and prayed constantly for his safe return.

'I wonder where he is right this minute.'

It was too much for Ruth and she stood up. 'I'm going to get a glass of lemonade,' she said quickly. 'Do you want one, Louisa?'

She brought back two glasses of the home-made lemonade after a few minutes and managed to compose herself during that time. Perhaps Louisa did not mean to be unkind.

She put a glass on the table in front of her friend, took a

25

long draft herself and then picked up the sock and resumed the turning of the heel, the part she liked knitting the best.

'Can I ask you a question, Ruth?' Louisa asked. Her voice dripped with curiosity. 'It's about Mr Allerton. Do you love him?'

Ruth compressed her lips, trying not to be annoyed at her friend's prying, especially in the crowded hall. 'No,' she said at last.

'But you must at least like him or you wouldn't be marrying him.'

'I neither like nor dislike him,' she answered airily.

It was true. She felt nothing, except perhaps a little unease at the intense way Edwin looked at her sometimes when they were alone, which was not often. Her father saw to that.

'He's very polite and attentive,' she went on. 'He always brings me a posy and one for my mother when he calls at our home or when we have tea at the Manse.'

'Has he ever kissed you?'

'Certainly not!' Ruth was angered.

Louisa giggled. 'I can't imagine the pastor kissing anyone.'

'Louisa, you go too far.'

Ruth was glad when it was time to leave the hall and say goodbye to her friend. Everyone took their knitting home with them to do in their spare time. Ruth did the same, although she hardly had any spare time. Olive kept her occupied every minute she wasn't sleeping.

Her mother was in the kitchen making pastry. 'I hope you didn't dawdle, chatting with that Louisa Morrison,' Olive said as Ruth appeared. 'You know full well I don't approve of her.'

'No, Mam, I didn't dawdle.'

'That girl has very outlandish ideas,' Olive said severely. 'She told her mother she's going to be a nurse when she turns eighteen.' She clicked her tongue. 'I've never heard anything so outrageous. I have serious doubts about her morals.'

'You're behind the times, Mam,' Ruth ventured. 'Nursing is respectable and patriotic nowadays. There are nurses at the front line, remember, risking their lives, and what about

Florence Nightingale, nursing in the Crimean War? She was revered for her work then.'

Olive sniffed. 'She was upper crust and the upper crust can do all kinds of things and get away with it.'

'Mary Seacole wasn't upper crust?'

Olive frowned. 'Don't be absurd, Ruth'

'There's no harm in Louisa, Mam,' Ruth defended. 'I grant you she can be a bit silly at times, but that's all.'

'Well, you won't be able to associate with silly girls when you're the minister's wife. Very responsible position that is.'

Ruth said nothing, but put on an apron and taking some cooking apples from a bowl nearby, began to core and peel them.

'I was talking to Mr Allerton's housekeeper this morning at the butcher's.' Olive went on talking, her hands busy with the pastry mixing. 'Mrs Cardew was telling me that an old uncle of the pastor's has just died leaving Mr Allerton a sizable legacy. What do you think of that?'

'Mrs Cardew is a terrible gossip,' Ruth ventured. 'She loves making mischief, that one.'

'What nonsense!' Olive tossed her head.

'Yes, well, I wonder what the pastor would say if he knew she was spreading his private business far and wide.'

'I don't know why you've taken against her,' Olive said. 'Mrs Cardew is a poor widow woman, and I'll thank you to show a bit of Christian charity, Ruth.'

Ruth pursed her lips and was silent.

'As I was saying,' Olive went on tetchily. 'Mr Allerton's uncle was his last living relative, except for a distant cousin living in Scotland. The pastor is well-to-do now, Ruth, and you'll be his wife.'

Ruth shrugged. 'It's of no importance to me, Mam. I don't want Mr Allerton or his money.'

'Oh, don't be a foolish girl,' Olive snapped. 'A husband who is comfortably off, and living in that substantial stone house, it's a good match for anyone.'

'The Manse belongs to the chapel,' Ruth reminded her mother. 'The pastor will have to move out in due course.'

'I dare say, but now he'll have enough to buy another

good house and keep servants, too, I shouldn't wonder. No cottage life for you, my girl.'

'I'd live in a mud hut quite happily,' Ruth retorted angrily, 'if I could be with David.'

'There'll be no more talk like that.' Olive's lips narrowed. 'David Beale obviously thinks nothing of you. He hasn't written you one letter since he's been in France.'

'How do you know that?'

'Because I've been keeping a careful watch on the post,' Olive said sternly. 'He won't be allowed to jeopardize your future as the minister's wife.'

Ruth lowered her head. 'I'm the last one he'd write to under the circumstances.'

But Olive's bitter words made her think. If David did really love her, nothing should have kept him from writing. Perhaps she was making a fool of herself over him. Perhaps he never really cared, not with the depth of feeling that she did. Perhaps it was only physical love he had ever wanted from her.

The apple pie was out of the oven and cooling when someone knocked at the front door of the cottage. Ruth was washing up so Olive went to answer. She could hear her mother's flustered tones and went to see who it was.

Edwin was standing in the passage. As a rule he only ever called when her father was at home and never unannounced.

'Oh, Mr Allerton,' Olive began. 'Jacob is not at home at present.'

'It's Ruth I've come to see,' Edwin said. 'I have some grave news for her.'

Olive looked even more upset, her hands shaking.

'Come into the parlour.' She led the way and he followed and so did Ruth, wiping her hands on a tea-towel.

'Sit down, Mr Allerton,' Olive invited.

'I'd rather stand, considering the news I bear.'

He was looking at Ruth intently, and a cold shiver ran down her spine.

'I was just paying a pastoral call on Mr and Mrs Beale,' he continued. 'When a telegram arrived for them.' He paused. 'Sit down, Ruth.'

'No, I'll stand,' she replied quietly although her legs began to tremble uncontrollably. 'What is it?'

'I felt it right that you hear the news from me, your future husband . . .'

'What have you come to tell me?' Ruth blurted out, although she was suddenly afraid to hear what he had to say.

'It's about David Beale,' he said, confirming her dread. 'The telegram informed his parents that he is missing in action believed killed. His regiment was fighting on the Somme at the time of his death.'

'No!' Ruth turned away, her hands flying to clutch at her head. 'No, David isn't dead. You're lying.'

'Ruth!' Olive's tone sounded shocked that she would speak to the pastor in such a way, but Ruth didn't care.

'You have to face it, Ruth,' Edwin said calmly. 'Undoubtedly it's a living hell out there and the newspaper reports tell us that the offensive is still going on. Twenty thousand British troops were reported killed in the early stages. No doubt there'll be thousands more before it's over. David was one of them. I'll pray for his soul.'

She turned to him, her heart full of hatred.

'You've come here to gloat, haven't you?' she accused him. 'You're pleased that the man I love is dead.'

He took a step back, his expression showing clearly that he was shocked at her allegation.

'Ruth, you wound me deeply,' he said in a hushed tone. 'I wish for no man's death. I am a man of God.'

'You're a man first and foremost,' Ruth flared. 'Your rival for my love is dead . . .'

Ruth stopped, her hand going to cover her mouth. David was dead. She had spoken the words herself and now she believed them. It had been her constant dread since he had enlisted. Somehow she knew at that time that she would never see him again.

'You do me an injustice,' Edwin said. His voice had the slightest touch of anger in it now. 'David Beale was not my rival. He never had a claim on you. You are promised to me, and you will be my wife.'

'Please go!' Ruth cried out. 'I don't want to see anyone at the moment. I'm in mourning.'

'You will *not* go into mourning!' he exclaimed loudly. 'I forbid it! I won't allow you to make a fool of me in the community.'

'You're not my husband yet, Edwin,' Ruth retorted. 'I answer only to my father.'

'Jacob will not tolerate such behaviour,' Edwin answered confidently. 'David Beale was not related nor connected to you in any way. Your mourning for him is inappropriate.'

'I should think it would be,' Olive butted in forcefully. 'You must forgive her, Mr Allerton. Young girls are head-strong and full of silly notions.'

Ruth stared from one to the other. Her heart was breaking for David, but all she could see were the stony expressions of two people who didn't care a jot for him.

'I'll call on Mrs Beale straight away,' Ruth said defiantly. 'With my condolences.'

Edwin lifted a hand of warning. 'I wouldn't do that, Ruth. Your name was mentioned in my presence which, inciden-tally, caused me some embarrassment.' He shook his head. 'Mrs Beale still blames you for David enlisting. You'll find no solace there.'

With a sob, Ruth turned and ran from the room. She scur-ried up to her bedroom and collapsed on the bed, letting the tears burst out, but no matter how long she cried the pain of grief in her heart remained sharp and unremitting.

Ruth knew nothing but grief and regret during the six weeks that followed the news of David's death. She could not help bursting into tears on any occasion when it came home to her that she would never see him again.

Her parents were impatient with her, offering her nothing but rebuke and criticism for moping around. Olive was par-ticularly caustic. Living with her unsympathetic parents, Ruth felt she was caught in a trap from which there was no release, and as the weeks went by, she became more and more desperate to be free of them. She had to escape from their merciless censure and repression. Marriage was the only way out.

What did it matter who she married now that David was gone? As Edwin Allerton's wife, she might gain a small measure of independence. She would be mistress of her own house, and there was the prospect of children of her own. She would love them unreservedly even if she could not love Edwin.

She came downstairs early at the start of the last week of September, the morning she had made a firm decision, and set about her chores with gusto.

She would marry next March, in six months' time. In the meantime, once her parents knew she had capitulated to their wishes they might cease their carping and life might be just about bearable.

By the time Olive appeared Ruth had black-leaded the range, set the fire, put the big iron kettle on to boil and had eggs and bacon sizzling in a pan above the fire.

Her mother stopped short at the sight. 'Well! I'm glad you've come to your senses, my girl.'

'I've been thinking,' Ruth said calmly. 'It's time I started planning my trousseau, especially my wedding dress. We should see Mrs Parker the dressmaker as soon as we can.'

'We'll go this afternoon,' Olive said, her tone lightening. 'Your father will be generous I know. After all, it must be a trousseau befitting a minister's wife.'

Ruth turned away to tend the frying food, her throat tightening as her thoughts turned to David, but she fought back the threatening tears.

She was about to embrace a loveless marriage so could hardly expect happiness under those circumstances. She would probably be lonely for a while until a baby came. After that she would devote herself to her son or daughter and live through her children. But she would never forget David. He would always be alive in her heart.

Four

They were in the sitting room after dinner, as Edwin preferred to call the evening meal. She had prepared it herself as she did all their meals, having taken the first opportunity after the wedding to dismiss the garrulous Mrs Cardew.

'Thank you for my birthday gift, Edwin,' Ruth said. 'The pearls are beautiful.'

She thought them a little pretentious for a minister's wife, but had learned in the twelve months since their marriage not to contradict him or speak her mind too freely.

Edwin was not much company she had found to her cost; too serious and studious and not given to general conversation, spending most of his time in his study.

She soon discovered, too, that the passion he demonstrated in the pulpit when preaching his sermons was a façade; he showed little emotion or warmth in private. Ruth would have welcomed any show of feelings, even anger.

Always controlled, he never lost his temper outright, but if crossed would sulk and not speak to her for days. At such times she felt extreme loneliness which visits to Louisa or her parents could not alleviate.

Curiously, his sulking silence did not prevent him from turning to her in their bed for nightly lovemaking; a loveless, joyless duty which she had steeled herself to endure for the sake of having a child of her own.

With a sigh, Ruth took the pearls out of their blue velvet box.

'They look expensive,' she ventured, letting the strand twist around her fingers, admiring the lustre of each pearl.

She would not suggest that he could not afford such extravagance, because of course he could. Man of God or not, Edwin didn't stint himself of the pleasures money could bring. And to be fair he was more than generous with her. Her household allowance was above adequate, although wartime shortages meant that they often had to do with what they could get. He gave her a generous dress allowance, too, which she carefully saved.

'I'll wear them at Louisa's wedding tomorrow.' She was matron of honour. 'I'm glad you are officiating at the ceremony, Edwin.'

He merely grunted, his head hidden by the daily newspaper he was reading. She wondered briefly if she had upset him in some way. He was in one of his brooding sulks, but she could not think what she might have done.

'I'm sure it's a relief to her mother that Louisa has chosen marriage over nursing,' she persisted lightly. 'I dread to think what damage she could have done at the front line. She's so frivolous at times.'

He remained silent.

Ruth ran her tongue over her lips. 'How goes it at the front? What do the newspapers say?'

He rattled the newspaper. 'According to this report the Germans have started a massive offensive, but the arrival of American troops in France might just tip the scales in our favour,' he said evenly. 'Time will tell.'

Putting the pearls back in their box, Ruth felt tension leave her. At least he was speaking to her.

'How many more lives must be lost before the end?' she murmured.

He lowered the paper and stared at her, his mouth a tight line. She was surprised at this unexpected show of emotion. Usually he maintained a restrained expression.

'David Beale is like a dark shadow between us,' he said morosely. 'You're my wife, Ruth. I forbid you to even think of him.'

Ruth was taken aback. 'What?' She could not believe her ears.

'You think I don't know that you are forever mooning

about his memory?' he said. 'I'm tired of it, Ruth, and won't stand for it.'

'That's not true, Edwin.' Ruth felt the injustice. Of course she would not forget David, but she was never maudlin over his memory. 'And totally unjust. I've given you no cause to think that.'

To her astonishment he crumpled the newspaper and threw it on the floor beside his chair and then stood up.

'We've been married a year and still you're without child,' he said accusingly.

She stared at him suddenly understanding his quarrel with her.

'And you think that's my fault?' she asked sharply. 'Are you suggesting that this mooning over David, as you call it, is preventing me from conceiving?'

'It has crossed my mind. You are wilfully denying me an heir.'

'It's absurd. And it's not possible,' Ruth cried. 'Has it ever occurred to you that *you* might be at fault?'

For the first time she had known him he looked incensed. 'How dare you question my manhood, woman? This is insufferable.' Dark colour suffused his face. 'I've had a bad bargain with you,' he went on grimly. 'One that I'm beginning to regret.'

'Then in God's name why did you marry me?' Ruth flared. 'There's no love in you for me and never has been. I can tell that when you turn to me each night like some automaton. How do you think that makes me feel?'

'Are you complaining of my attentions? I'm your husband. Your submission is my conjugal right.'

Ruth shook her head. 'No, I'm not complaining, Edwin. I am equally disappointed that I have not caught. I want a child as much as you do.' Her lips twisted in bitterness. 'What else is there for me in this bleak marriage?'

He looked at her for a moment and then turned and strode from the room.

Ruth collapsed on to a chair nearby, her legs shaking with anger and shock. That was the first real quarrel they had had, and for the first time she had spoken of the suspicion

34

in her mind. She had been troubled at her failure to conceive, but was convinced it was not her fault.

Her shoulders drooped. She could look forward to perhaps weeks of his silence after this outburst, and yet she had no doubt that tonight he would expect her compliance when he turned to her for ritual, almost desperate, lovemaking. And she would comply and pray; and ask God for the gift of a child, for how could she go on in this marriage alone and without love?

Five

R uth was pleased to see that Louisa had made a comfort-able home for herself and her husband in the rooms above the haberdasher's shop on the main road.

The handsome young shop assistant on whom Louisa had set her sights ever since his family arrived in the village three years before turned out to be the proprietor's son, Mervyn Jenkins.

'I couldn't stand living in the same cottage as his mother,' Louisa confided when Ruth went to tea there on the last Sunday in August. 'So Mervyn persuaded his father to let us have these rooms. Mrs Jenkins criticizes everything I do.'

'That's mother-in-laws for you,' Ruth joked with a smile.

'You're lucky not to have one,' Louisa retorted pertly.

Ruth felt her smile falter. An interfering mother-in-law might have been a welcome diversion from the monotony of her life with Edwin.

'Perhaps so,' she agreed, carefully keeping regret from her voice. She would tell no one of her unhappiness, especially not Louisa who enjoyed spreading gossip. And there was no one else to talk to, certainly not her mother, Olive.

'No, I won't have Mrs Jenkins telling me how I ought to do things, particularly now,' Louisa said and then grinned widely. 'Ruth, you're the first to know. I believe I'm in the family way already. In fact, I'm sure!'

'Oh, Louisa!' Ruth was so pleased for her friend.

'Mervyn's delighted, of course,' Louisa rushed on. 'But I've warned him not to say anything to his mother just yet. I don't want her around here taking over our lives.'

'When will the happy event be?' Ruth felt a spasm of envy. If only the same joy could be hers.

'I reckon I'm two months gone,' Louisa said eagerly. 'So round about the end of March should be right.' She reached forward and put her hand on Ruth's arm. 'Oh, Ruth, I'm so happy.' She gave Ruth an old-fashioned look. 'I thought you'd get there before me. After all, Ruth, you've been married over a year now.'

Ruth held her smile with difficulty. 'It's in God's hands,' she replied.

'Is that what Edwin says?'

Ruth turned her head and reached for her purse and gloves. 'I must be off now, Louisa. Edwin prefers a light snack before he leaves for evening service. I mustn't keep him waiting.'

Ruth stood up and Louisa moved quickly to get her coat from a nearby chair.

'Speaking of happiness . . .' Louisa began.

'Were we speaking of happiness?' Ruth interjected sharply. Perhaps Louisa was more intuitive than she realized.

'Well, I'm happy about the baby,' Louisa said as she helped Ruth into her coat. 'And so is Mervyn. But I'm referring to someone else's happiness. The Beales. Have you heard their latest news?'

Ruth paused, whirling around to stare at her friend. 'No, what about them?'

'Well, it's a miracle, isn't it?' Louisa said. 'They've just been informed by the War Office that their son – you remember David Beale, don't you? Well, he's been found alive in France.'

'What?' Ruth started violently, her legs suddenly failing her and she clutched at the back of a chair for support. 'What did you say?'

Louisa nodded. 'Mervyn explained it to me. It was during this latest big offensive by the Allies last month, driving the enemy back towards their Hindenburg Line or something.' Louisa made a face. 'Funny names they've got haven't they . . .?'

'Louisa!' Ruth couldn't stop herself from crying out. 'What about David?'

'Well, hundreds of British prisoners of war were found by the Allies in the first few weeks. David was one of them.' Louisa shook her head. 'He's alive but in poor health apparently. He received wounds to both legs.'

'Oh, God!'

'Yes, it is awful, isn't it?' Louisa nodded. 'Mervyn wanted to enlist, you know, but they wouldn't have him, not with his fallen arches. I'm glad, too.'

'Is . . . Is David home yet?' Ruth could hardly speak for the pounding of her heart.

'Early September they say. It could be next week. It'll be hard for him I expect.' She paused. 'I wonder if he's badly disabled. But still,' Louisa went on in a practical tone, 'he'll inherit his father's business, so he won't starve. Mrs Beale is so happy the doctor had to give her a sedative.'

Ruth dared not move or try to walk, fearing she would fall, her legs were shaking so. Louisa seemed not to notice her predicament, but was moving fussily towards the staircase that led down to the street door.

'I'll find these stairs a trial when I get bigger,' she observed as she descended. 'If only we could get a cottage in the village. Ruth? What's the matter? Where are you?'

'I'm looking for my gloves,' Ruth called out. 'Won't be a minute.'

With an effort she managed to walk to the top of the stairs, and descended towards the waiting Louisa, clutching desperately at the banister as she went, knowing she must pull herself together or her friend might suspect something, for although Louisa was often silly she was no fool.

Louisa pecked a kiss on Ruth's cold cheek. 'Don't tell anyone my secret yet, will you?' she said. 'I don't want it getting to Mother Jenkins' ears.'

Ruth assured her friend that her lips were sealed. She had almost forgotten Louisa's interesting condition anyway. Only thoughts of David filled her mind now. He was alive and he was coming home. She could hardly believe it was true.

She made her way back to the Manse as quickly as her failing legs would let her and went straight to the bedroom where she lay on the bed, still too shocked to even cry, although her mind was in turmoil.

David was to return but it could mean nothing for her. She was Edwin's wife now. It was too late.

She lay there for a while, praying thankfully for David being spared, and yet her heart was full of pain for a love that is lost.

She wondered if her parents knew and then sat up with a jerk. Edwin must have known about David. The pastor was always the first to be told of these important village matters. He knew, but he had said nothing to her.

At that moment the bedroom door opened and Edwin stood there.

'You've not prepared my usual snack, Ruth,' he complained.

She realized almost an hour had passed as she had lain there.

'I'll have to do without now or be late for chapel,' Edwin went on. 'You know my routine, Ruth. We should never have let Mrs Cardew go. She was very reliable.'

She stared at him in silence.

'What's the matter?' he asked. 'Are you ill?'

'Why didn't you tell me about David Beale being found alive?' she asked in a hard voice. 'Did you think you could keep it from me?'

He stood there still holding on to the door knob, his face expressionless. 'I didn't think the news would be of any concern to you, Ruth. You're *my* wife now.'

'Yes.' Ruth got up from the bed and faced him. 'You keep reminding me of that fact, Edwin, although I don't know why you feel the need to.'

'You're being facetious, Ruth.' His tone was even, but she thought she saw a spark of anger behind his eyes, and had the urge to goad him further.

'Did you think I'd rush into his arms at the first opportunity?'

'Now you're being sardonic,' he said coldly. 'And it ill-suits you.' He turned as though to leave. 'Perhaps you'd better rest further. I'll manage without my snack this once.'

'Are you made of stone, Edwin?' Ruth asked desperately. 'Do you imagine that because I'm your wife my feelings for David cease to exist?'

He turned back to look at her, his lips tightened. 'They should, Ruth.'

'I'm just a human being, Edwin. I can't help my feelings.'

He stepped further into the room. 'Ruth, I forbid you to see David Beale. Do you understand? I don't want a scandal.'

'Why would my seeing David cause a scandal?' Ruth exclaimed. 'As far as the village is concerned he's merely an old friend.'

'But *I* know he's an old lover – there's the difference, Ruth.'

'David and I loved each other, Edwin, but our relationship never came to that step.' How she wished it had now.

'I'm glad to hear it,' he said, but his tone was disbelieving. 'That makes it all the more advisable you should have no contact with him. Pity can make women do foolish things.'

'Pity?'

'A man who has been though hell and back; a hero, and a cripple at that. It would be easy for him to seduce you.'

Her mouth fell agape in shock. 'You think that of me?' she said at last. 'I do regret marrying you, Edwin, but I regard my marriage vows as sacred. I may feel love for David still, and perhaps I shall feel pity, too, but I'll never forsake my vows.'

'That remains to be seen,' he answered sceptically. 'The world is paved with good intentions.'

She thought she detected scorn in his tone. 'Now you're being facetious,' she said. 'I'll be your faithful wife, Edwin, until death. I pray to God that He'll send me a child of my own before long in recompense for disappointment in my husband.'

She saw she had hit her target when his face suffused with colour. He did not speak again, but left the bedroom, slamming the door behind him.

'The war seems to be swinging our way at last.' Edwin was reading the newspaper at the breakfast table, a habit Ruth disliked.

She looked up, surprised. It was the first time he had uttered a word to her since their bitter quarrel over David Beale the week before. His tone sounded so normal as though no words of anger had ever been spoken between them.

'Really?' She could not see his face hidden by the paper but presumed he was in a better mood. 'What do the papers say?'

'The Allies are pushing the Hun back even harder,' he went on. 'I hazard a guess that we'll see the end before this year is out.'

'I pray fervently that it will be,' Ruth said with all her heart. It was September already and winter would be on the poor troops again before they knew it.

'Well, the Hun can't resist the onslaught much longer.' He rattled the paper. 'It says here that many of the German troops are already surrendering.'

Ruth thought about David. At least he was home, safely out of danger. And if what Louisa had said about his being wounded was true, the war was already over for him. She thanked God for that. He was out of harm's way at last.

Edwin lowered the paper and looked across the table at her, his expression showing no emotion.

'I suppose you already know Beale arrived at his parents' home yesterday,' he said.

Ruth felt a catch in her throat. 'No I didn't know,' she answered quietly. 'Thank you telling me, Edwin.'

He raised his eyebrows. 'The only reason I tell you is that you will be wary of meeting him as you go about the village. There will be no contact, you understand?'

Ruth lifted her chin. 'You've already made that clear, Edwin.' Then she nodded her acquiescence. 'I doubt David would welcome meeting me anyway. We didn't part on the best of terms. He believes I betrayed him in favour of you.'

'Then let the matter rest there.' He put the paper aside and rose from his chair. 'I have some pastoral duties to perform this morning.' He took out his pocket watch and glanced at it. 'I'll return for my midday meal at the usual time.'

When he had left Ruth quickly washed up the breakfast

41

crockery. Then she put on her coat and hat, and fetching her purse and wicker basket, she set off for the butcher's shop on the main road, opposite Beale's bakery to get their weekly ration of meat.

She wasn't surprised to see the 'closed' sign put up on the inside of the bakery door. David would hardly be there, of course. He would be at his parents' cottage recuperating. She imagined his family would be celebrating their son's miraculous return from the grave.

Ruth paused a moment before going into the butcher's shop, gazing longing at the bakery. If only she could glimpse David for just a moment; look once more on the face of the man she loved.

She did still love him; she couldn't deny it, and only time would cure it; must cure it, for nothing else was possible.

Edwin was unfair in suspecting her of intrigue with David, but at the same time, she knew he was right about keeping her distance. The love she and David had shared was gone, lost in the past. And she was certain, judging by their last encounter before he went to war, any feelings he had for her were now just cold ashes.

Ruth walked home to the Manse through the back lanes. Her wicker basket was not heavy. Apart from the ration of meat, she had managed to get a little butter and some real potatoes. They would be a change from the substitutes they had been enduring for the past few months.

As she approached the back of the Manse through the shrubbery she glimpsed the tall figure of a man in infantry uniform standing at the back door. Men home on leave in the village often sought out the pastor, looking, Ruth supposed, for some kind of hope or comfort after the ordeals they had experienced, but they usually came to the front door.

Ruth walked up the path towards him, pity in her heart for this soldier whoever he was. 'Pastor Allerton is not here this morning,' she said kindly. 'I'm sure he'll see you this afternoon though.'

The man turned. 'Ruth, it's you I've come to see.'

42

She stopped dead in her tracks, astonished that the man called her by her first name. She gazed at him more intently, not recognizing him. Then he spoke again.

'You're looking very well, Ruth. Oh, it's good to look on your lovely face once more. It was the image of your face that kept me alive in the trenches and in that hellish camp.'

Ruth felt her mouth go dry. Her throat closed up and she struggled to speak his name. 'David!' She could not believe it. 'David.'

'Yes, it's me, Ruth,' he said, stepping nearer.

He was very much changed she saw and her heart was wrenched with pity. He was so thin, a shadow of the man he had once been. The planes of his face were sharpened and darker making him look older, hard and worn. David's eyes as she remembered had always gleamed with joy of life, now she saw only pain and despair there.

'David, I can hardly believe it is you.' She saw then that he leaned heavily on a walking stick. 'Oh, my dear! You've been hurt.'

'It's all healed now. It happened just before I was captured,' he said dully. 'The German doctors patched me up. Sometimes I wish they had let me die.'

'Oh, David, don't say such things, please.' Ruth could not help herself, but rushed forward to embrace him. 'Think of those who love you.'

His arms closed around her fiercely, desperately; she felt his dry lips on her cheek and suddenly realized she was behaving recklessly. This was not an embrace of friendship – friendship could never be theirs.

Gently she pushed herself away from him. 'David, I thank God you were spared,' she said breathlessly, feeling her heart pounding. 'Your parents must be ecstatic at this miracle.'

'Yes,' he said quietly. 'They are.' He grasped her hand, and his tone was tense when he spoke. 'Ruth, can you forgive me for the way I behaved when we parted? I was a fool. I've regretted it every moment since.' He looked towards the door. 'Can we go inside? I must talk to you.'

Ruth hesitated. She wanted to talk to him, too, learn all

she could about the horrors he had been through, but Edwin's warning was echoing in her head.

'I don't know, David . . .'

'Please, Ruth. I've been though hell . . .'

'All right.' Ruth opened the back door and went in. Perhaps it was better they spoke in private. Anyone passing along the lane might see them.

'Sit down, David. I'll make some tea.'

'No.' He stayed her by grasping her hand again. 'Just sit with me,' he said urgently. 'Let me look at you. Oh, Ruth, I love you so. I've never stopped.'

Her heart turned over in her breast to hear such an impassioned declaration after all that had happened, and she felt confused and upset, and sat down because her legs were unsteady.

'David, please. You shouldn't say these things to me now. I'm a married woman.'

He stood up and stepped towards her and she rose too.

'But you wouldn't have married him, would you?' he said throatily. 'If I hadn't spoiled things by being a jealous fool?' He shook his head. 'You can't tell me you don't still love me, Ruth,' he said. 'I can see it in your eyes. You can't hide it from me.'

Ruth swallowed hard. She could not lie to him and yet neither could she compromise herself. 'I think the world of you, David, and always will. But I have taken vows. I can't dismiss them.'

'But, Ruth,' he cried. 'We were always meant to be together. I knew that from the start and so did you. You can't dismiss me either.'

His words were upsetting. 'But you didn't fight for me, David,' she said unable to keep reproof from her voice. 'You ran off to war without giving me a chance.'

'Ruth, I've said I'm sorry and you promised you'd wait until I returned. Well, I'm back now and . . .'

'I did wait,' she interrupted quickly. 'I tried to resist my father's wishes, even though you had made it clear that you despised me.' A sob caught in her throat and she could not go on for a moment. 'When I heard you'd been killed I gave

44

up all hope,' she said at last. 'I also gave way to the pressure on all sides. I married Edwin.'

'It's not too late for us, Ruth,' he said urgently. 'You could leave him; come away with me. My father is talking about opening a second bakery in Swansea. I'll be managing it.'

'David! What are you asking me to do?'

He clasped her hand tightly. 'You don't love Edwin Allerton, I know you don't.'

Ruth bent her head and was silent. No, she did not love Edwin and could never learn to. But that was her misfortune.

'I'm his wife,' she murmured. 'And I will be until death.' She looked up into his face, hardly able to see his beloved features for the tears that were brimming in her eyes. 'Of course, I love you, David. I've never stopped. But there can be nothing between us now, nothing. You must see that.'

'No, I don't see it,' he said harshly. 'I've lived through a nightmare, Ruth. I feel I deserve some happiness now, but there will be no happiness for me without you at my side.'

'It can't be, David.' She gazed up at him, her heart breaking to have to hurt him further after all he had been through. 'In fact, we can never see each other again.'

'Don't say that!'

'I must! My marriage vows are sacred to me.' Even though they were empty, she thought miserably. 'And not only that. I won't bring disgrace to my parents and Edwin. And what about your family? How would they hold their heads up in the village?'

'Never mind about others,' David said. 'I can only think of us and our happiness. My God! I think I've paid for it through and through.'

'Yes, yes you have,' Ruth said gently. 'You've paid a terrible price. But if we did as you suggest, run away, bring shame and humiliation on our families, we would never be happy together.' She shook her head. 'It would come between us, David. We could end up hating each other.'

'But, Ruth . . .'

'You must go now, David,' Ruth said, her throat constricting. 'I'm sorry, my dear. I think you're doing the right thing in leaving the village. You'll make a new life for yourself in Swansea. You might meet someone else.' She could not go on with that thought.

'My parents want me to marry my step-cousin,' he said dully. 'My Uncle Sydney never had a son of his own. Since his wife died some years ago he has only her daughter, Esther, the child of her first marriage.'

He was looking at her pleadingly, but Ruth was silent keeping her eyes downcast, giving him nothing he could interpret as encouragement.

'Uncle Sydney has a thriving coal merchant's business in Swansea. He wants it to stay in the Beale family, that's why they want me to marry Esther. Everyone thinks it'll be a good match.'

Ruth lifted her gaze to him, holding back tears with difficulty. 'You see, David,' she said carefully controlling her voice. 'Life goes on, and you'll probably find happiness with your cousin.'

'I love you, Ruth.'

Ruth feared her control would break at any moment and felt as though demons were tearing at her heart. She looked up into his face.

'It will pass, David. I promise you.' She realized she did not sound convincing. How could she when she still suffered herself. She went to the door and opened it. 'You must go now. I'll never forget you.'

He stood for a moment looking at her. 'I'll do as you wish, Ruth, for now.' He stepped forward and through the door and then paused on the step, turning to gaze at her again. 'But I'm not going to give you up just like that,' he went on. 'The war taught me how to cling on. I clung on to life and I'll cling on to love.'

'David, it's no good.'

He shook his head. 'I won't rest until you are mine again, Ruth.' His lower lip jutted stubbornly in the way she so fondly remembered. 'You'll see me again soon. One day we will be together and that's *my* promise.'

Six

In the surgery, Ruth dressed quickly, her fingers made awkward by suppressed excitement. She was with child. She could feel the difference in herself, but she would not allow the excitement to burst out until her hopes were confirmed by the doctor.

Ruth stepped out from behind the screen. Dr Rowlands was sitting at his desk. He looked up at her and smiled.

'Congratulations, Mrs Allerton,' he said jovially. 'You're two months' pregnant.'

'Oh! How wonderful!' Breathlessly Ruth sat on a chair before the desk. 'I've been praying for this, doctor.'

'There shouldn't be any difficulty,' he went on. 'You're a healthy young woman; but just the same, this is your first so no lugging heavy furniture about or getting on your knees scrubbing floors. No over-exertion. Otherwise live a normal life. Yes, a normal life.'

'I'll be careful.'

'Come back and see me in two months' time just to check everything is going well.' He smiled. 'Give my congratulations to Pastor Allerton for me.'

Ruth felt she was walking on air as she made her way back to the Manse. Her prayers had been answered. A child would make marriage to Edwin worthwhile after all. She could put up with anything now and perhaps his distant attitude might change. Excited, she was anxious to tell him the news. He would be relieved as well as pleased, and so was she.

She let herself into the kitchen through the back door and

47

glanced at the clock on the mantelpiece over the range. Edwin was on pastoral duties in the neighbouring village of Waunarlwydd, but was due home in an hour for his midday meal.

Quickly fastening an apron around her waist, she began to prepare the food. They ought to be celebrating with some special dish, she thought regretfully, but rationing precluded that. Nevertheless, she would make something tasty with what she had in the larder and tell him he was to be a father at last as they sat at the table in the dining room. Perhaps this was the beginning of a new start for them. A child of their own would make all the difference.

She was busy at the range when someone tapped at the back door. Before she could answer the door opened and David Beale stepped quickly inside.

'David!' She was dismayed to see him. 'You shouldn't just walk in like that. Edwin might've been here. There would have been an awful row.'

She noticed that today he had dispensed with the walking stick.

'I'm not a fool, Ruth. I made sure he wasn't here,' David said. 'I had to see you.'

He moved purposely towards her and Ruth drew back, shaking her head. 'David, these visits must stop. I've asked you so often not to come here. Someone will notice.'

'I'm very careful,' he said confidently. 'I've been thinking about you constantly, Ruth, my dear. I think of little else. It's driving me mad.'

'David, please!' It was two or three weeks since he had last called and she had hoped he had given up. She found their meetings painful. Feelings for him always flooded back, and left her wracked with guilt. 'You know this is wrong.'

'Loving you is wrong?' He shook his head. 'No. My love kept me going; kept me alive all those terrible years.'

Pity as well as love was in her heart, but she quelled her feelings.

'That's not fair, David,' she said. 'I'm sorry that you suffered, but you're not making things easy for me, either, sneaking in to see me like this.'

On more than one occasion when they met alone, when he pleaded with her to leave Edwin and come away with him, she was tempted to rush into his arms, to know again the love and warmth that had been theirs before Edwin came into her life. But she steeled herself to resist. There would be no turning back from that step once taken. And now there was her baby to think of.

'You must stop loving me,' Ruth said quietly. 'And I must stop loving you. You see, David, I'm carrying Edwin's child.'

His mouth went slack and he looked at her as though she had struck him across the face.

'Dr Rowlands confirmed it this morning,' she said, turning her gaze away from his stricken face. 'I'll tell Edwin when he comes home later.'

'How could you do this to us?' David asked. His tone was heavy as though she had mortally wounded him.

'I'm Edwin's wife,' Ruth cried, astonished that he should take such an unreasonable attitude. 'You speak as though I've done something shameful.'

He looked angry. 'This is the second time you've betrayed me for Allerton's sake, Ruth.'

Suddenly she was angry too for his unfair rebuke. 'Edwin is my husband. We both want a child. What passed between us years ago is over, David. It has to be put aside.'

His lips tightened. 'You don't belong to him,' he said. 'You belonged to me long before he came on the scene. You'll always belong to me.'

'Things have changed, can't you see?'

'Once you swore you loved me,' he interrupted quickly. 'Was that a lie, Ruth?'

'No, of course not! I still . . .' Ruth hesitated, swallowing her words. It seemed like a betrayal of her unborn child to admit her feelings for him. 'David, please go now. We shouldn't be talking like this.'

'Ruth, my dear, listen,' David said persuasively, stepping closer. 'It doesn't matter about the child . . .'

'What?'

He shook his head. 'What I mean is I accept it. You only

married Edwin because you thought I was dead. None of that matters now.'

'David, how can you dismiss my marriage just like that?' Ruth cried. 'And you're being stubborn, and selfish, too. We can't just do as we please and to hang with the consequences.'

He stood looking at her solemnly for a moment.

'Why not? Our happiness is at stake, Ruth.' He held up a hand as she opened her mouth to protest again. 'Look,' he continued. 'I'm begging you to leave Edwin. He need never know about the baby. Don't tell him. I'll take you away. We can go to Swansea. My uncle will give me work. We can be together.'

'That would be madness,' Ruth said aghast. 'The scandal would destroy us and our families. We'd never be happy, David, don't you see that? We'd always be ashamed.'

'Ruth, I'm begging you, don't make your mind up at this minute,' David said urgently. 'I know it's a big step, but think about it.'

Ruth swallowed hard. 'I don't need to think about it, David,' she said gravely. 'I know my duty. No matter what has gone before, I have a husband and will soon have his child. My place is here in his house.'

His expression showed anger. 'You never loved me. I see that now. I'm a fool to love you.'

With those bitter words he turned and hurried to the back door. He paused for a moment before opening it, she sensed he wanted to say more. Then he gave a low growl and was gone.

Ruth sank on to a kitchen chair. Her love for him was pitted against her strict Christian upbringing, and her principles had won through. But it was a sad victory, for her heart ached for the kind of love that was absent in her marriage and which only David could provide.

With a sigh Ruth rose to see to the stew simmering on the range fire and at that moment a knock came at the back door again. She rushed to open the door, expecting to see David again.

'David!' she blurted out. 'There's nothing more to say!'

She stopped short, her hand flying to her mouth in dismay to see Mrs Cardew standing on the step.

'Morning, Ruth,' the older woman said familiarly, a mean smile twisting her thin lips.

'What do you want, Mrs Cardew?' Ruth asked, confused. She hadn't spoken to the woman since terminating her employment as Edwin's housekeeper, and wondered what business she could have at the Manse.

'It's a funny thing.' Mrs Cardew paused and then glanced back along the path to the back garden gate. 'I'm sure I saw David Beale leaving a moment ago.' She turned her gaze back to Ruth, her gimlet eyes alight with curiosity. 'What did your old sweetheart want here, I wonder?'

'I beg your pardon!' Aghast, Ruth was on her metal. Mrs Cardew was notorious for her nosiness and her gossip-mongering. She liked nothing better than to stir up mischief. 'What on earth do you mean?'

Mrs Cardew gave a little chuckle. 'Nothing much gets past me, my girl,' she said. 'I saw you two up by Prosser's farm on more than one occasion years ago . . .'

Ruth was furious. 'How dare you suggest . . .' She swallowed hard, trying to regain her composure. 'As you say that was years ago when I was a single girl and we did nothing wrong then. I've nothing to be ashamed of.'

'So you say!' Mrs Cardew sneered. 'I saw you coming out of that old cowshed more than once. Up to no good, I said to myself.'

'You were spying on us!' Ruth gasped. She was startled and suddenly afraid.

'I was doing no such thing.' Mrs Cardew sniffed and tossed her head indignantly. 'Going about my own business I was, getting some extra eggs from the farm.' The older woman gave a mocking smile. 'There'd have been ructions if your parents had found out, eh?'

'You're being impertinent, Mrs Cardew!' Ruth ground her teeth in anger. 'Please leave. You have no business here.'

'I've as much right to call at the Manse to see the pastor as anyone else,' Mrs Cardew said firmly.

'Then why didn't you come to the front door if it was

Mr Allerton you want to see?' Ruth asked sharply. 'No. Instead, you skulk around at the back.'

'I never skulk!' Mrs Cardew looked highly offended. 'If people have shameful things to hide that's not my fault.'

'This is outrageous!'

'Aren't you going to ask me inside?'

'Certainly not!'

'I see. Guilty conscience is it?'

'How dare you,' Ruth flared. 'Pastor Allerton will hear of this.'

'Oh, I don't think you want that, Ruth, not after what I've just seen.'

'There was nothing to see.'

'Well, for one thing, I saw you coming out of Dr Rowlands' surgery earlier, and very pleased you looked with yourself, too.' She gave Ruth an enveloping glance. 'You're in the family way, by the looks of you. I can always read the signs.'

Ruth was flabbergasted and stared at the older woman with her mouth open.

'I'd better come inside,' Mrs Cardew went on. 'We've a bit of business to talk over.'

'We have no business.' Ruth felt her mouth go dry. 'Please leave. Pastor Allerton will be home for his midday meal shortly. He won't be happy to see a visitor.'

'I want my old job back,' Mrs Cardew demanded imperiously, pushing Ruth aside to step into the kitchen. 'I should never have been sacked in the first place. The pastor and I got on very well indeed before you came.'

'Why on earth would I take you back?' Ruth stared helplessly at the other woman standing determinedly in the kitchen. 'You're not trustworthy.'

'I could take offence at that insult, but I won't because I've got the upper hand.' Mrs Cardew gave a smirk. 'The pastor wouldn't be pleased if he knew you've been entertaining the likes of David Beale behind his back. And it's not the first time, I'll be bound.'

Ruth lifted her chin. 'Mr Allerton knew from the beginning that David and I were friends once . . .'

'Friends!' Mrs Cardew laughed. 'That's a polite way of

putting it. He doesn't know about the goings-on in the cowshed.' She gave Ruth a crafty glance. 'What would he believe now if he knew the baker's son has been setting foot over his threshold regularly to see his wife – especially now you're expecting.'

'That's an evil thing to say!' Ruth cried. 'You're a wicked woman, Mrs Cardew!'

'Huh! The pot calling the kettle black.'

'What? Get out!'

'You'd better give me my job back, Ruth,' Mrs Cardew said, her expression grim. 'I'm a poor widow woman. I need the money, but I know how to keep my mouth shut if I'm well paid.'

'Blackmail!' Appalled Ruth put her hand to her mouth.

'Call it what you like,' the older woman said smugly. 'Either I'm reinstated as housekeeper at the Manse, or Pastor Allerton gets to know you've been diverting yourself with David Beale.'

'It's not true. You're making it up for your own ends. You're a monster.'

'You'll pay me two shilling a week more than I was getting before,' Mrs Cardew went on. 'And I keep the scraps.'

'The war may be over, but foodstuffs are still in short supply,' Ruth snapped. 'There won't be scraps.'

'There'll be some leftovers I'll be bound.' Mrs Cardew straightened her shoulders determinedly. 'Now, have you got a place for me here, or do I have to tell what I know?'

'It's all lies!'

Mrs Cardew was silent, her expression smug and Ruth didn't know what more to say. Even though there had been no wrong-doing, she had felt guilty over these last few months for allowing David to enter the kitchen when no one else was in the house.

The gleam in the Mrs Cardew's eyes told her it was no use arguing or even pleading. She would get her own way. Ruth turned her back unwilling for the older woman to read the expression on her face.

'I suppose with the child coming I'll need some help,' she said carefully. 'You're used to the running of the house and the pastor's ways. You can start next Monday.'

'I'll start tomorrow, I think,' Mrs Cardew said firmly. 'And I'll have a week's wages in advance.' She held out her bony hand.

'I have no money,' Ruth said triumphantly. 'Only what the pastor gives me day to day for food. You'll have to wait and get your money from him, although I doubt he'll give you wages in advance.'

Mrs Cardew's lips pinched in frustration. 'All right, but I want that extra two bob a week, mind. You'd better make that right with him or else.'

With a final haughty look and the toss of her head, Mrs Cardew left.

It was almost half an hour later that Edwin made an appearance. Ruth was waiting anxiously for him in the hall. She was still upset over her spat with Mrs Cardew, but tried not to let it show in her face.

'Is luncheon ready, Ruth?' Edwin put his hat on the hall stand and looked at her expectantly.

'It's vegetable stew. I'm about to serve it,' she said.

'What? No meat again?'

'I managed to get a small shoulder of lamb. I intend to serve that at dinner.'

'Huh! These dreadful shortages,' he murmured absently. 'Although, I hear there is food to be had in Swansea, but at a price. When will this government do something?'

He strolled into the dining room, never deigning to eat in the kitchen and Ruth hurried to fetch the tureen of stew. As they sat down at the table together Ruth knew she must tell him straight away about Mrs Cardew.

'Edwin, I've taken the liberty of engaging Mrs Cardew as housekeeper again,' she began. 'I hope you approve.'

He looked up from his meal, brows raised in surprise. 'You hadn't a good word to say for her the other day. Why the change of heart?'

Ruth hesitated, touching her lips with a napkin. She had so looked forward to telling him he was to be a father, but Mrs Cardew's avariciousness had tainted the moment. Her stomach churned to realize that the woman now had some power over her and could cause mischief for her with Edwin at any time.

'I'll need more help about home in the coming months.' She smiled at him. 'You see, Edwin, you're to become a father at last.'

He sat upright in his chair, soup spoon halfway to his lips and stared at her. The look of surprise on his normally expressionless face was all she had hoped for.

'Ruth! Are you telling me you're expecting a child?'

'Yes, Edwin. We're to be parents at last.'

'My dear!' The spoon rattled back on to the plate and he rose hurriedly from his chair and came around the table to her. 'This is stupendous news.'

Ruth rose too, anticipating a warm embrace. Instead he caught her by her shoulders, put a quick kiss on her cheek and then held her away from him, his gaze searching her face.

'You're sure? There's no mistake.'

'Dr Rowlands confirmed it this morning.'

'When is the birth to be?'

'Dr Rowlands says next June,' Ruth said. 'A summer baby, Edwin. Isn't it wonderful?'

'Yes, wonderful!' There was a tremor in his voice. He whirled away to walk quickly in laps around the room. 'I must prepare,' he said as he trod the lacquered boards. 'I'll have the spare room turned into a nursery.'

He turned to her, his face more animated than she had ever seen. 'It will be a boy, of course,' he said. 'A son to carry on the line.'

'It might be a daughter,' Ruth ventured.

He paused for a brief moment and then shook his head. 'No,' he said firmly. 'It's a boy. There are only boys in my family. No girl child has been born to the Allertons for three generations.'

He came towards her and placed her again in her seat.

'Our meal is cooling,' he said almost genially. 'You must take as much sustenance as you can, Ruth, and rest, too. You did a wise thing reengaging Mrs Cardew. How very sensible of you.'

Ruth wetted her lips. 'I promised her two extra shillings a week, Edwin. Was I wrong to do that?'

He sat down again and picked up his spoon. 'No, I think that's fair. We'll rely on her a great deal in these coming months.' He paused and looked at her keenly. 'Ruth, I'm very pleased with you.' He touched his lips with his napkin. 'I must now amend my will.'

'Your will?' Ruth moved uneasily in her chair. 'Must we talk of that? It's so morbid.'

'As a prospective father it's my duty to think of such things, Ruth,' Edwin said. 'My son must be provided for should anything happen to me.'

'But you're young yet, Edwin.'

'We are all in God's hands, Ruth. He may deem to call any one of us at any time. A man with a son must be prepared.'

Ruth and Mrs Cardew were in the kitchen preparing the midday meal two weeks later when the older woman suddenly mentioned David's name.

'Have you heard the latest about David Beale?' Mrs Cardew began. 'I know you're interested in that young man.'

Slicing carrots at that moment, Ruth's hands trembled but she steeled herself not to show any other response and did not answer. Since Mrs Cardew had started work at the Manse she had been under considerable tension which had made her feel quite ill and she was worried for her baby.

'The baker's son has gone to live in Swansea,' Mrs Cardew went on. 'Gone for good, he has.'

This was unexpected news but among her mixed feelings there was a sense of relief. No more clandestine visits and nothing for Mrs Cardew to gossip about.

'Really?' she said in an even tone. Knowing the older woman was concentrating on her face, Ruth was careful to keep her expression neutral. 'By the way, Mrs Cardew, did you manage to get some more potatoes at the grocer's?'

'They're in the pantry,' Mrs Cardew said. 'Talk in the village is that he'll marry his cousin.'

Despite her resolve not to be affected, Ruth felt a pang of disappointment in her breast and chided herself for it. As a married woman she should not still have feelings for him. But they were there still buried deep.

'There's money there, you know, with the Swansea Beales. The girl's step-father owns a prosperous coal merchant's, so I'm told.' Mrs Cardew sniffed disparagingly. 'David's got his head screwed on the right way, hasn't he?'

Ruth rallied. 'There's no time for gossip, Mrs Cardew,' she said sharply. 'The pastor will be here directly.'

'Don't you get on your high horse with me,' the older woman snapped. 'David Beale may be gone, but I know what I know. You remember that!'

Ruth bit back a retort, wondering why Edwin had not mentioned David's departure. It must be a triumph for him to know David was to marry someone else.

The thought of that made her heart ache despite her resolve not to let her feelings get the better of her. David had gone out of her life, but Mrs Cardew was still an ever present threat, and there was nothing she could do about that.

Seven

'It's unwise to get up just yet,' Olive said fussily. 'You gave birth only a week ago, remember. You must stay off your feet another week at least. It's common sense.'

'But I feel fine,' Ruth objected. 'Besides, I'm stifled in bed in this hot weather.'

Olive clicked her tongue disapprovingly. To Ruth's surprise her mother had been very helpful and considerate during the confinement, but was now spending far too much time at the Manse. She had even clashed with Mrs Cardew who showed plainly that she resented interference in the running the house.

Ruth turned back the bedclothes and swung her legs out of bed.

'It's such a lovely day. I want to take my baby son for a walk in his pram.'

Olive threw up her hands. 'Let yourself be seen in public in the middle of your confinement? I've never heard the like!'

'Mam, this is the twentieth century,' Ruth retorted impatiently. 'Those ideas are outdated. Besides, it's time I took control of the household again. Goodness knows what Mrs Cardew has been up to.'

'Mrs Cardew is a good housekeeper,' Olive said albeit grudgingly. 'The place is spotless.'

'Ask her to fetch me some hot water,' Ruth insisted.

She was determined to get up today. It was time she took sole charge of her baby son. Her mother had been very good, but now Ruth wanted him all to herself.

*   *   *

58

When Edwin returned midday he looked surprised to see her dressed and in the sitting room nursing their child. 'You're up. Is this wise, Ruth?'

Ruth stood up and showed the baby off to his father. 'Isn't he beautiful, Edwin?'

He touched the child's head gently, his expression softening.

'He's perfect.' There was pride in his voice. 'My son; God's beneficence.'

'I've pleased you at last then?'

'You've done well, Ruth,' he said.

She was gratified and realized she had not felt so happy since falling in love with David. She quickly smothered that memory. The past must be buried and forgotten. She would revel in what she had now, a beautiful baby son.

'We must decide on a name,' Edwin went on. 'We'll call him Andrew.'

'Andrew is a good strong name,' Ruth agreed with pleasure. 'Whatever made you chose that. Is it a family name?'

Edwin was silent for a moment and when he spoke Ruth thought his voice was breaking with emotion and was surprised at the uncharacteristic show of feeling.

'My younger brother was named Andrew,' he said in a low voice. 'He died tragically many years ago.'

She waited for him to explain but when he remained silent she said: 'Our son should be christened as soon as possible.'

Edwin rallied. 'I'll see to it myself,' he said with alacrity. 'Next Sunday, perhaps.'

Edwin took the child from her and cradled him in his arms.

'You can't know what this means to me, Ruth,' he said, his voice quivering a little. 'My long cherished wish to have a son has come true. My life has some meaning at last.'

Ruth was taken aback. It was on the tip of her tongue to ask why his calling and his faith did not give his life meaning, but she hesitated, fearful of provoking his displeasure just when things were easier between them. But the remark gave her an insight. She was beginning to understand him better.

Ruth watched him stride about the room, the baby in

his arms. Andrew would bring them closer together, she was sure of it. Perhaps love would blossom for them both in time. She yearned for love and prayed it would be so, but at least the love between mother and child was hers. Nothing could take that away, and her heart glowed at the thought.

'Three weeks to Christmas!' Louisa exclaimed excitedly. 'Think of it Ruth, the first Christmas with our babies.'

Her friend had called in for a chat and a gossip as she usually did mid week and Ruth was entertaining her in the sitting room at the Manse. Since both becoming mothers they had grown even closer, and Ruth looked forward to Louisa's visits, when she could relax and be herself.

Louisa balanced her nine months old baby daughter, Rose, on her lap, and laughed. 'Oh! I'm so looking forward to it.'

'So am I.' Ruth felt just as excited. 'I'll make it the best ever.'

Which wouldn't be hard, she reflected. Christmas in her childhood had never been anything special; prayers, hymn singing and attending chapel. The only highlight had ever been the Christmas dinners, because Jacob enjoyed his food. Seasonal gifts were invariably bibles, hymn books or a new coat for Sunday chapel. She had seen how other children were treated and could only envy them. Andrew would never know that. He would never want for anything.

'Would you and Mervyn like to visit us on Boxing Day,' Ruth invited impulsively. 'We could spend the afternoon together; watch the children with their Christmas gifts.'

Louisa looked at her doubtfully. 'What would Edwin say? He doesn't know Mervyn very well, him not being a big chapel goer. Perhaps Edwin wouldn't approve.'

Ruth lifted her chin. 'The Manse is my home as well as his,' she said and then realized that sounded strange. 'I know he'll want to please me,' she said lamely.

'Well, if you're sure, we'd love to come,' Louisa said.

'Good!' Ruth was delighted and began to plan the treat. She would persuade Edwin to give her more housekeeping money than her usual amount to get extra provisions in. It

60

might mean a trip or two into Swansea to visit provisioners and the market there. She would make it a Christmas to remember.

She held Andrew closer to her. 'Oh, Louisa, I can't remember when I've felt happier.'

It was true. Her love for David was still there, but now the love for her child consumed her, outshining everything else. Andrew and his future was all that mattered in her world.

'You don't regret marrying Edwin, then?' Louisa was looking at her keenly. 'I remember you once said you never would marry him.'

'I was young and silly,' Ruth said, feeling the smile on her face stiffen. 'I have a beautiful son. What more could I want?'

On the morning of Christmas Eve, Ruth was in the sitting room busy ticking off items on her lists, feeling pleased with herself.

The goose would be delivered later today. Several hams, two pieces of beef and a large piece of pork, all found at great expense because of continued food shortages, were already stored in the larder. The Christmas cake had been made weeks since, as had the several puddings. Everything was ready for the best Christmas ever.

Ruth looked up as Olive came in tutting in high disapproval.

'I've just been inspecting your larder,' she said. 'The amount of foodstuffs you've stored there is ungodly. It's gluttony, Ruth, a deadly sin. Your father wouldn't approve.'

'Edwin is quite happy with my arrangements,' Ruth answered mildly. 'After all, he can well afford a good Christmas. Louisa and her husband are coming to dinner on Boxing Day . . .' Ruth hesitated. 'I've been meaning to ask you Mam. You know you and Father are very welcome to join us.'

Olive drew in her chin. 'I think not,' she said stiffly. 'Overindulgence and excesses of all kinds are blasphemy at Christmas time. You've been brought up to know better, my girl.'

'Mam, that's nonsense. There's no harm in enjoying yourself.' She wanted to add that she had had little enjoyment in the past, but refrained. 'Besides, Edwin has invited some important guests for dinner on Christmas Day; the minister of Calfaria chapel in Fforestfach and the pastor of Mount Calvary in Manselton. We must show a good table for them.'

'Gluttony!' Olive repeated. 'I counted two hams alone. You'll be serving strong liquor next.'

'Two?' Ruth frowned. 'There should be three hams.'

'Ooh!' Olive was scandalized. 'I'm surprised the pastor allows it.'

Ruth put her lists aside. 'I'd better check the larder myself. I've been leaving too much for Mrs Cardew to see to.'

Ruth was astonished when she had finished her inspection. Several items were missing; beside the ham the smaller piece of beef had also disappeared, together with one of the Christmas puddings she had made.

When Ruth went into the kitchen, followed by Olive, she found Mrs Cardew at the table rolling pastry for the steak and kidney pie Edwin was to have for his midday meal.

'Mrs Cardew, there are foodstuffs missing from my larder,' she burst out. 'Only you could've taken them.'

Mrs Cardew dropped the rolling pin, her cheeks flushing deep red. 'I never did!'

'Ruth!' Olive exclaimed. 'Mrs Cardew is as honest as the day is long. She's a staunch chapel member.'

'Mam, keep out of this,' Ruth snapped. 'You don't know her as I do.' She turned to the housekeeper. 'She took that food all right, and I want an explanation.'

Mrs Cardew's crafty eyes flashed a warning. 'Don't you go accusing me of thievery. I'm not the guilty one around here, remember. You should watch what you're saying. People in glass houses shouldn't throw stones.'

'What's she getting at?' Olive asked.

'Never mind, Mam,' Ruth said hastily. 'Leave this to me. Go and see to Andrew.'

Olive left reluctantly and Ruth turned on Mrs Cardew.

'I've had enough of you and your empty threats,' she said angrily. 'You're a thoroughly dishonest woman, Mrs Cardew, and I suspect you've been robbing Mr Allerton's larder for years.'

'Slander! That's what it is,' the older woman shouted. 'You'd better not insult me again otherwise you'll be very sorry.'

'Not as sorry as I'll be if I let you stay. You're sacked, Mrs Cardew, as from now.'

'You can't sack me. I know too much.'

'Get your hat and coat and go now,' Ruth responded furiously. 'And I want to look in your basket before you leave here too.'

'But it's Christmas!' Mrs Cardew exclaimed. 'You can't sack me at Christmas. It's not Christian.'

'Thievery and blackmail are not Christian either,' Ruth said. 'Don't worry, you'll get what wages that are coming to you next week. I don't want to see your face here again. Now go!'

Mrs Cardew's face creased into an expression of malice.

'You'll be very sorry for this, believe me. There'll be no happy Christmas Day for you.'

'Get out!' Ruth shouted. 'I've had enough of your threats.'

Mrs Cardew snatched at her hat and coat behind the back door, her eyes sparking as she glared at Ruth.

'Before tomorrow dawns the wrath of hell will be down on you for this. I'll see to it that you're shown up for the harlot that you are. You and that brat of yours will be out on the street.'

Mouth gaping in shock Ruth stared speechless at the woman as with one final glance of spite Mrs Cardew threw open the back door and stomped out.

Eight

Christmas Eve, 1919

The chapel was full for the midnight service and when the last hymn was finished and the last prayer intoned Edwin stood in the pulpit a moment longer surveying the congregation.

Even though it was half past midnight most people were hanging back from leaving and were exchanging seasonal greetings and invitations with neighbours and friends. Watching them Edwin envied their easy exuberance. They had no need to check every mood and feeling in case they lost control.

He felt a sudden wrench of his heart strings as he remembered that Christmas so many years ago, when his brother Andrew had died aged only seven years. And it had been his fault.

Standing there in the pulpit Edwin once again felt bitter grief and a wretched sense of guilt grip him; the guilt that was never far from his conscious mind and acted as his bridle.

Unable to keep control of his temper in his childhood years his unbridled fury at his younger brother had caused the accident on that terrible day. Escaping Edwin's onslaught Andrew had lost his balance and tumbled down the staircase at their home, to fall in a heap at the bottom, neck broken.

His father never spoke to him again from that day onward until his death and his final words had been a rebuke. As if Andrew's death had not been enough, their mother died two years later of a broken heart, it was said. Edwin saw his loss as a punishment and a warning. From that time, through his teenage years into manhood, Edwin exerted an iron control over his emotions, even to the extent that he denied he had any feelings at all. Now his control was second nature.

It was only at the birth of his son that he allowed love to come through. Andrew's birth seemed to repay in some measure his debt to his brother. His heart swelled with joy at the thought of his child, and at the coming few days of celebration when he could lavish love and attention on his son.

'Happy Christmas, Pastor.'

A cheery call from someone in the congregation brought Edwin back from reverie. With a return wave he climbed down from the pulpit and walked to the chapel door to shake hands with as many worshippers as possible as the congregation filed out.

Edwin stood patiently as each one shook hands. The last worshipper to leave was a surprise.

'Mrs Cardew! I'd have thought the midnight service would be too late for you to be abroad and in this cold weather, too?'

'So it is, Pastor,' Mrs Cardew said. 'But I wanted to have a word with you away from the Manse.'

Edwin frowned. There was nothing Mrs Cardew would want to discuss with him except her wages, but the early hours of Christmas Day seemed an inappropriate time to pursue such matters. He longed to get home to kiss his son goodnight before retiring to bed and he felt a sense of irritation, which he quickly smothered.

'Surely my wife has paid you, Mrs Cardew.'

'She's sacked me that's what she's done,' Mrs Cardew said surprisingly, her tone waspish. 'Sacked me on the spot and at Christmas time too.'

'But why?' Edwin was perplexed.

'Because she doesn't want me anywhere near the Manse,' the woman said. 'I know too much. I see what's going on.'

'What are you talking about, Mrs Cardew?' Edwin felt the chill December wind pierce the material of his jacket and shivered involuntarily. 'I'm sure you've misunderstood my wife.'

'Oh no I haven't.' Mrs Cardew shook her head vigorously. 'She ordered me out on a trumped up charge of stealing.' She sniffed and lifted her chin defiantly. 'I've never stolen a crumb in my life.'

Edwin shivered again. 'Mrs Cardew, this is hardly the time or place to be discussing domestic matters . . .'

'I'm trying to do the Christian thing,' Mrs Cardew interrupted him sharply. She glanced about her as though wishing not to be overheard although they were completely alone on the windswept steps of the chapel.

'Mrs Cardew . . .'

'It's my Christian duty to warn you, Pastor.' She peered up at him. 'It's about your wife and the baker's son. You ought to know what's going on under your very nose.'

'What?'

'It's a disgrace, that's what it is,' she rushed on. 'Them carrying on like they have been doing since he came back from the dead and under your own roof too.'

'David Beale has been at the Manse?'

Mrs Cardew nodded. 'I've seen him going secretly in the back way on more than one occasion when you were on your pastoral rounds. Them, alone in the house together.'

Edwin lifted a hand to his head, feeling suddenly dizzy.

'It's been going on for months.' Mrs Cardew's words bore into his head like a drill hammer. 'And then all of a sudden she's in the family way.'

'Oh my God!' Edwin backed away from her, stumbling down the steps. 'I've been betrayed!'

'Oh, you have, Pastor, and wickedly, too.' Mrs Cardew came down the steps to him. 'What are you going to do?' Her voice was filled with excitement.

Edwin edged away from her, putting both his hands to his head. He felt disorientated, as though in some nightmare. He had never consciously acknowledged it, but his one deep-seated dread had always been that as punishment for his brother's death God would never allow him to sire a child. The idea had haunted him all his adult life. At Andrew's birth he had rejoiced that his fear was unfounded. But now it came back in full force. The child he had loved so deeply

66

as his own over these last six months was the progeny of another man. Ruth had betrayed him, humiliated him.

Edwin stood at the chapel gates. The cold wind did not touch him now. He was boiling hot with rage and anguish. Ruth had taken his new found happiness away from him; his future was bleak and empty. She was a Jezebel and she would pay dearly. So would her bastard child.

He walked swiftly towards the Manse, only vaguely aware of Mrs Cardew trotting along at his side.

'About me being sacked, Pastor,' she twittered. 'I can come back to my work after Christmas, can't I?'

Edwin whirled around to face her. 'No, you can't,' he howled in his fury. 'Be gone from my sight, woman.'

He strode on.

'But it's not my fault your wife is a harlot,' Mrs Cardew squealed behind him. It was as though the Devil were laughing behind his back.

Edwin turned in to the carriageway of the Manse, striding to the front door to let himself in. The gaslight was still on in the hall, awaiting his return from the service.

The house was in silence, Ruth having gone to bed. Sandwiches and ale would be waiting for him in the dining room as a snack before retiring to bed, but this night Edwin went straight to the staircase taking the steps two at a time and hurried across the landing to their bedroom. He flung the door open and strode in.

The gaslight was turned low. Ruth was asleep. At the sight of her slim form laying there he thought of David Beale taking his pleasure of her, perhaps in this very bed; their bed.

Towering rage like flowing molten lava, searing, scorching consumed him and exploded like an uncontrollable volcano in his breast. He strode forward and wrenched the bedclothes away from her.

'Wake up!' he shouted. 'Wake up, you Jezebel and face my wrath.'

Ruth opened her eyes and sat up, staring around her and then up at him. 'Edwin! What's happening?'

'You adulteress!' Edwin stormed in a thundering voice. 'Did you think I wouldn't find out?'

'What are you talking about?'

'You thought to deceive me into believing that Andrew was my son,' Edwin accused. 'But now I discover he's the son of your lover, David Beale.'

'No, Edwin,' Ruth cried out. 'Who's been telling you these awful lies?' She shook her head vehemently. 'It's not true.'

Unconvinced at her protests, he could hardly bear to look at her. 'My eyes have been opened to your vileness; your baseness,' he roared on. 'You've deprived me of my son, you harlot!'

'Andrew is your son, Edwin,' Ruth tried to struggle off the bed. 'I'll swear on the Bible if you like. He *is* your son.'

'Silence! No more lies.'

Again he had a mental picture of David Beale and Ruth writhing together in this bed. A red mist seemed to envelope him while one thought pierced through his anguished mind. Ruth must be punished for inflicting such torment on him.

'Beale took what was mine by right, mine alone,' he shouted. 'I demand my conjugal rights, woman. You'll submit to me, now this minute.'

He pushed her back on to the bed and threw himself on top of her.

'Edwin! For God's sake! Don't do this.'

Her struggles enraged him even more, and he felt savagery in his heart. With his open hand he struck at her face.

'I'll take you for the harlot that you are.'

Andrew was grizzling. The familiar sound brought Ruth to sudden awareness from a fitful dozing, and as she tried to move she found her body was stiff and aching in every joint from being curled up in a chair for hours in the chilled air.

She rose with difficulty and going to Andrew's cot, lifted him up into her arms. He was fretful. She had disturbed his slumbers when she had finally escaped from Edwin in the early hours, to find refuge in the nursery.

She was still horrified at what had happened. Edwin, her husband, had taken her by savage force against her will. She

68

could hardly believe it of him. He had gone mad. That was the only explanation.

She glanced at the chair-back wedged under the knob of the nursery door. She'd been so appalled and frightened at his violence she believed he might attack her again. Even now she did not feel safe.

Andrew whimpered. He was hungry and wet too. She must see to his needs immediately. That meant leaving the comparative safety of the nursery and venturing down to the kitchen.

The clock on the mantelpiece said half past seven. There was worship at the chapel this Christmas morning where Edwin should be officiating, but where was he now? She was afraid to face him again, uncertain at what he might do.

A sob caught in her throat. She had planned this Christmas day so eagerly, expecting it to be the happiest she had ever known, but now it was a nightmare.

Andrew struggled in her arms, crying in his misery. She must see to him. Ruth removed the chair-back from the door, and easing it open, listened. The house was quiet.

Their bedroom was next door, the door was standing ajar. Her heart in her throat, Ruth cautiously put her head around it. To her relief the room was empty.

Putting Andrew safely on the bed she looked in the mirror. An ugly bruise darkened her left cheekbone where Edwin had struck her. At the memory of the blow she relived those awful minutes when he had savagely forced himself on her, and felt nausea. She could never forget or forgive him for what he had done.

Rallying, Ruth dressed quickly and then carrying Andrew went quietly downstairs. The study door was open and she glanced in as she was about to pass on her way to the kitchen. Edwin was inside slumped in a chair asleep, still dressed as he had been the night before.

Ruth moved quietly on to the kitchen. She bathed Andrew in the stone sink, found a clean nappy, dressed him and set about preparing his breakfast rusks. When he had been fed she took him back to the nursery and placed him in his cot.

Ruth sat on the chair, clasping her hands tightly together. What should she do now? How could she stay with Edwin after what he had done; after his monstrous accusation? She would take Andrew and go to her parents' home. They must believe her when they saw the bruising and how distressed she was.

Now that she had a plan she felt her courage return. She would face Edwin and voice her disgust at the way he had treated her, and once again she would declare her innocence of the charges he had brought against her. It dawned on her that Andrew's future was at stake. If Edwin persisted in believing these lies about her he would disown the child and Andrew would lose his birthright.

Gathering her courage, Ruth went determinedly downstairs to the study. Edwin was just stirring, sitting upright in the chair. Ruth stood in the doorway. Throughout their marriage she had felt no enmity towards him; he had given her no cause, but now watching him she felt intense dislike, bordering on hatred, knowing what he was capable of.

'I'm surprised you're not down on your knees, asking for God's pardon,' she burst out. 'You should certainly beg my forgiveness.'

He rose from the chair at the sound of her voice and turned to look at her. His expression was cold and without emotion – there was no sign of the violence of the night before. His glance went to the bruising on her cheek and then he looked away.

'Yes, this is your handiwork,' Ruth said bitterly. 'You took me by force. How could you, you so-called man of God?'

'I took what was mine by law.'

'You raped me, your own wife. That a coward's way. You're despicable!'

'It was not rape!' Momentarily there was rage in his eyes, but it died almost as quickly as it ignited. 'I have every right to your body. You left me no choice.'

Ruth was speechless at his self-deception.

'I have a service to conduct at the chapel,' he went on coldly. 'I'll need breakfast served immediately.'

'What?' Ruth was astounded that he believed life could go on as before. 'You expect me to run your house as before after the abominable way you mistreated me?'

'It's your duty, Ruth.'

She stared at him. 'Duty? What about your duty to your calling and this parish? How can you in all good conscience walk into the house of God and stand before a congregation preaching the scriptures after what you did? You hypocrite!'

'Silence! You, a fallen woman, are hardly in a position to criticize me.' He put on his jacket. 'Besides,' he went on. 'There's not a self-respecting man in this village, including your father, who would blame me for my actions after discovering his wife is a harlot.'

'It's untrue, I tell you!' Ruth exploded. 'And since you refuse to believe me, your own wife, I'll not stay here in this house with you an hour longer. I'll take Andrew and go to my parents' home.'

'You'll do no such thing! You'll stay here and do as I command.' He stared at her, his glance vindictive. 'Mrs Cardew is already spreading her gossip. I'll not have it confirmed by you leaving me.'

So, she had Mrs Cardew to thank for this.

'You can't mean we're both to stay under this roof, Andrew and me?' she said. 'I'm surprised you don't want to be rid of us immediately if you're so sure I've betrayed you. Why don't you throw me out?'

'Because I intend to punish you myself.'

'What?'

He took a step towards her, his eyes flashing in a feverish way and Ruth flinched, her fear returning to realize that his apparent calmness was merely a façade. Violence was still there just beneath the surface.

'It's God's will that you be punished for your sins and I am God's instrument.'

'You're insane!' Ruth backed away into the hall.

'Your child is an abomination!' Edwin thundered advancing on her. 'And God has charged me with the task of smiting it; smiting it from the face of the earth!'

'Edwin! What are you saying?' Ruth was terrified by his tone and expression as much as his awful words. 'Andrew is your own son. You must believe me.'

71

'No, he's the spawn of the Devil himself,' Edwin ranted. 'He must be destroyed. It's God's command to me.'

'You're unhinged!' Ruth screamed. She backed away. 'I'm going to my father's house immediately.'

'He'll not take you in nor your Devil's brat,' Edwin declared triumphantly. 'When he learns of your degradation he'll cast you off. You have no money, nothing. You'd both starve.'

She knew what he said was only too true. Edwin, as their pastor, could very easily turn her parents against her.

'Edwin, this is madness,' Ruth cried. She had to try to pacify him somehow. 'How can you believe Mrs Cardew above me?'

'She's been loyal to me for years.'

'But I'm your wife,' Ruth burst out angrily. 'While Mrs Cardew is a thief and a liar!'

'Why would she cause mischief for no reason?'

'There is a reason. I sacked her for stealing food,' Ruth said. 'She's been robbing you for years. She's told you these lies to spite me.'

'Ruth, you admitted to me that you love David Beale.'

She shook her head.

'David and I love . . . loved each other, but we were never lovers as you mean it, not in the past or now.' She took a tentative step towards him, reaching out a hand to touch his chest in a desperate appeal. 'Please listen, Edwin. Andrew is your son; your flesh and blood. I'm a faithful wife, I swear it.'

'Don't try your harlot's wiles on me, woman,' Edwin stormed, moving back, his eyes glowing with a kind of madness. 'I was a fool to believe I would ever be allowed to find happiness after . . .'

Ruth was puzzled. 'After what? What're you talking about?'

'Be quiet!' He seemed to regain control momentarily and moved away from her. 'Get me my breakfast now,' he commanded. 'I'll decide how you'll be punished after I return from chapel. In the meantime, there'll be no celebration of Christmas for you.'

'But your friends are coming to dine . . .'

'I've sent word that there is illness in the house.'

Ruth shook her head. 'But all the food I've bought . . .'

'I'll distribute it to the poorer families in the parish this afternoon.'

She should feel upset by this, but Ruth found she wasn't. Christmas was ruined so it didn't matter. She was glad someone might have some joy out of the provisions she had bought. There could be no joy for her or Andrew.

'I'll visit my parents, give them my greetings,' Ruth said defiantly.

She intended to tell her mother exactly how Edwin had mistreated her. Olive would not want to hear anything against her pastor perhaps, but Ruth was determined to expose him as an abuser and Mrs Cardew for the liar that she was.

'No! You're not to leave this house.'

'What? But that's absurd!' Ruth exclaimed. 'They'll expect a visit from Andrew on Christmas morning and they'll wonder why we weren't in chapel.'

'I'll give them your excuses.'

'No, I want to see them myself. You're afraid I'll expose you after what you did,' she said, giving him a meaningful look. 'But you can't keep me from speaking to them.'

'I did nothing wrong!' Edwin exclaimed angrily. 'You're the adulteress. You'll remain locked in the nursery while I'm out.'

'I will not!' Ruth flared. 'How dare you try to confine us? It beggars belief.'

'Don't defy me, Ruth,' Edwin said in a heavy warning tone. 'Now get upstairs out of my sight.'

Afraid that he might turn violent again, Ruth did as she was told.

She did not know there was a key to the nursery door and when she heard it turn in the lock her heart sank. She sat on the chair again, her head in her hands. How could she make Edwin understand that Mrs Cardew was lying for her own ends? It was almost as if he wanted to believe she had been unfaithful. But what frightened her most was his threat against Andrew. Surely he did not mean to do the child actual harm?

It seemed an eternity before she heard him return, but he did not come up to the nursery to let her out. Andrew was grizzling again probably hungry and so was she, as she had had no breakfast.

In anger at the extreme treatment of herself and Andrew Ruth pounded her fists against the panelling of the door, and shouted. Finally she heard his feet on the staircase and he unlocked the door.

'How dare you treat me and your son like this? It's cruelty, that's what it is,' she burst out as he opened the door. 'You have no right to keep us prisoners.'

'I'm your husband and this is my house. I can do as I please,' he told her.

She was wary of his coldness. She had seen how quickly it would turn to uncontrollable rage.

'I have every justification to punish you any way I see fit,' he went on.

'I'm innocent of any wrong-doing,' Ruth said desperately. 'I can't go on like this, Edwin.'

'You have no choice.'

'But Louisa and her husband are coming to visit Boxing Day,' she reminded him. 'What am I to do?'

'I spoke to them after chapel,' Edwin said. 'I told them we wouldn't be receiving guests.'

'But Louisa must have wondered why Andrew and I were not at chapel.' Jacob and Olive Williams must have wondered at it, too. 'Did my parents ask after me?'

Edwin turned away without answering her question. 'It's midday,' he said, his back turned to her as he left the room. 'I expect some sustenance provided for me. That's your duty.'

For the rest of the day, apart from meal times, Edwin stayed closeted in his study. Ruth had the freedom of the house, although she found that the front and back doors were locked and the keys not to be found.

At the usual time, Ruth put Andrew to sleep in his cot, and then busied herself making up a bed in a bedroom further down the passage. There was no point in remaining up any longer, so as soon as the bed was ready, she undressed and slipped between the sheets. But what with worrying over her situation and listening for any cry from Andrew she could find no sleep.

The clock in the hall chimed ten and then she heard Edwin's tread on the stairs. There was silence for a few minutes as he went into their bedroom and then she heard his shout down the passage.

'Ruth! Where are you?'

A great fear swept over her. She sat up in bed her hand over her mouth, as she waited tensely. Within minutes he was at her door and threw it wide open sending it crashing against the chest of drawers.

'You can't hide from me, you whore,' he shouted at her. 'Get to our bedroom where you belong.'

Frightened, Ruth cringed back at the sight of his face white with anger. He was shaking and sweating as though with ague, while his gaze was feverish, too. The change in him from a man who never showed his feelings to this threatening figure of simmering emotion, was stark, and Ruth felt her fright mount to terror.

'No, Edwin,' Ruth cried out. 'I refuse to share a bed with you ever again.'

He strode forward and leaning over grasped her arm roughly.

'You'll submit to me as you always have or that bastard brat of yours will suffer for it by my hand.'

'Edwin!' Ruth cried out appalled. 'You don't know what you're saying. How could you hurt your own son?'

'He's not my son!' He dragged her from the bed and hustled her roughly from the room. 'He's a vile thing spawned in sin and foulness,' he shouted. 'The brat is an affront to God and he's an affront to me and I will rid myself of him.'

Ruth stumbled along the passage in Edwin's tight grasp. When they reached their bedroom he threw her unceremoniously on the bed.

'I demand my conjugal rights, Ruth,' he said. 'Now submit willingly or I will take what's mine again and again until you do.'

'Oh, God have mercy!'

'God has no mercy for me or you, Ruth,' Edwin rasped as he mounted the bed and forced her down. 'We have both offended His laws.'

'I don't know what you mean, Edwin,' Ruth uttered the words, appalled at what must come next. 'I've done nothing wrong. My conscience is clear.'

'You are a fornicator and I am already responsible for one innocent life lost,' he said harshly. 'It's justice that I rid the world of the abomination you and Beale created between you.'

He threw himself on top of her.

'No, let me be!' Ruth shrieked, and struggled wildly. This could not be happening again. She could not let it happen.

'Don't struggle,' he warned in a harsh voice. 'Or I'll go at once to the nursery. A pillow over the bastard's face will take no effort.'

Terrified at his words Ruth stopped struggling immediately.

'Edwin, that's murder,' she whimpered. 'You would murder your own child? You're insane!'

'I'm God's instrument of justice. Now will you submit?'

Ruth let out a sob of wretchedness. He gave her no choice.

Nine

The Sunday After Christmas

Ruth woke early on Sunday morning, wretched in mind and body. Edwin was not in the bed beside her and in sudden mind-numbing dread she raced to the nursery.

Andrew was in his cot, already awake, kicking his legs happily. He gurgled at the sight of her face as she bent over him. She picked him up and held him tightly against her, offering prayers of thankfulness for his safety. She also chided herself. How could she have slept when her child was in danger?

She heard a step behind her and whirled to face the door. Edwin stood there, already shaved and dressed.

'You and the child will attend the service at the chapel this morning,' he announced in a tone that brooked no argument, although Ruth had no intention of objecting.

'I'm glad you're being reasonable at last,' she said tartly. 'But I warn you, Edwin, I doubt I'll be returning to your house afterwards.'

He regarded her steadily. 'We'll see.'

'Why this sudden change of heart?'

'After worship on Boxing Day evening I noticed a change in attitudes towards me,' he said, an angry edge to his voice. 'Parishioners I have known for years could hardly look me in the eye as I shook hands with them after the service.'

Ruth's lip curled disdainfully. 'Mrs Cardew has been at work spreading her lies,' she said. 'Why can't you see her for what she is, Edwin? She's your enemy as well as mine.'

'The looks I did receive were ones of pity,' Edwin snarled. 'I will not be pitied! Everyone knows your shame, Ruth.

There's nothing for it, but that you show your face in public. This humiliation must be dealt with.'

The morning worship began at half past ten. Edwin went on to the chapel beforehand as usual. Ruth bathed and dressed Andrew and then got ready herself. Putting him in his pram she walked down the main road through the village to Soar Chapel. Other villagers were also making their way, but no one acknowledged her as they usually did, and Ruth began to worry that her parents had also heard Mrs Cardew's gossip. She wanted to curse the woman for her spite and enmity.

Ruth left the pram outside the chapel and carried Andrew inside. The chapel was full to capacity. The general hum of many voices in conversation ceased as she made her way down the aisle, making her feel conspicuous and very uncomfortable.

She saw her parents sitting several pews back. Normally they joined her in the front, for as the pastor's wife she and her family had precedence. She tried to attract their attention, but they stubbornly kept their heads turned away. So today Ruth sat alone.

The silence in the chapel was complete as Edwin made an appearance from a side room. He seemed an even more solemn figure today in his black suit as he leisurely mounted to the pulpit and then faced the congregation, to utter the hymn number that was to be sung. There was a rustle of paper as people sought the correct page in their hymn books even though they probably knew the words off by heart.

Mr Ferris, the chapel organist, struck up the opening chords and the congregation rose to their feet and loosed their voices in worship. Ruth did the same, holding Andrew in the crook of one arm and grasping her hymn book with the other hand. In giving voice she felt some relief from the misery she had suffered over the last few days. She would make the most of her freedom today and was determined not to return to the Manse. Andrew must be protected.

The hymn was finished and the congregation sat. Edwin stood in the pulpit, his head bowed and there was general shuffling of feet and coughing as the congregation waited.

Edwin raised his head. 'Today,' he intoned in that ringing

voice of his. 'I cannot go on with the service as usual. Instead I have a grave task to perform.'

There were gasps and whispers around the chapel. Edwin raised a hand and there was silence again. Ruth felt a dreadful foreboding as she looked up at the hardened planes of his face.

'I am commanded by the Lord God to expose an abomination. We have an adulteress in our midst.'

Ruth was terrified at his words. 'Edwin, what are you doing?' she called out to him.

'Yes, my friends it is true.' He carried on as if she had not spoken. 'And it is a matter of great sorrow for me, for that foul adulteress, that wretched sinner, is none other than my own wife, Ruth.'

'No!' Ruth cried out into the silence of a stunned congregation. 'None of this is true!'

She stared up at Edwin. His gaze was on her, cold and unfeeling and she felt a fearful chill rise throughout her body at the awful denunciation. She wanted to run from the chapel but could not move; it was as if she was turned to stone.

'As I expose her,' he went on in a censorious tone. 'I must also denounce the man who is as guilty as she in this dreadful sin of adultery and fornication.'

'Edwin, for God's sake don't do this. It's wrong and unjust.'

Edwin ignored her and looked out over the silent people in the chapel. 'The blameworthy man is David Beale of this parish.'

There was an anguished cry from someone in the congregation and Ruth guessed it was David's mother. She glared up at Edwin. How could he be so cruel? Anger rose in her breast and she hurriedly sprang to her feet and swung around to face the people gathered, Andrew in her arms. The usual familiar faces of family, friends and acquaintances stared back at her.

'It's all lies I tell you!' she cried out passionately. 'You must believe me. I'm innocent. David is innocent.'

'The pastor would hardly lie,' someone said from the congregation and Ruth saw Mrs Cardew sitting a few pews back, smirking at her.

'No, but *you* did, you witch,' Ruth shouted at her angrily. She lifted a hand and pointed a finger at her enemy. 'Mrs Cardew there is the author of this monstrous lie.' Ruth went on in echoing tones. 'She's done this vicious thing because I caught her stealing and sacked her.'

'Liar yourself!' screeched Mrs Cardew rising to her feet. 'The baker's son has been visiting her at the Manse. I saw them! We all know what that means.'

'Uttering untruths in the house of God,' Ruth shouted back furiously. 'Aren't you afraid to be struck down dead?'

'Silence!' Edwin roared. 'Sit down both of you.'

Stubbornly, Ruth remained on her feet and turned to face the pulpit. To run from the chapel now would be like admitting that the charge was true.

'I am falsely accused,' she cried out to Edwin in the silence of the chapel, clutching Andrew to her. 'You, my own husband, have humiliated me in front of the whole village. I'm innocent of any wrong doing, and so is David Beale.'

Edwin's face clouded and he pointed a finger at her. 'You stand brazenly there holding Beale's bastard son in your arms and deny it? Oh, worthless woman, you are without shame or self-respect.'

'Andrew is your son,' Ruth called out desperately. 'Edwin, how could you brand your own child in this way?'

Edwin's gaze swept around the silent congregation.

'My friends, you have seen with your own eyes the degradation into which my wife is downcast,' he said lifting up both his arms as though pleading with them. 'I ask you, in the name of the Lord, to shun this woman and her illegitimate child. Let her family and friends have nothing more to do with her from this moment on.'

'You can't do this to me, Edwin!' Ruth shrieked. 'It's inhuman. Man of God! Where is your Christianity?'

'My Christianity will be shown by the fact that I'll not put you out on to the streets to starve as you deserve,' Edwin replied magnanimously. 'You and your child will remain under the roof of the Manse, but in excommunication, not only of worship but of daily village life. That is my edict as pastor of this parish.'

There were murmurings and excited chatter among the congregation and Edwin lifted his gaze to them again. 'Please let every one of you depart now; go your separate ways and remember my diktat.'

She had to get outside in the fresh air. Carrying Andrew, Ruth hastily left the pew and ran down the aisle to the door. She could not help the tears that flooded her eyes. Never in her life would she have believed such a humiliating thing could happen to her. And to have her child publicly ruined was the worst thing of all. She could live through being shunned, but Andrew's whole future was destroyed.

Ruth hurried away from the chapel as quickly as she could and not knowing what else to do went straight away to her parents' cottage to await their return. She must convince her father of her innocence and he must intercede with Edwin on her behalf. The damage that had been done must be put right.

She was holding Andrew in her arms when her parents finally arrived home. They stopped in their tracks and both looked disconcerted to see her.

'What are you doing here, Ruth?' Olive asked sharply.

'Olive!' Jacob rebuked. 'She is shunned.'

'Yes, and I want to know what she's doing here,' Olive insisted. 'Hasn't she brought enough disgrace without forcing her presence on us like this? The whole village will be against us.'

'You must both listen to me,' Ruth exclaimed in desperation. 'I am innocent of these charges.'

'Huh!'

'Mam, I tell you I've done no wrong,' Ruth declared heatedly. 'Father must go and speak to Edwin this minute; make him understand that Mrs Cardew has been lying to him.'

Her father strode past her without a word and putting the key in the lock opened the door and went inside. 'Olive! Leave her,' he said curtly.

Ruth caught at her mother's arm as she was about to follow him.

'Mam, please listen to me. You don't have to speak. Edwin is out of his head with hatred at these lies. He . . .' She could

81

hardly find the words to tell her what happened. 'He raped me in the early hours of Christmas morning,' she said in a lowered voice.

Olive paused and looked at her, her brows raised. 'You're his wife,' she said. 'He has every right.'

'He has no right to do that,' Ruth burst out. 'I can never forgive him for it and I won't return to the Manse.'

'Then you'll be on the streets,' Olive said. 'You being shunned has caused your father such mortification.' She shook her head. 'There's no place for you here, not after that.'

'And my son, is he to go on the street?' asked Ruth. 'I know you love Andrew. Surely that hasn't changed.'

'It's no good,' Olive said flatly. 'I know your father wouldn't hear of it. We can do nothing for either of you.'

'If my own parents won't help me, who will?' Ruth cried out.

'Go back to the Manse,' Olive said firmly. 'You're lucky the pastor takes his Christian duty seriously. Any other man would put you out without a second's thought.'

'What about my father's Christian duty to his own child?' Ruth asked. 'He forced me to marry Edwin. I did as he wished and now when I'm in need he turns his back on me.'

Olive gave a sigh of impatience. 'Jacob has had a severe blow today. As deacon his self-esteem has been dented. He may be asked to stand down; a great humiliation for him and you are the cause of it.'

'No! Mrs Cardew's spiteful mischief-making is the cause of it,' Ruth said angrily. 'I find it hard to bear that my family believe an outsider over me.'

'You made no bones about your feelings for David Beale in the past,' Olive said huffily. 'You've always been a wilful girl; never prepared to submit to your father's authority. Nothing you do surprises me.'

Ruth ground her teeth in anger. 'Christian charity begins at home, but I've seen little of it,' she burst out. 'If I had money I'd leave this village for good. You'd never see me or Andrew again.'

Olive blinked. 'Perhaps it would be better if you did go,'

she said stiffly. 'You're shunned and therefore dead to the rest of us.'

'Ooh!' Ruth stepped back feeling as though her mother had struck her across the face. 'How could you say that to your own daughter?'

Olive sniffed and tossed her head before turning and entering the cottage to slam the door closed.

Stunned, Ruth stood like a statue outside for a moment. They had washed their hands of her. There was no one else she could turn to for help. She had told Edwin she would never return to the Manse, but now she must for there was nowhere else to go, and even though Andrew was in danger there they needed a roof over their heads.

She put him in the pram and with heavy steps made her way back to the only home she had.

Edwin was standing before the fireplace in the sitting room when she walked in, carrying Andrew. He glared at her, his face tense.

'Where have you been?'

'My parents' home.'

'They ignored my edict?'

Ruth sat down on a chair nearby feeling exhausted. 'No,' she said dully. 'They would have nothing to do with me.'

He seemed to relax a little. 'As it should be,' he said with some satisfaction. 'You are a tarnished soul, Ruth. There's no hope for you.'

Ruth compressed her lips. 'I'm sick of your sermonizing and false piety, Edwin,' she said heatedly. 'I told my mother what you did to me.'

He looked startled for a moment, and Ruth felt pleased.

'I'll deny everything,' he said.

'Oh, you've no need to worry,' Ruth replied bitterly. 'My mother is of the same narrow opinion as you. I'm your wife, so you may treat me like a street woman if you wish it.'

He looked angry. 'You brought it upon yourself by your adultery with Beale.'

Ruth rose to her feet. 'Pass me a Bible, Edwin and I'll gladly swear my innocence on it.'

'I'll have none of that blasphemy!' he said. 'You are an adulteress – your word is valueless.'

Ruth sat down again in silence, feeling weary with the misery of the last few days. She had little energy or hope left to fight with.

'You're free to go about as you will,' Edwin said. 'But you will be spurned by all. Understand this; I do not consider shunning sufficient punishment for your sins. You have taken my child away from me, Ruth. I intend to take yours.'

She jumped to her feet in alarm. 'What do you mean, Edwin?'

He turned his back on her. 'I can't bear to set eyes on the child. God has given me licence to do with him as I see fit. I'll cast out this vile thing. You'll never see him again. That will be your punishment.'

'Cast him out?' Ruth cried, holding Andrew closer. 'What in God's name do you mean? What're you going to do, Edwin?'

He turned to look at her with a stony gaze. 'I believed God had given me a child as forgiveness for . . .' He hesitated, swallowing hard. 'Instead,' he went on in a low voice, 'the only happiness I've ever known was snatched from me by your evil-doing. This child of yours was not meant to be. There is no place for him – anywhere.'

'Listen to yourself, Edwin,' Ruth sobbed out. 'You're insane! You can't harm Andrew and not pay for it. God has not commanded this. It's your own thirst for revenge.'

'It's God's law, I tell you!' Edwin thundered.

'And what about Man's law?' Ruth howled. 'They hang men for murder.'

'God will protect me,' Edwin said with certainty and she knew he truly believed what he said.

Ruth spent the remaining hours of the day in constant fear, Andrew always just an arm's length away from her. When night came Edwin insisted that she share his bed and she complied with his demands for fear of his wrath against her child.

Monday morning, when she thought her father would have left for his shop, she went again to see Olive, though doubting she would get a hearing. Olive opened the door and tutted impatiently at the sight of her with Andrew in her arms.

'Mam, listen please,' Ruth pleaded desperately. 'You must help me. No, no, not for me,' she went on hastily as her mother shook her head and began to close the door. 'Edwin is threatening Andrew's life! He's insane.'

Olive opened the door wider then and came out on to the step to stare at her.

'Wicked lies!' she said in a shocked voice. 'The pastor wouldn't do anything like that. He's a godly man. You should be ashamed, Ruth, maligning the man you've cruelly betrayed.'

'He's uttered threats, I tell you,' Ruth said. 'There's no mistake at what he means to do. He's out of his mind.' She held out her child. 'Mam, please take Andrew in. He's just an innocent baby in all this. Keep him safe and I promise I'll never bother you again.'

Olive hesitated, her face softening as she looked at Andrew, and Ruth's spirits rose.

'Please, Mam.'

'Who's at the door, Olive?'

Ruth was startled to hear her father's voice and the next moment he came into the passage. His expression turned thunderous when he saw her. Grasping Olive's arm he pulled her inside and with one final angry glance at Ruth he slammed the door in her face.

Holding Andrew close, Ruth turned away, a lump in her throat and her heart heavy not only with misery at what she must do to save her son, but also with disappointment and fear. Edwin never ceased to beleaguer her with threats against Andrew as though he found some pleasure in tormenting her.

How much longer would he wait before acting? The law would make him pay, but Edwin seemed beyond caring about that. She would die if anything happened to her son.

She must find refuge for him. With determination in her mind Ruth set out for where Louisa lived. Surely her friend would help her.

She was surprised as she walked along the main road to see that the Beales' bakery shop was boarded up. The family had been shamed, but surely abandoning their business, their livelihood was an extreme reaction.

She was still pondering it when Louisa answered her knock

at the side door. Her friend looked astonished to see her.

'Ruth!'

'Please, Louisa, I'm in desperate trouble. Can I come in?'

'Well . . . I suppose so.'

Louisa led the way up the stairs to the rooms above the haberdasher's shop. Ruth climbed eagerly. Louisa was a mother herself and would understand the terror she was going through, and besides they had been friends for so long.

As they went into the living room Ruth saw that Mervyn was there. His eyebrows were raised to see her and he looked somewhat taken aback.

'Ruth, I'm surprised to see you under the circumstances,' he said stiffly.

Ruth noticed she wasn't invited to sit. 'I wouldn't bother you if it wasn't so important,' she answered. There was no time for small talk, so she plunged into explaining her mission. 'Louisa, I've come to beg you to take in Andrew. He's no longer safe at the Manse.'

'What?'

Ruth bit her lip, trying to hold back tears. 'Edwin is threatening our child's life. He intends to do him harm.'

'You can't mean that,' Mervyn said sceptically. 'It's absurd. Mr Allerton would have to be mad.'

'Edwin *is* out of his head,' Ruth agreed earnestly. 'Mrs Cardew's vile lies have affected his mind and his judgement. You don't know what I've been going though these last days.'

'Oh, Ruth . . .' Louisa looked sympathetic, but Mervyn straightened his shoulders and lifted his head to an authoritative angle.

'We can't help you, Ruth,' he said in a harsh voice. 'You must leave now.'

'Mervyn!' Louisa stared at him in chagrin. 'Don't speak to Ruth like that. What's the matter?'

'Self-preservation, that's the matter.' Mervyn took a deep breath. 'I don't mean to be heartless, Louisa,' he said seriously. 'But I can't afford to offend Pastor Allerton, the foremost member of our community. I have the business to consider.'

'I'm concerned about my child's life,' Ruth burst out. 'That's more important than anything else. I'm prepared to be parted from him rather than let Edwin hurt him.'

'I think you're overreacting to your husband's natural wrath, Ruth,' Mervyn said. 'Mr Allerton won't do anything drastic, I'm certain of it.'

'Are you?' Ruth burst out angrily. 'Well, I'm not. I know differently.'

It was on the tip of her tongue to reveal that Edwin had raped her, but she felt too ashamed to admit it. No one knew Edwin Allerton as well as she did. But now she realized everyone seemed to fear him for the power he had in the parish.

She glanced at her friend standing by. 'Does Mervyn speak for you too, Louisa?'

'Louisa will do as I think best,' Mervyn answered for her, his tone sharp. 'Enough damage has been done. The scandal has ruined George Beale already. You must've noticed his shop is boarded up.'

'I'm surprised by it.'

'Huh!' Mervyn gave her a sharp look. 'Are you? Mr Allerton made it plain to George that his business had little future in the village.'

'Oh no!' Ruth was stunned. 'There! You see how vindictive he really is!' she exclaimed. 'And you say Edwin won't take drastic action against Andrew. It's only a matter of time.'

'Like I said, Ruth, we can't help you,' Mervyn continued. 'There is too much at stake; my family's livelihood.'

Ruth saw his uncompromising expression and the regret in Louisa's eyes, and knew it was hopeless.

'The Beales are leaving Gowerton for good on Thursday, New Year's Day,' Mervyn went on. 'It's terrible. Their family have been in business in this village for three generations, and now this scandal . . .'

'You believe these lies, don't you?' she accused the couple, a catch in her voice. 'And I thought you were my friends. Well, I won't put you in jeopardy any longer.'

Ruth turned and left the room, hurrying down the stairs as quickly as she could. Louisa called out something from above, but Ruth did not hesitate. There was no help to be had here or anywhere. How much longer could she protect Andrew from Edwin's madness?

Ten

New Year's Day, 1920

R uth woke stiff, cold and weary, having spent yet another night in the chair in the nursery. She had been in constant fear for her son all the week, and each night, having endured Edwin's attentions, waited until he was soundly asleep before slipping from their bed and making her way to the nursery to keep guard for the rest of the night.

But this could not go on, she knew that. She must take desperate measures. She had pondered on the news that the Beales were leaving the district. Perhaps she could persuade Mrs Beale to take Andrew with her.

It broke her heart to realize that if David's mother agreed, she would probably never see Andrew again. But if her sacrifice could keep him from harm that she must suffer it for his sake.

There was early morning worship at the chapel so Edwin was up and gone. Ruth got dressed, attended to Andrew and then found a large carpet bag. Quickly she packed it with Andrew's clothes, nappies and other things he might need, and then set off for the Beales' cottage.

There was an open wagon at the roadside outside the cottage. It was filled with various pieces of furniture and household objects. The driver, a man she did not know, was tending the horse's head. Ruth breathed a sigh of relief. She was not too late. She went hesitantly up the path to the open door and knocked.

A flustered-looking Mrs Beale came to answer, but her expression turned from fluster to anger at the sight of Ruth.

'What do you want?' Sarah Beale asked in a high pitched voice. 'Come to gloat, have you?'

'No, Mrs Beale,' Ruth said still hesitant, but determined. This woman might be Andrew's last hope. 'I've come to ask a favour of you.'

'What!' Sarah Beale looked astonished. 'You've got some brass neck, I must say,' she said, disbelief in her voice. 'I've had to give up my home; my husband has had to desert his family business after three generations and all because of you. You'll get no favour here.'

'Please, Mrs Beale, I'm in desperate circumstances,' Ruth said. 'I want you to take my child with you; I beg you to take him.'

'Are you mad?' Sarah Beale took a step back.

'My husband has threatened to do him harm,' Ruth said desperately. 'I must get him to a place of safety, away from the village. You could take him to Swansea with you; make him your own.'

'And why pray would I agree to do that?' asked Sarah Beale huffily.

Ruth bit her lip. She had to lie now, a lie that might destroy her completely but there was no sacrifice she would not make for her child.

'Because Andrew is David's son,' she said in a low voice. 'This boy I hold in my arms is your grandson.'

Looking shaken to the core Sarah Beale took a staggering step back, and raised a hand to her throat. 'Then it's true what they've been saying about you,' she said in a shocked voice.

Ruth was unwilling to say anything more to confirm the lie.

'My husband has sworn to destroy my baby,' she said distraught. 'He's lost his reason, Mrs Beale, and is full of mad vengeance. He could strike at the child at any time. I beg you to take your grandson with you to keep him safe.'

Sarah Beale was silent for a long moment. Then she sent the waiting driver a cautious glance before speaking.

'Come inside,' she said, her voice trembling. 'We must talk in private.'

Hopefully Ruth followed her into the living room now bare of furnishngs. The room rang emptily as Sarah Beale spoke again.

'You swear this child is my grandson,' she said.

Ruth swallowed hard. 'I have said so, haven't I? Would I admit such a thing if it weren't true?'

'But David said nothing of this to me.'

'I haven't told him,' Ruth said. She was getting in deeper and deeper. 'I didn't want him to know.'

'That was wrong of you,' accused Sarah Beale. 'He has a right to know he has a son.'

'Well, if you agree to take Andrew, David will have his son.'

Sarah Beale's eyes narrowed. 'How do I know you won't suddenly change your mind and want him back?'

'While Edwin Allerton lives I cannot have my child with me,' Ruth said, feeling close to tears at the thought. 'You're Andrew's only hope, Mrs Beale.'

Sarah Beale was thoughtful for a few moments more.

'All right,' she said at last. 'I'll take him. And you'd better call me Sarah from now on. After this we are, in a way, related I suppose.'

Ruth swallowed down her tears, determined that she would not jeopardize Andrew's one chance of escaping Edwin's wrath.

'Thank you, Sarah. I'll always be indebted to you.'

'Hold your horses,' Sarah said quickly, lifting a hand. 'I'll take the child, but there are conditions.'

'What?'

'I'm no fool, Ruth Allerton,' Sarah said. 'You've been devious, and I'd never have believed it of you, but now I see you for what you are.'

'Please, Sarah . . .!'

'No, I insist on conditions,' the older woman said firmly. 'You're to give up all claim to the child from this day forward.'

Ruth could only take in a tortured breath.

'And that means,' Sarah went on decisively. 'You must never come in search of him. Do you swear to keep these conditions, Ruth?'

It was the most terrible moment of Ruth's life. She knew more sorrow now than when she had learned of David's death; more anguish than when she had been abused by her own husband. But she was prepared to suffer death itself to save her child.

'I swear, Sarah,' Ruth uttered, her voice strangled.

Sarah Beale reached out her arms. 'Then give him to me.'

Ruth involuntarily clutched Andrew closer to her breast. It was such a cruel thing in life to lose one's child, but it was better to give him away than to see him hurt or even dead.

'If you've changed your mind, Ruth,' Sarah began sharply.

'No, I haven't,' Ruth answered dully, and with a heavy heart, she released her son into Sarah Beale's arms. 'Take care of him, I beg you,' she said tearfully. 'He's so precious to me.'

'He'll have a good life with me,' Sarah said, and then she looked pensive. 'There's only one problem . . .'

'What?' Ruth was startled. 'Will your husband object?'

'No. It's David's wife Esther I'm worried about,' Sarah said. 'I wonder how she'll take the news that David has an illegitimate son.'

'Don't call him that!' exclaimed Ruth in distress.

'That's what he is.' Sarah shook her head. 'And some people might have a worse name for him.'

'No!'

'Well, it's none of your concern now, is it?' Sarah said sharply. She indicated the carpet bag at Ruth's feet. 'Are those his things?'

Ruth nodded, grief and pain making her dumb.

'I must get going,' Sarah said. 'George went ahead earlier with the rest of our things. He'll worry if I delay longer, and the wagon driver is kicking his heels.'

'Write to me,' Ruth begged. 'Let me know how my boy is.'

Sarah looked stern. 'That's not a wise thing,' she said. 'It's best for you if you give up all interest in him. He's no longer your child'

'I can never forget him!'

'You'll be a happier woman if you try,' Sarah said firmly. 'Now I must go and I suggest you go too before the wagon leaves. You don't want to make a spectacle of yourself, Ruth. You don't know who may be watching.'

Ruth put a hand to her mouth to hold back sobs, knowing she must stay strong for her child's sake. His safety was all that mattered now. She must smother her feelings so that he might survive Edwin's vengeance.

'On your way out tell the driver to come in to fetch this bag,' Sarah said sharply, obviously dismissing her.

Ruth stumbled towards the open door, not daring to look back at her son. Sarah Beale was right. She had given him away. He was no longer hers, and her heart was in torment at the truth of it.

The house was silent when Ruth returned home. Edwin was still absent and she was glad of it. Instinctively she went straight to the nursery, but stopped at the door shaken at the emptiness of the room and she could not bear to step inside. It would always be empty from now on. She closed the door, wishing she had the key for the lock. She did not want anything disturbed.

She made her way to the other bedroom and collapsed on the bed, knowing that a part of her was missing. She had given her child away and she would never be whole again.

A memory of Andrew's little face wreathed in smiles whenever he looked at her came into her mind, and the weeping started, great gales of tears and shuddering sobs. In her misery time seemed to stop and she knew only pain and grief at her loss.

It was not until the bedroom door was thrown open and Edwin strode in, his expression irritated that reality began again for her.

'Ruth, you have not prepared my midday meal,' he said gruffly. 'I demand to know why.'

She looked up at his face, his anger unconcealed, and she was suddenly struck by the strangeness of it. Edwin had never shown any emotion before or after their marriage, but now, it seemed, he could not hide his feelings at all, as though emotional flood gates had opened and he was totally at the mercy of his emotions.

'I'm not feeling well,' she said, pushing herself up from the bed, hiding her tear-stained face with one hand.

'What's wrong with you?' He raised his eyebrows, his expression disdainful. 'Guilty conscience perhaps?'

His mocking tone set her teeth on edge and then she realized that now Andrew was out of harm's way, she could freely respond to Edwin's abuse with anger of her own.

'Be quiet, you sanctimonious hypocrite!' she screeched at him, struggling off the bed to face him.

'What?' His face flushed deeply and his hands trembled.

Ruth was pleased to see him shaken. Giving vent to her own anger at last brought a small measure of relief from her heartache.

'You shame your calling,' she went on shrilly. 'You shame the pulpit you stand in each Sunday, and the very chapel itself.'

His jaw worked angrily. 'Have a care, Ruth,' he said at last. 'You're piling grievance upon grievance and you'll be punished for it. So will your brat.'

'You can do nothing more to me now,' she cried. 'And as for Andrew you'll never see him again.'

He stared keenly at her and she was conscious of the ravages weeping had brought to her face.

'You've been crying.' His tone made the words seem like an accusation. 'Where's your bastard child?'

'Don't call him that, damn you!'

'Where is he?'

Ruth gave a sob. 'Where you can't reach him.'

He took a hard breath. 'Your parents have taken him in against my edict.'

Ruth shook her head. 'No. They turned him away. They're as stiff-necked and without any real Christian charity as you are.'

'Then where is he? I demand to know.'

'You can demand all you want, Edwin,' Ruth flared at him. 'Andrew is long gone from this village. I gave him to . . .'

Ruth hesitated, unwilling to betray Andrew's whereabouts to the man who would harm him. 'I gave him away to strangers passing through the village early this morning.'

'Tinkers?'

'I didn't ask,' Ruth said. 'But better with tinkers than in your house, with your threats hanging over him and me. He's safe from you now, and I've won.'

He stared at her for a moment. 'No you haven't, Ruth. I've won. You've lost your child. Your grief for your loss will be your punishment for betraying me.'

'I never betrayed you, Edwin,' Ruth declared lifting up her chin in defiance. 'That's the pitiful irony of it. My betrayal is just a notion in that twisted brain of yours. It has no substance. Andrew's your rightful son, so it's your loss as well as mine, and you brought it on yourself.'

Edwin took a step back. 'So the child is gone, and is dead to you,' he said. There was satisfaction in his voice. 'But nothing has changed as far as you're concerned. My edict stays in place.'

'I don't care!' Ruth shouted angrily. 'Do you think anything matters to me now? So do as you like, Edwin.'

She tried to rush past him to leave the room but he caught at her arm. 'You're still my wife, Ruth and you'll do as I say. Attend to your household duties as a wife should.'

Ruth pulled her arm free. 'I intend to leave you, Edwin,' she said triumphantly. 'How will that look to your flock?'

'You can go nowhere,' Edwin said. 'You're destitute without me.'

Ruth said nothing but hurried from the room. It was not quite true that she was without some money. She had secretly saved most of her dress allowance. It would not have been enough to keep both she and Andrew if she had broken away from Edwin earlier, but if she found work somewhere she could manage on her own, albeit frugally.

But the time to leave was not just yet. She must wait where she was for now because Mrs Beale could relent in the next few weeks or months and might send word of Andrew.

And it would be better to quit the Manse when the warmer

weather came later in the year. Ruth felt a little better at the thought. She had plans and did not feel so helpless now.

Undoubtedly Edwin would continue to demand her submission to his needs and she must suffer his attentions as best she could for the time being, knowing that soon she would be free of him. Though what the future could hold for her without her child she did not know.

In the back of her mind was a hopeful thought. No matter what she had promised Sarah Beale, one day she would be in a position to get Andrew back. In the meantime she was sure he was safe with David's mother.

Eleven

Swansea, New Year's Day, 1920

'Sarah! What in God's name . . .?'

George Beale was staring up at her as she sat next to the driver on the wagon's passenger seat, the child in her arms.

'George, don't stand there with your mouth open looking *twp*,' Sarah said crossly. She was uncertain that she had done the right thing in bringing this baby with her. Self-doubt and guilt always sharpened her tongue. 'Help me down. Can't you see I'm hampered with the baby here?'

He held up his arms and took hold of the child, still looking perplexed and worried as he watched her clamber down on to the pavement outside the home of her brother-in-law, Sydney Beale, where they were to stay until they found a place of their own to rent.

Sarah felt flustered already at the prospect of living with their well-to-do relatives instead of being the mistress of her own small kitchen as she had been since she married George. And now she had taken the step, perhaps a foolish step, of taking responsibility for another woman's child.

'This baby,' George said when she had two feet on the ground. 'Where did you find it? Who does it belong to?'

'It belongs to us,' Sarah said firmly. 'This is your grandson, George. His name is Andrew.'

'What!' George boomed.

The wagon driver was already busy emptying the things from the wagon on to the pavement. Sarah was conscious that he might be listening to their conversation.

'I'll explain later,' she said sharply, taking the baby from

96

her husband's arms. 'Get about shifting our things inside. It might rain.'

Sarah hurried into the house her mind now in a whirl of worry. She realized now that she had been precipitous in taking in the child, but there had been desperation in Ruth's voice and face. And it must have cost her to admit the truth about her and David.

And there was the problem Sarah thought with misgiving. How would she find the words to explain the situation to David's wife? She could not help feeling she had brought trouble to her son's marriage.

Esther would have to get over it, Sarah thought with asperity. The child was a Beale; their grandson. It was only right that Andrew should be with his father and David must face up to his responsibilities.

Besides, the whole business cast a dark shadow over Ruth's character and Sarah was inclined to think now that she wasn't a fit mother.

She took the child up to the bedroom that was to be hers and George's for the foreseeable future. Making a nest of pillows on the floor, Sarah placed Andrew there in safety until the family were all together and she could reveal her actions and introduce him to his father.

As she went downstairs she was still uneasy despite her determination. Esther was pretty, and as sharp as a tack when it came to Sydney's coal merchant business in which she took an active part in running the office, but she was also a rather sullen girl. Sarah was unsure she even liked her daughter-in-law.

The bulk of their furniture and fittings had been put into storage in the town to be retrieved when they found a house to rent, and they had brought with them today only the day to day essentials. Luckily, Sydney's house in Brynmill west of the busy port and town of Swansea was a large one, as befitted a businessman of his wealth and standing. There was plenty of room so they would not be under each other's feet, and for that Sarah was thankful, but it was also a far cry from the cottage life she had always known.

Feeling a little at sea, Sarah went to the large sitting room where George was alone waiting impatiently for her; Sarah was glad that Sydney and Esther were still at the coal yard. She needed time alone with her husband and son to sort out Andrew's future.

'Sarah, I want an explanation now,' George blustered as soon as she appeared. 'This damned baby . . .'

'George! I'll not have you swearing! This is a Christian household.'

'Poppycock!' George exclaimed irritably. 'We've left all that sanctimonious nonsense behind us.'

Sarah sniffed. 'You may have,' she said. 'You were never a willing one for chapel anyway, but I haven't fallen by the wayside.' She lifted her chin. 'I'll soon find a nice little place of worship around here.'

'Never mind that now,' George said brusquely. 'This baby, whose is it and what are you doing with it? The last thing we want is another scandal, especially while we're staying here with Sydney so I hope you haven't done anything stupid, Sarah.'

Sarah bit her lip, wondering what Esther and Sydney would say to learn that David had done that very thing. Esther would eventually inherit a considerable fortune and now perhaps David's foolishness with Ruth Allerton would ruin everything. Nevertheless, they all had to face up to it.

'Listen to me, George,' she began tensely. 'All that talk about our David and Ruth Allerton is true.' She shook her head. 'I'm ashamed to admit it but I had it from Ruth's own lips. The child is David's son, our grandchild.'

He stood with his mouth open again, and Sarah felt irritation. Sometimes George acted so gormless. It was no wonder to her that Sydney Beale, his older brother, had done so much better in business.

Of course, she pondered, in all fairness to her husband, Sydney had had the luck to marry the widowed daughter of Joshua Rawlings, a wealthy coal merchant while George had married the daughter of a dairyman who was as poor as a workhouse mouse.

'Well?' she snapped, annoyed more at the vagaries of fate than at him.

'I don't believe it!' George said at last. 'David has always been straightforward with me; always has come to me for advice. He'd have told me if he was in trouble of this kind.'

'David doesn't know he has a son,' Sarah said. 'It's going to be a shock.'

'A shock!' George stared at her. 'Damn and blast it, Sarah! Do you realize what you've done in bringing this baby here? You've most likely ruined our boy's marriage.'

Sarah shook her head stubbornly. 'It won't come to that.'

'Oh won't it?' Normally a placid man, George's lips tightened in anger. 'David could lose everything, Sarah. His wife is set to get her grandfather's money after Sydney's days. What do you think she'll say when she learns David has an illegitimate son, eh?'

Sarah wrung her hands. 'I had no choice,' she said earnestly. 'Ruth was desperate to part with him. What could I do?'

He turned away with a groan to face the fireplace. 'How could you be so foolish, woman?' he asked. 'Our David marrying Esther was the best thing that could have happened. It took long enough to persuade him. Foisting this baby on them will make Sydney and Esther believe we deceived them.'

Sarah tutted, struggling to make less of it. 'Sydney's a man of the world. He'll understand. It happens in the best of families.'

'Listen to yourself, will you?' George said, rounding on her. 'Chastizing me for swearing one minute and condoning adultery the next.'

'No such thing!' Sarah flared. 'Our son made a mistake. Good heavens, he's been a war prisoner for years. Who can blame him for one little weakness?'

'Oh, I give up!' George said with anger. 'There'll be ructions, I'm telling you. There could be a divorce.'

'Oh, no! Not that! It would be a disgrace for both families.'

'Our Sydney is old-fashioned, but Esther is a very modern-minded young woman,' George warned. 'They might ask us to leave and then where will we be?'

'George, you're always looking on the black side,' Sarah said more calmly than she felt. 'David and Esther will work things out. They must. Where is David anyway?'

George flopped into a nearby armchair. 'He's gone to inspect the new bakery premises I've rented in the town. It's well equipped, so I understand. We're lucky we haven't got more expense than we can handle.'

He gave a deep sigh that sounded almost like a sob.

'It broke my heart to leave our old place in Gowerton,' he said sorrowfully. 'It suited me fine.'

'I know,' Sarah said sympathetically, coming forward to put her hand on his shoulder. 'And I'll miss the kitchen in our cottage; been there since we were first married.' She shook her head sadly. 'So many happy memories.'

George gave a grunt. 'If Pastor Allerton hadn't seen fit to name our David we'd be there still,' he said, his tone bitter. 'There was no need for it.'

'I blame Ruth Allerton,' Sarah said harshly. 'She led our David on, of course she did. She's not fit to bring up a child.'

David returned to the house in time for the midday meal. It would always be another's house, he reflected wearily; Uncle Sydney's, Esther's, never his, but Esther would not even consider buying a place of their own. It was she who had the money, but he had married her and he wanted the marriage to work so he gave in to her wishes. What else could he do?

His parents were still in the sitting room, looking uncomfortable and out of place. They both stood as he came into the room.

'Have you both settled in?' he asked, giving his mother a hug and a kiss, and shaking his father's outstretched hand. 'I'm sorry no one was at home to greet you.' He took out his pocket watch. 'Any sign of the meal being ready yet.'

'I haven't dared go near the kitchen,' Sarah said huffily. 'There's some woman in there banging about with pots. Who is she?'

'Mrs Cooper. She's our housekeeper and cook.'

Sarah sniffed. 'In my day wives did their own housekeeping and cooking,' she said, still huffy. 'I'd have thought it was Esther's place to stay at home and look after things.'

David swallowed a sigh. He had suspected for some time that his mother didn't approve of Esther, despite urging him to marry her. He had been pushed into this marriage and he felt like reminding them of it at this moment, but held back.

'This is the twentieth century, Mam,' he said patiently. 'Many married women work these days.'

'Yes, they have to if they have kids and are short of a bob or two,' Sarah retorted. 'Esther is hardly poor. She doesn't need to.'

'It's not a matter of need, Mam,' David said. 'It started in the war when there was a shortage of men. Esther helped out in the office. It suited her and when the war ended she was determined to continue. Uncle Sydney says she's the best office manager he's ever had.'

'Huh!'

'She'll probably give it up if we start a family,' David said trying to placate her.

His mother gave a little cough and turned away.

David paused, wondering at the strange tension in the room.

'I'm sure you'll get used to living here, Mam,' he said to her turned back. 'And it won't be forever, will it?'

'Tell him,' George said abruptly to his wife. 'Tell him what you've done.'

'What's going on?'

Sarah turned back to face him. 'Sit down, David, boy,' she said gently. 'There's something I have to tell you.'

David sat obediently waiting uneasily. Had they changed their minds about moving to Swansea? He hoped not for the new bakery premises his father had agreed to rent were perfectly situated in a narrow street behind the market in the town centre. It could be a little gold-mine.

'Before I left Gowerton early this morning, Ruth Allerton came to our cottage.'

David felt a little jolt in the region of his heart at the mention of Ruth's name, but quelled it, determined that the old longing should be buried. Ruth had made it plain at their last meeting that she no longer cared for him. She had chosen Edwin Allerton once again.

'She confessed everything, David.' His mother sat down next to him, and put her hand on his arm. 'Your father and I don't blame you.'

'What?' He stared at her mystified.

She patted his arm. 'Obviously Ruth led you on when you were at your weakest.' She shook her head. 'I blame her. A married woman carrying on like that. It's a disgrace.'

'Mam, what are you blathering about?'

Sarah sniffed, and pulled in her chin in annoyance. 'Now there's no need to take that tone with me, David, when I'm trying to help,' she said sternly. 'Ruth confessed to me that the child is yours.'

David stood up. 'Ruth did what?'

'She looked desperate, as well she might, being shunned,' Sarah said. 'But I can understand Pastor Allerton not wanting anything to do with the child. What right-thinking man would?'

David glanced at his father feeling more bewildered than ever.

'Dad, what's this all about?'

George Beale shrugged and turned away, but David knew him well enough to see that his father was very uneasy and would not hold his gaze.

'At least she had a bit of sense at the last,' Sarah continued as though David had not spoken. 'And it's only right that the boy should be with his father.'

'Who should be with his father?' David asked impatiently.

'Andrew, your son,' Sarah said. 'He's upstairs in our bedroom. I'll take you up to him.'

David sat down again and held up his hands for silence from his mother.

'Now, let me get this right, Mam,' he said. 'You've brought Ruth Allerton's baby here with you. In heaven's name, why?'

'Well, it's plain, isn't it?' Sarah said impatiently. 'Ruth probably wants to run off, but she'd be hampered with a baby and that's why she confessed her sin to me.'

'Confessed?'

Sarah made a sound of impatience. 'David, you know full well Ruth was publicly denounced and why.'

David sat forward suddenly in silence, elbows on knees. Of course he knew what had happened to Ruth; his mother had written to him in full detail, but he had left the village long before the scandal broke and had settled in Swansea.

He might have returned to the village to deny the charge, but he doubted it would have helped, and besides, he had Esther to consider. He did not love her as he had loved Ruth, but Esther was his wife. Ruth had clung to her marriage vows despite everything, despite all his pleading, and now he must respect his vows.

'What did Ruth say exactly?' he asked carefully.

'That you fathered her child, David,' George Beale roared. 'Is it true? I demand to know.'

David glanced at his mother. 'Ruth voluntarily gave you the child?'

'Begged me to take Andrew,' Sarah said. 'Your son, David, how could I refuse?'

David rose and paced the room. He had to think. Why would Ruth do such a thing; confess to something that never happened? They had never once been intimate, not even before he went to war, although he had done enough begging. Ruth must have had good reason, so he would neither agree or deny for the time being.

The only problem was Esther. How would she take this news? Not well, he judged. They had discussed having a family, but she made it plain she was in no hurry. She liked the freedom of working in the family business too much.

'This needs careful handling,' David said at last. He glanced at his parents. 'I beg you to say nothing of this to Esther. I must tell her myself in my own way.'

'What about the baby?'

'He'll have to stay in your room. You'll have to look after him for the time being, Mam.'

'But I have nothing in the way of nappies or anything.' His mother looked even more flustered. 'Except what Ruth gave me.'

'Then you'll have to go into town and buy some,' David said flatly. 'We have an account with David Evans in Castle Street. You can use that. I'll give you a covering letter.' He looked at his father. 'You best go with her, Dad. Mam's not used to busy streets and traffic.'

George shook his head. 'I knew I'd get roped in somehow. Your mother will have me in an early grave.'

'George, please!'

Esther came home with her stepfather an hour before the evening meal was to be served. She walked into the sitting room and with a sigh dropped her fashionably slender frame into an armchair before the fire.

'Get me a glass of sherry, David,' she asked. 'It's so cold. I'm sure it'll snow tonight.'

David handed her a glass straight away and watched speculatively as she sipped it, feeling agitated, uncertain how to bring up the subject of Andrew.

Hoping he and Esther would be alone he had asked his parents to wait in their bedroom until Mrs Cooper sounded the gong for dinner. Uncle Sydney, a teetotaller, always went to his study before dinner.

Esther took another sip from her glass and looked at him over the rim. 'Did your parents arrive?'

He nodded. 'They're upstairs.'

She smiled thinly. 'Afraid to show their faces?'

'Why should they be?' His tone was sharper than he intended.

She looked surprised. 'It's a joke, David,' she said airily. 'It's only natural they'll feel out of place at the start. I mean cottage living is so limiting . . .'

'You promised you wouldn't be snide.'

'Good Heavens! You are on edge. What's the matter?' she asked. 'Your war wounds giving you jip again, are they?'

'No, it's not that,' he said. 'I have something to explain, something serious.'

He went to the chiffonier and poured himself a whisky and soda which he rarely drank at this time of day, but now he really needed it.

'Dutch courage?'

He turned to look at her. Sometimes he felt she could read his mind. 'Something like that,' he said and hesitated.

'What've you been up to?'

David ground his teeth. Esther could be so patronising, as though reminding him of their different upbringing. But then again, he thought, it is only a marriage of convenience after all.

'My mother has brought a baby here from Gowerton.'

'Whatever for?' She looked astonished.

'The mother is a young woman named Ruth. She told my mother that the child is mine.'

'What!' Esther almost spilled her glass of sherry. 'David, you'd better explain yourself.'

He had not seen her disconcerted before. Now she was paying serious attention to him for the first time since their marriage began.

'I'm just reporting what Ruth told my mother,' David said evasively. 'Ruth maintains I'm the father and has sent the child to me.'

'But is it true?'

'What if it were true, Esther?' he asked out of curiosity. 'What would you do?'

Esther put her glass on a side table and stood up. There was anger in her expression now. 'Have you been seeing this woman?'

'Not since I came to Swansea to live, just before the war ended.'

Esther looked confused. 'Then she's lying. Why would she do that?'

David had been asking himself the same question. 'It's not entirely impossible, of course,' he said. 'As I understand it the child was born in June last year. I *was* in Gowerton until the end of September.'

She looked at him from under her eyelashes. 'David, don't play games with me. Are you the child's father or not?'

He could not prolong the deception. 'No, I'm not. Ruth and I were in love years ago, but we were never intimate.'

'Do you swear it?'

He frowned. 'Don't take that attitude with me, Esther,' he said sharply. 'You always make it plain you believe you've married beneath you. It's insulting.'

She gave an impatient sigh. 'It's your imagination, David.' She gave him a penetrating glance. 'I still want reassurance from you that there was nothing between you and this woman, Ruth.'

'There was love,' he said bitterly. 'But nothing physical. Now, are you satisfied?'

She sat down again and took up her glass of sherry. 'I believe you,' she said. 'And, of course, the child cannot stay here in this house.'

He had half expected that decision. 'The child can stay until my parents find a house to rent. Andrew can go with them.'

'You actually want them to keep him?' She looked at him steadily. 'Why are you so protective of this child if he is nothing to you?'

'I believe Ruth had a very good reason for parting with him. I believe she was worried for the child's safety.'

Esther laughed scornfully. 'What possible reason could you have for thinking that?'

David shook his head in silence. He had a picture of Edwin Allerton's austere face in his mind. The man had denounced his own wife so publicly and so cruelly. What else was he capable of?

'Well, your parents had better find a place soon,' Esther said flatly. 'I won't tolerate that child under this roof.'

'Be reasonable, Esther . . .'

Esther looked angry. 'Don't think you can foist another woman's child on me, David,' she interrupted. 'I won't be tied down. This is the twentieth century when women can strive for careers instead of endless pregnancies. I intend to take over and run the family business eventually. Nothing will stop me.' She gave him a challenging look. 'Certainly not children.'

Twelve

B itterly cold though it was Ruth could not remain in the house. She needed the coldness to numb her mind, deaden the ache in her heart for her lost child. She had spent hours outdoor over these last weeks, dreading her inevitable return each day to the Manse.

She avoided the village. In the first few weeks she had tried to carry on as normal. Everyone knew by now that she had given her baby away. At the butcher's or the green-grocer's they had served her, but always in silence, never meeting her eye. No one spoke a word to her other than Edwin, and only then to demand she cook his meals or submit to his needs in bed.

Over the last few days she had stopped going into the village shops altogether. Let Edwin rant and rave, she decided, but she would neither shop, cook nor clean his house.

For herself, she did not care if she starved. In fact some-times she felt like going out into the fields in the freezing night, lying down in the damp grass and letting the cold take her, but one thing stopped her. The thought that one day she and Andrew would be reunited. She never gave up that hope.

It was growing dark now and she could sense snow in the air and so, reluctantly, she turned her steps towards the Manse.

She was about to let herself in through the back door, but stopped in surprise to see the gaslight was on and to hear someone bustling about in the kitchen. Surely not Edwin.

Ruth went in and stared about her, dismayed to see an old enemy at the stove where saucepans steamed.

'Mrs Cardew! What are you doing here?'

'What does it look like?' There was a disdainful smirk on the older woman's face.

'How dare you come here? Get out!' Ruth screeched at the woman who had done so much harm; who had been the cause of losing her child.

'I've every right to be here,' Mrs Cardew snapped. 'The pastor has given me my job back. If there's anyone who doesn't belong it's you.'

Ruth could not believe it. After Mrs Cardew had delivered her poisonous news to Edwin at Christmas time he too had dismissed her, refusing her return; shooting the bringer of bad news, Ruth thought, but now he had obviously relented.

Ruth was furious. It was just another way to heap humiliation on her. This time she intended to fight back if she could.

'I said get out,' she shouted at Mrs Cardew. 'You're sacked.'

'You're whistling against the wind,' Mrs Cardew said with a sneer. 'You can't sack me.' She gave a narrow smile. 'I could have told you giving your baby away would make no difference. Once a harlot always a harlot.'

'What does the Bible say about those who give false witness?' Ruth asked angrily. 'Mark my words, Mrs Cardew. One day you'll be shown up for the conniving scandalmonger that you are.'

'Oh! Don't you talk to me like that, you hussy,' Mrs Cardew hooted. 'This is my kitchen now, so get out yourself!'

Fuming Ruth stalked out, going down the passage to the front of the house. Edwin would answer for this new ignominy.

She found him in the sitting room, a room she rarely entered these days. He was reading the paper but glanced up as she entered and then immediately turned his attention to his paper again without even acknowledging her.

'Edwin,' Ruth said loudly, standing in front of him. 'What is that woman doing in my home?'

He continued to read, ignoring her presence.

'Damnation to you, Edwin! Answer me!'

With a sudden uncontrollable spurt of anger, Ruth snatched at the newspaper, tearing it from his fingers. He recoiled back in his chair in surprise and then leapt to his feet.

'How dare you do that!' he bellowed. 'You forget yourself, Ruth.'

'And how dare you humiliate me by bringing Mrs Cardew back here? Am I not punished enough? I won't stand for it, Edwin.

'There can never be enough punishment for what you've done,' Edwin rasped. 'You must be punished for your sins until the day you die.'

Ruth gave a sob. 'I've already given my child away. Isn't that enough for you?'

'No, not nearly enough,' he said adamantly. 'I want you to suffer as I've suffered.'

'Only your pride has suffered, Edwin,' Ruth flared. 'Isn't pride a deadly sin? Don't tell me your heart is broken because you have no heart.'

He turned away from her and resuming his seat picked up the newspaper where it had fallen on the rug. It was an act of dismissal and Ruth was infuriated.

'Get that woman out of my home, Edwin,' she shouted. 'I demand it.'

'She stays,' he said. 'And what's more, Mrs Cardew will take over the running of my house. She may even live in if I decide it suits me.'

'What?'

'Since you have failed in your duties to me, I've arranged that Mrs Cardew has charge of the housekeeping money. From now on she'll purchase all my provisions and manage my meals and my home.'

'Edwin, you're a fool,' Ruth exclaimed furiously. 'The woman is a thief and a liar. She'll rob you blind.'

'And you have not robbed me, I suppose,' he said.

Ruth was silent knowing the futility of arguing with him.

'There's nothing more to be said,' Edwin went on, a finality in his tone.

She left the sitting room, head bent in dejection. How

would she bear it if Mrs Cardew did take up residence? Life would be impossible.

She thought again, as she often had lately, of leaving Gowerton. A motor coach service had started to run between Swansea and West Wales, the vehicle passing through the village once a week. But the winter promised to be severe, and she doubted the service would continue if snow fell making the roads impassable. It would be better to wait until spring.

Ruth went up to the second bedroom. It was so cold for it had no fireplace, but she wrapped a blanket around herself and huddled on the bed. Edwin would come for her later, demanding she made herself available for his nightly needs, but until then she would lie down and think about spring.

She would go to Swansea and claim her son from Mrs Beale. Ruth thought about the lie she had told her regarding the boy's father. David knew it wasn't true, but what had he told his mother? And how had his new wife taken it?

Mrs Beale could not refuse to hand Andrew back, surely. Ruth prayed that soon, within months, she would be happy with her child once more. Until then, she must bear the heartache and the regret.

Thirteen

I n the sitting-room David helped himself to another whisky and soda. He could feel his mother's disapproving expression, and knew that lately he was drinking too much. The whisky eased the pain in his legs and it also eased the pain in his heart for his empty marriage.

Avoiding his mother's gaze he stood in front of the warm hearth to drink and took out his pocket watch to glance at it.

'It's almost seven,' he said. 'Time to go up and dress for dinner.'

'Tsk! Dressing for dinner again,' Sarah scolded. 'It's a lot of old swank that's what it is. And another thing, having a big meal in the evening is playing havoc with my digestion.' She sniffed. 'Why can't we have dinner at midday like everybody else?' She nudged her husband sitting next to her on the sofa. 'Isn't that right, George?'

He had been dozing and came to with a start. 'Eh?'

'Oh, you're no help at all, George.'

'I'm tired, woman,' his father said irately. 'I've been at the bakery since early this morning. I'm not as young as I used to be.'

'Then you should let David take more responsibility. After all, the business will be his eventually.'

'I'm not ready to be put out to pasture yet,' George answered with alacrity, straightening up in his seat. 'I intend to struggle on to my dying day.'

David grinned at his father. 'That's the spirit, Dad.'

George rose awkwardly from the sofa stifling a yawn.

111

'Who are these people coming here tonight?' he asked. 'Do we have to meet them? I feel like going to bed now.'

David ran his tongue over his lips. 'I wish you'd both make an effort this evening,' he said, trying to keep irritation from his voice. 'The Hamilton family and the Rawlings have been friends for years, back to the time of Esther's grandfather, Joshua.'

'I don't think they're our kind,' Sarah put in. 'We're plain folk, we are, and all this swanking goes against the grain.'

'Richard Hamilton owns coal mines in the Neath Valley and he's a friend and an important business associate of Uncle Sydney,' David said. 'While you are under his roof, I think you both should make an effort.'

George grunted. 'My brother always did think himself a cut above.'

'Uncle Sydney has been pretty successful, Dad, and he knows how to talk to wealthy people like the Hamiltons.'

His father frowned, looking angry. 'Meaning that I'm a failure because I'm a lowly baker?'

'You know that's not what I meant.' David put his empty glass on the mantelpiece. 'I'm going up to dress,' he said shortly. 'I suggest you both do the same.'

When David returned to the sitting room later, Esther was there together with her stepfather Sydney Beale, who sat in an armchair reading the newspaper. His uncle glanced up when David came in.

'How was business at the bakery today?' he asked.

Sydney Beale was a big florid-faced man, despite being a teetotaller, who was always ready to talk about business even if it wasn't his own. David liked and respected him.

'Promising,' David said. 'The site is ideal, so close to the market. Passing trade is well up.'

'Good, good,' Sydney said and then returned to his paper.

'I hope your parents won't keep dinner waiting,' Esther said with asperity.

She was wearing a gown of emerald damask. The colour suited her dark eyes and her black hair was cut in a fashionable bob. She was a handsome woman, and he suddenly realized many men would envy him such a wife.

'The Hamiltons aren't here yet,' David quickly pointed out, angered at her tone. He suspected that Esther would be glad to see Sarah and George Beale gone. 'I think you might be more civil to my parents,' he continued as he handed her a glass of sherry.

She took the glass from him, giving him a sharp look of surprise.

'I'm always civil,' she said, taking a sip. 'But I do wonder when they'll find a suitable house to rent. After all, it's been over a month; and that baby . . .' She gave him a challenging look. 'I hear it crying at night. I can't put up with it much longer.'

'Be reasonable, Esther. My mother is doing her best.'

'He should go back to Ruth,' Esther said.

At that moment Sarah and George entered the room, his mother wearing the same old-fashioned black gown she always wore, the only one she had.

'What's that?' Sarah asked harshly. 'Are you talking about Andrew?'

'As a matter of fact, yes,' Esther said. 'Sarah, you should be sensible. That baby is getting too much for you.'

'No such thing!'

'Well, he's getting too much for me,' George said. He went to the chiffonier to pour himself a drink. 'Why you ever took him in the first place, beats me.'

'You know why, George.'

'Yes, but now you know David is not the father,' George pointed out. 'The child is no kin to us.'

'Exactly,' Esther agreed. 'He should go back to his mother.'

'No!' Sarah sat down on a sofa opposite her daughter-in-law, a determined expression on her face. 'Ruth is an unfit mother. And even if Andrew isn't a Beale I won't see him go back there to her.'

'I agree with my mother,' David said quickly. 'He can't go back.'

Not for one minute did he believe Ruth to be unfit to care for her son. It must have been agony for her to part with

113

him, and he was certain she had good reason. He was still convinced it was something to do with Edwin Allerton. The man was a strange bird indeed.

'Then he'll have to be placed elsewhere,' Esther said resolutely. 'I'll look into it.'

'That's presumptuous of you!' Sarah exclaimed. 'It's not your concern, Esther. This is Sydney's house. I think he should have the last word.'

Uncle Sydney rattled his newspaper. 'Please don't involve me in this,' he said.

'I think it is my concern,' Esther replied. 'My husband was falsely accused of being the father, and I have to suffer being under the same roof as the child. I don't see why I should be inconvenienced.'

'Ruth placed the child in my care,' Sarah said stubbornly. 'I'm responsible for it. I have a right to decide his future.'

The front door bell sounded at that point and David heard the maid go to answer.

'Our guests have arrived,' Uncle Sydney said hurriedly. 'Let there be no unpleasant atmosphere in the room.'

'We'll discuss this tomorrow,' Esther said, rising to her feet in readiness to receive their guests. Sarah's chin jutted stubbornly, but nothing more could be said then.

A tall, fashionably dressed man about thirty years of age entered the room in the wake of the maid. David had met him once before at his business premises in Neath when he had accompanied his Uncle Sydney. He had formed a good opinion of the man, who was down to earth in spite of his wealth.

While Richard Hamilton smiled a greeting at all present, there was a sombre air about the man that David immediately recognized as sadness and perhaps regret, and was surprised. He knew those feelings himself, but was curious. Hamilton had known only wealth and privilege all his life, so why did he appear so solemn?

Introductions were made. Richard's grasp of David's hand was strong and self-assured despite his air.

'Annette sends her apologies, Esther,' Richard said regretfully. 'I'm afraid she is not well enough for social events.'

'I'm sorry,' Esther responded, but David detected a softer tone in her voice than usual as if Annette Hamilton's indisposition suited her. 'Please tell her how we regret her absence.'

While they waited for dinner to be announced there was conversation about business in general and the price of coal in particular, a subject dear to Sydney's heart.

'Richard owns several coal mines in the Neath Valley,' Esther explained to Sarah and George.

She occupied the same sofa as Richard and seemed to lean towards him in a way that made David pause to watch her. He knew they were old friends, at least their families had a long history, but he was somewhat taken aback at how, when she looked at Richard, her features softened along with her voice which took on a light huskiness.

With sudden insight he saw Esther for the first time and realized she was in love with Richard Hamilton. He sat back in his chair unsure how he should react, but at that moment they were called to dinner.

Esther went in on Richard's arm, clinging to him in an intimate way that made David feel uncomfortable, wondering if his parents had also noticed her behaviour.

His discomfort lasted throughout the meal and he was relieved when their guest left at about ten o'clock. After he had gone they gathered in the sitting room again for a nightcap except Esther, who had excused herself.

'Splendid fellow, Richard Hamilton,' Sydney said.

'Esther seems very fond of him,' David said bitterly.

He could not help making the observation although still unsure how he should feel. He could not deny his marriage to Esther was merely one of convenience for both families. Yet she was his wife and the knowledge that she loved another man made him feel cheated.

'Joshua Rawlings and Richard's father were great friends. Esther and Richard saw a lot of each other as children; you might almost say grew up together even though there are seven years between.'

'It's a wonder they didn't marry then,' Sarah said. She glanced at David as she spoke and he knew his mother had understood Esther's behaviour also.

'Joshua wanted that,' Sydney said, nodding thoughtfully. 'But Richard's father sought a connection with the wealthy Kreppel family of Cardiff. He made no bones about it and Richard being a dutiful son married Annette Kreppel just before his father died three years ago.'

'Tsk! These arranged marriages . . .' Sarah said disparagingly and then stopped, staring at her son. 'I mean, sometimes they work.'

David stood up abruptly and went to the chiffonier to get a whisky and threw the liquid into the back of his throat. Now he felt like a fool and was determined to confront Esther that night.

'Goodnight,' he said brusquely as he strode from the room.

Esther was in their bedroom creaming her face. He hated her doing that in front of him. It was as though she did not care how she appeared to him.

'Pleasant evening, wasn't it?' she began, wiping some of the cream away on a soft cloth.

'Was it?' he returned huffily. He took off his jacket to fling it on a nearby chair and removed his bow tie.

She turned from the mirror to look at him. 'I thought you liked Richard?'

He stared at her glistening face. 'I'm not sure I like to see my wife acting so . . . friendly with another man.'

She sat perfectly still gazing at him. 'Why, David!' she said at last, surprise in her voice. 'I might think you're jealous.' She turned back to the mirror. 'But I know that's not possible. After all you made it plain you loved Ruth Allerton before we were married.'

'Why did you marry me then?'

'Same reason why you married me,' she said frankly. 'My love belongs to someone else.'

'You've made me feel a fool, Esther,' David said gruffly.

She rounded on him angrily. 'Now you know how I felt when your mother brought that child here, claiming he was your son.'

'I explained about that . . .'

'You could be lying as far as I know.'

116

David was silent for a moment. 'Are you having an affair with Richard?'

'No. Not that I haven't tried . . .' She paused. 'Richard has principles. He's married and that's it.' She bowed her head. 'Besides, I know he doesn't love me.'

David did not know what to say for a moment. Esther had never opened up to him like this before. But then he had never given her a chance.

'He loves his wife even though it's an arranged marriage?' he asked at last.

'No. He admitted to me that he doesn't love Annette, in the proper sense,' Esther said dully. 'He's very fond of her and respects her. He'd never leave her or betray her now she's so unhappy.'

'Unhappy?'

'Their child died at the end of last year,' Esther went on, wiping her face clean of the remaining cream. 'A boy aged six months. It's destroying Annette apparently. She was never strong; one of those women who are always ailing. I suspected from the start that she's consumptive. Richard is suffering the loss too. He wanted an heir so much.'

'I'm sorry for their grief.'

She turned her head to look at him, intensity in her eyes.

'Are you, David? How sorry? Would you be prepared to give Andrew to Richard to bring up as his son?'

'What!' David took a step towards her, shocked by the idea.

She stood up, slender in her white satin negligee. 'I've been thinking about it for weeks,' she said quickly. 'It would be the answer to everything.'

'Now wait a minute . . .'

'You said yourself that Ruth doesn't want the child back. Richard and Annette are desperate for a child. And it would be wonderful for Andrew. Think what Richard can do for him. He'd be Richard's heir.'

David felt his jaw clench spasmodically. 'You've actually discussed this with him before consulting me?' he asked angrily.

'I sounded him out. I told him that the father is dead

and that Andrew is unwanted by his mother. He's thinking about it.'

'I don't like the way you're taking everything into your own hands, Esther,' David said forcefully. 'Ruth gave Andrew to my mother. We should consider her wishes, not to mention Ruth's.'

'Your beloved Ruth has abandoned her son,' Esther said bitterly. 'Obviously she has no further interest in him. I'll not have the child stay here. He goes to Richard if he'll have him.'

'It's against the law surely.'

'We're not selling him, for heaven's sake,' Esther exclaimed irately. 'And Ruth wasn't very concerned about the law, was she?'

'I suspect she had no alternative,' David said defensively. 'In my opinion she married a religious fanatic. Heaven alone knows what she's been through.'

Esther lifted her chin stubbornly. 'It's in Richard's hands now. He'll let me know his decision in a few days.'

'Richard contacted me at the coal yard earlier,' Esther told David when she returned home from business the following week. 'He wants us to call on him at his home later this evening to discuss Andrew.'

He shook his head. 'I'm not certain about this, Esther,' he said. 'It's not what Ruth would've wanted.'

'Oh, I think we know what Ruth wants,' Esther said. 'She wants to be free of an inconvenience.'

'That's not fair,' David said angrily. 'We don't know her circumstances.'

'At least have the courtesy to meet with Richard,' she said. 'There's no harm in talking about it. Besides, I thought you wanted the best for Andrew. What better future than being the first son of a rich man?'

David was silent. He could not argue with that, but his thoughts were with Ruth. She would be broken-hearted if she knew her child was being bartered about like some unwanted dog.

*   *   *

Richard lived in a large house on Gower Road. The headlights of Sydney's big Humber motorcar played across the imposing frontage of the house as David manoeuvred the vehicle down the driveway. He was impressed by its size despite himself. The prospect of Ruth's son inheriting this grandeur one day gave him pause for thought.

He pulled up outside the front door, got out and then helped Esther descend from the car. The front door opened immediately and Richard stood there to greet them in person, his pleasant face all smiles for a change.

It was bitterly cold this mid-February night and David was glad to get inside the large hall.

'Come into the sitting room,' Richard invited. 'There's a good fire going there.'

They shed their coats and hats and followed him in.

'You'll take a drink of course. Whiskey for you, David? I know Esther will take sherry.'

She smiled at Richard warmly and David averted his eyes, wondering why he was feeling so put out.

They settled down with their glasses. David ran his tongue nervously over his lips.

'How is your wife?' he asked politely.

Richard hesitated for a moment before answering. 'Annette remains unwell. The doctor has attended her but I've called for a second opinion. Her family's doctor from Cardiff will be down tomorrow.' He looked down into his glass for a moment. 'I'm fearful though,' he went on quietly. 'She grows weaker with every passing month. Grieving for our son has taken a terrible toll on her.'

'I'm so sorry, Richard,' Esther said. 'You must be suffering also.'

There was so much real emotion in her voice that David stared at her. She was always so indifferent with him; always flippant. He wondered what she would do if Annette Hamilton died. Richard would then be free.

'Perhaps the child . . . Andrew would make a difference,' Esther went on eagerly. 'I know he can't replace her own child but . . .'

'I've mentioned your proposal to her,' Richard said.

'Perhaps it was unwise to do so before we had discussed it, but she's very keen to see the boy. His story has touched her heart.'

'His story?' asked David, glancing suspiciously at Esther.

'His being abandoned by an uncaring mother,' Richard said.

'That's an exaggeration,' David said quickly. 'I'm sure his mother cares a great deal.'

Esther gave a muffled exclamation of impatience but otherwise remained silent.

'She's known to you then?'

'Yes.'

'I have to ask this. Is the child illegitimate?'

Esther glanced at David. 'Well . . .'

'No,' David said emphatically. 'The boy comes from a respectable family; a Christian family.' He gave a bitter laugh. 'One might say a pious family.'

Richard raised his eyebrows obviously surprised at David's vigorous defence of the child's background. 'Then why did the mother part with her son?'

'She was falsely accused of adultery,' David said trying to control the tremor in his voice. 'I can only suppose she felt he was in some danger from her husband, a religious fanatic, who believed he had been wronged.' This was the only conclusion he could make to account for Ruth's decision. 'But there was no wrong-doing, Richard, I assure you.'

'Am I allowed to know the mother's name?'

'Richard, I'm sure you'll understand when I say no,' David said gravely. 'If this influences your decision then I'm sorry.'

Richard put his glass on a side table, stood up and began to pace the room.

'If I agree to take the child I may be breaking the law,' he said at last. 'A man in my position must be careful. If I do agree I must ask you both to say nothing of this to anyone.' He looked at Esther. 'Not even your stepfather, Esther.'

'My mother will have to know,' David said quickly. 'The child's mother entrusted him to her care.'

Richard shook his head. 'I can't risk it.'

'Not even for Annette's sake?' Esther asked. 'Richard, the boy might make all the difference to her and to you, too. I know you long for a son. David's mother will say nothing. You have my word on that.'

'Esther, you have no right to speak for me or my mother,' David said fiercely, rising to his feet. 'I think we should forget the idea altogether.'

'Let's not be hasty,' Richard said. 'Of course I'm cautious, David. It's a big decision and responsibility to take another man's child as my own.'

'He's an innocent, helpless baby,' David said. 'And he's from good stock. I know his family well. There'd be no risk for you, Richard.'

Richard took a deep breath and David could see that he had finally made up his mind.

'When can I see the child?'

'You could call at my uncle's house next week . . .' David began, but Esther interrupted him.

'We'll bring him to you,' she said swiftly. 'The day after tomorrow.'

David swallowed convulsively. That sounded so final. It was not that he didn't trust and respect Richard, but he felt guilty realizing he was about to give Ruth's baby away to a comparative stranger.

'You're still unsure, David,' Richard suggested.

David sighed. 'No, I am sure, Richard. We'll bring Andrew to you whenever you want.'

'Shall we say tomorrow afternoon early? Usually my wife does not rise until then.'

David nodded agreement and rose to his feet ready to leave. He could see Esther was inclined to linger and was annoyed at her undisguised eagerness to remain in Richard's company.

'We should leave Richard in peace now, Esther,' he said shortly.

She rose reluctantly. 'I'm so glad to be the one to aid you Richard,' she said softly. 'Please don't hesitate to call on me any time for further help.'

Richard nodded and then glanced at David, obviously embarrassed by Esther's warm tones.

'Thank you both,' he said. 'Annette is grateful too.'

As David had expected, his mother was very cut up and angry when he told her their decision about Andrew.

'You and she had no right!' Sarah exclaimed loudly, tears already brimming in her eyes. 'Andrew was given to me. I would've brought him up, now he's been taken from me without as much as a by-your-leave. That interfering wife of yours has a lot to answer for, David.'

'It's for the best, Mam. Andrew will have everything a child could want with Richard Hamilton. He'll have a real future ahead of him.'

'Will he have love, that's the question?' Sarah said tearfully. 'Esther couldn't wait to be rid of him. And I see no sign of you having children of your own.'

David turned away not wanting to discuss that.

'Now, don't carry on, woman,' George said gruffly. 'As David has said, we mustn't discuss it outside these four walls. I for one am glad it's all settled, and rightly so.'

David was not so settled in his mind that they had done the right thing. While he was aware of the advantages to Andrew in the arrangement, the idea that Ruth was in ignorance of her child's fate and would remain so troubled him greatly. He felt he had betrayed her.

Fourteen

E dwin left about five o'clock, driving the gig over to the hamlet of Penwern five miles away to take the midweek evening service. Ruth watched him from the bedroom window driving away through a thin flutter of falling snow flakes.

She went downstairs then to the sitting room where the only fire was lit in the house except for the kitchen range, but she would not step foot in the kitchen while Mrs Cardew was present.

Refusing to sit with Edwin to be ignored all evening she used the sitting room very rarely but she made herself comfortable there now. Usually she made do with going to bed early and trying to keep warm with a hot water bottle. The service at Penwern would not end until after seven thirty, so she could look forward to a good few hours of relative comfort.

At six o'clock Mrs Cardew came into the room. Ruth had lit one oil lamp although she neither wanted to sew or read, but the soft glow was comforting in the darkness.

'It's snowing heavy now,' Mrs Cardew announced imperiously. 'So I'm going home before it gets dangerous under foot. My old legs are not what they were.'

Ruth ignored her, keeping her face averted. She could not even bear to look at the woman.

'I've left sandwiches for the pastor when he gets back,' the woman went on, irritation in her voice at Ruth's lack of response. 'And there's some of that beef broth left.'

Ruth remained silent.

'I wouldn't be surprised though if the pastor has to spend the night at Penwern,' Mrs Cardew went on as though determined to get a reaction from Ruth. 'There's a blizzard blowing. The roads could become impassable for a gig.' She sniffed. 'Mr Allerton ought to get himself one of those new motorcars,' she said. 'It's not as if he can't afford one from what I've heard.'

It was too much for Ruth. 'You'd better go,' she said sharply. 'And I'll thank you to keep your opinions to yourself.'

'Hoity-toity!'

Ruth had no more to say and after a moment Mrs Cardew left. Ruth heard the front door close with a heavy slam and was thankful to be alone.

She sat for a long time curled up in a chair before the fireplace, thinking about Andrew, her heart heavy, wondering how he was. It was almost three months since Mrs Beale had taken him, and in all that time she had not bothered to send one word about his welfare.

Ruth continually considered writing to the woman to enquire, but remembering her promise she had made no move to find out her new address. Soon spring would be here and then early summer. When that time came she would go in person to Swansea to find her son, promise or not.

From time to time during the evening Ruth fed the fire with coal and a log. She did not envy Edwin out on a night like this, but he would do his duty, she thought bitterly, even if it killed him.

When it became late Ruth fetched a couple of blankets, deciding not to undress but to remain in the sitting room where it was warm instead of going upstairs. The bedrooms were chilled and it was difficult to keep warm even in bed. Ruth glanced at the clock on the mantelpiece before turning out the oil lamp and snuggling down. Nine o'clock. Edwin could arrive at any time if the roads were passable, but she thought Mrs Cardew was right. He would probably stay the night at Penwern.

She woke suddenly to complete darkness, certain there had been a disturbing sound outside. The fire had gone out and the room had chilled. She fumbled with the matches and managed to light the oil lamp before taking it to the window.

Pulling back the curtains she looked outside. It had stopped snowing. Cold moonlight was reflected off snow which lay thick on trees, hedges and piled in high drifts against the foot of stone walls. Everything was white and still and strangely clear.

As she let the curtains fall back into place Ruth heard the sound again. It appeared to come from the back of the house and she recognized it then; the whinny of a horse, a horse in distress.

Carrying the lamp Ruth hurried through the house to the kitchen and opening the back door stepped out into the yard and into deep snow. Shivering with cold she raised the lamp high and saw the animal moving frantically about near the stable. It turned to her as it saw the light, whinnying again, its eyes staring in terror. Its harness was still on and attached to one side was a splintered length of wood.

Ruth took in a sharp gasp, recognizing it as part of one shaft of Edwin's gig. Where was he? And where was the rest of the gig?

Anxious, she took a step towards the horse, but it reared up, screaming, and she hesitated. By the lamplight she saw blood glistening on its belly and flanks. She dare not attempt to restrain an injured animal on her own. She must get help.

Ruth hurried back inside the house, put on some thick shoes, hat, coat and warm muffler, and leaving by the back door started off making for her father's cottage. The snow was up over her ankles and made walking heavy going. She fell once but picked herself up and trudged on.

She was near tears with fright and dread when she reached her father's cottage. She hammered frantically on the door, praying she would be heard, but it was some time before a window opened above her and her father's voice called out.

'Who is it that wakes Christian folk at this ungodly hour?'

'It's Ruth, Father,' she called out on the edge of hysteria. 'I need help. Something has happened to Edwin. His horse has returned home without him and the animal appears injured. Father, please help me!'

The window was slammed shut and within a few short minutes Jacob, in his long white nightshirt, opened the door.

'What's that you say? The pastor is missing?'

'Yes,' Ruth sobbed. 'He went over to Penwern to take the service . . .' She hesitated suddenly realizing a new day must be dawning. 'Last evening. He didn't return.'

'Come inside,' Jacob ordered sharply. 'I must dress and raise the alarm. Make me a hot drink before I go.'

'Is there time for that?' Ruth asked, nervously twisting her hands together. 'We must search for him now. He may be lying injured somewhere.'

Her father did not answer, but went upstairs. Ruth went to the kitchen and put the kettle over the fire in the range that was always banked up with small coal at night and never allowed to go out. When Jacob came down again fully dressed, followed by Olive, Ruth had a steaming cup of tea waiting.

Hot as it was he drank it down almost in one swallow. 'Get back to the Manse,' her father told her brusquely. 'And be ready for the worst.'

Ruth put her hand to her throat. 'What?'

'Oh, dear me!' Olive exclaimed. 'Whatever has happened to our dear pastor?'

'I'll send someone for the doctor,' Jacob said as though to himself. 'Tom Bowen has a sleigh. We'll need that.'

'What about the horse,' Ruth asked anxiously. The thought of the animal in pain filled her with dismay.

'I'll rouse the farrier,' said Jacob. 'Get back to the Manse quickly. I'll send him straight there.'

Ruth and her mother struggled back to the Manse through the snow. Olive was out of breath by the effort but still talked incessantly while Ruth kept silent. Her mind was in a quandary. If Edwin was found injured or, God forbid, dead, what would happen?

They reached the house at last and had just gone inside and had lit a lamp when someone knocked on the back door. It was Dai Prosser, the farrier.

'I've had a look at the animal,' he said as he knocked snow off his boots before stepping over the threshold. 'Can't save the beast. Its belly has been gashed open by something like a jagged rock. I'm fetching my shotgun.'

'Oh, no!' Ruth exclaimed. If the horse had been injured Edwin must be also.

'Can't be helped, Mrs Williams,' he said looking at Olive and ignoring Ruth, which annoyed her.

'Do what you must then,' she said to him shortly.

With only a flickering glance at her he left.

'Sit down, Mam,' Ruth said, straining to keep her voice under control.

She was facing the grimmest situation a woman could find herself in, the loss of a husband. Still villagers treated her as though she was a pariah and she was heartily tired of it.

'How long do you think they'll be finding the pastor?' asked Olive.

'Hours possibly. The roads are difficult,' Ruth answered wearily. 'I'll get a fire going in the range. The doctor may need boiled water.'

She was surprised how calm she felt now when on the walk home she had been confused and frightened. Whatever had happened to Edwin she must face it with fortitude. If he was badly injured and needed care then she would shelve her plans to leave until he recovered.

Olive took a seat near the range still wearing her hat and coat against the chill of the kitchen. 'It's a terrible thing to be widowed so young,' she said mournfully. 'A punishment for your sins.'

'Mam, you're talking utter rubbish!' Ruth burst out angrily. 'If I'm the sinner why would Edwin's life be taken and not mine?'

With shaking fingers she added small pieces of coal to the paper and wood in the range grate and then put a lighted match to it.

'Besides, I haven't sinned,' she went on sharply. 'God knows that even if my family and neighbours believe other-wise.'

'You gave the child away,' Olive said. 'That speaks for itself.'

'I gave Andrew away because Edwin, his father threatened

127

his life and for no other reason,' Ruth snapped. 'You think because Edwin is pastor he can do no wrong.'

'Tsk! Tsk! Speaking ill of the dead. Ruth, how could you?'

'You're jumping to conclusions, Mam,' she said impatiently. 'Edwin may well be alive but injured.'

As she spoke two loud reports sounded from outside, making them both jump.

Ruth hurried to the back door. Dawn was just breaking to give just enough light to see what was happening in the yard. The poor horse lay on its side near the stable door, the snow around its head turning almost black with its blood.

Ruth turned away appalled and shocked and stumbled back into the kitchen. Dai Prosser followed her to the doorway.

'I'll tow the carcass away now,' he said matter-of-factly and left.

Ruth went to tend to the fire, piling more coal on. She felt detached as though it was all happening to someone else.

'We'd better be ready with hot drinks once the men return,' Olive said. 'They'll be chilled through and through.'

'They've not been gone long enough yet,' observed Ruth. It would take longer than a couple of hours to search the five miles of road between here and Penwern. 'Plenty of time for that when they get here.'

It was past seven o'clock when someone hammered on the front door. Ruth hurried to answer. Her father stood there with a group of men behind him.

'We've found him,' he said in a low voice. 'He's badly injured.'

'But he's alive!' Ruth put her hand to her throat, relieved. She could not bear the thought of Edwin dying before knowing the truth that Andrew was his son. 'Oh, thank God.'

'Yes, amen to that,' Olive put in. 'I feared the worst.'

'He needs our prayers for he's only just alive,' Jacob said solemnly.

He turned to the waiting men and waved his arm and Ruth saw that they were supporting a makeshift stretcher between them. The four men carried Edwin through the door and

Ruth rushed forward to go to her husband, but Jacob held her back.

'Stand aside, Ruth,' he said harshly and then spoke to the men. 'Take him upstairs to the front bedroom.'

They quickly followed his instructions.

'I must go to him,' Ruth said in agitation. 'He needs me.'

'No. He's in great pain. The doctor has given him morphine,' Jacob went on. 'He's gone home to fetch more.'

'What happened?' Olive asked.

'It looks like the gig slipped off the road into a ravine about two miles outside Penwern,' Jacob said. 'We were lucky to spot him in undergrowth.' He looked at Ruth gravely. 'Your husband may not last the night.'

'Oh, no!' Ruth was unable to believe it. 'It can't be true.' She had a sudden sense of relief that Edwin was no longer a threat to her child, but just as quickly she felt deep shame at her reaction. She had never wished her husband dead.

'The doctor believes he has serious internal injuries. He'll know more when he's examined him in his own bedroom.'

Ruth was filled with dread. Edwin could not die still believing she had betrayed him. She had to see him; let him know he had been badly misled by a spiteful woman.

'Is he conscious?' she asked anxiously. 'I must speak with him, Father. Andrew is his true son, and Edwin needs to know that before the end.'

'Edwin is dying, Ruth,' Jacob said brusquely. 'He'll not want to spend his last hours on earth looking at the face of the wife who wronged him and means to deceive him still.'

She knew it was no good protesting her innocence against her father's closed mind. She needed to see Edwin.

'But he's my husband,' Ruth said. 'I have every right . . .'

'No,' Jacob interrupted. 'You squandered all rights as his wife when you sinned with David Beale.' He began to ascend the stairs and then turned to look down at her. 'The men will need hot drinks after the hours they've spent in the cold. Make yourself useful, Ruth and see to it.'

Wringing her hands with frustration, Ruth hurried back to the kitchen, her mother hard on her heels. She quickly made tea and put the steaming cups on a tray and then moved towards the passage to the front of the house.

'I'll take those up,' Olive said quickly moving to take the tray from her.

'No, Mam.' Ruth stepped aside. 'I've got to see Edwin.'

'It's no place for a woman up there. Leave it to the men.'

'But Edwin has to know the truth before it's too late,' Ruth burst out passionately. 'He must not die still believing that awful lie.'

'Tsk!' Olive looked angry. 'There's no point in raking that up again, not with the man breathing his last.'

'There's every point,' Ruth retorted. 'Edwin desperately wanted a son and he doted on Andrew until that viper spewed her poison. He can't die believing a lie. It isn't right, Mam.'

'Oh dear!' Olive looked flummoxed. 'I don't know what your father will say if you go upstairs now.'

'I don't care what Father says,' Ruth burst out.

Pushing past her mother Ruth headed for the stairs and climbed them quickly. She nudged open the bedroom door and went in. Immediately her father came forward to take the tray from her.

'I forbade you to enter this room, Ruth,' he said forcefully. 'How dare you disobey me?'

'This is *my* home, Father,' Ruth said fiercely. She was conscious of the other men looking on, but ignored them. 'How dare *you* dictate to me here?'

She put the tray on a table and hurried to the bedside. Jacob tried to intercept her, but she was determined and pushed his hands away.

'Jacob,' the doctor said in a low voice. 'Let there be no commotion. The pastor is very weak.'

Ruth stood at the bedside, her hands twisting together in distress. Edwin lay there very still, his complexion ashen. There were cuts and bruises about his face, but Ruth knew that the fatal injuries were hidden.

'Edwin,' she said softly. 'Edwin, it's me, Ruth, your wife.'

His eyelids fluttered and opened so slowly as though he found it hard to lift them.

'Ruth.' His voice, the voice that had boomed out many

sermons in the chapel, was a mere hoarse whisper. 'I'm glad you're here.'

'Edwin, I must tell you something,' Ruth said hurriedly, sensing there was little time left. 'Something vitally important to you.'

'At last you confess?' he asked in a tired tone. 'Confession is good for the soul, Ruth, and here on my deathbed I forgive you your sins against me and against God.'

'But I did *not* sin,' Ruth said. She heard her father's angry murmur behind her but ignored him. 'Edwin, before you die you must believe me when I say that Andrew is your true son.'

'Ruth . . .' There was a weak protest in his tone. 'Please!'

'Listen to me, Edwin!' Ruth cried out. 'Do you think me such a wicked woman that I'd lie to you, my husband, on your . . . your deathbed?'

He stared up at her and she saw uncertainty kindle in his eyes for the first time and perhaps a gleam of hope.

'I was never false to you, Edwin, never,' Ruth said earnestly. 'I was never even tempted to be untrue. My marriage vows are sacred to me and I would never scorn them.' She took hold of his hand and held it against her heart. 'Andrew is your son, your true son, and no other man's. Let the world know this as God's truth.'

'Ruth!' Edwin tried to rise from the bed, but she gently pressed him back. 'You must forgive me for what I did,' he whispered. 'I'm so ashamed of it.'

'Edwin, you must not distress yourself. You don't know how ill you are.'

'I know I'm dying, Ruth, and I need your forgiveness,' he said hoarsely. 'I've done you a great disservice which must be put right.' He looked past her to Jacob. 'Jacob, fetch Mr Bromage, my lawyer in Sketty before it's too late.' Weak as it was there was urgency in his voice. 'I must change my will again.'

'The roads are blocked with snow,' Jacob said in agitation. 'It would take hours, I doubt you have . . .' He broke off in confusion, glancing at the doctor and the other men for support.

'I'll go, Pastor. I'll borrow the sleigh,' one man said and left the room immediately.

'Ruth,' Edwin said, his voice barely a whisper now. 'I've done a terrible thing. I instructed Bromage to write a new will, leaving my money and all worldly goods to my cousin in Scotland.'

Ruth shook her head, clutching at his hand. 'Edwin, don't think of that now. It doesn't matter. Conserve your strength.'

Edwin lifted his other hand towards the doctor, and spoke urgently. 'Doctor, Jacob and you there Tom Bowen, be witnesses that I rescind my current will in favour of my wife Ruth and our child Andrew.'

'Don't agitate yourself, Pastor,' the doctor said quickly.

'Swear that you will support my wishes,' Edwin said. His voice was so faint that Ruth, standing nearest to him, could hardly hear his words.

'Edwin, please,' Ruth said gently, a sob in her throat. 'You must lie still.'

He sank back. His lips were moving but now Ruth could hear nothing at all. She bent and put her ear against his mouth. It was a sound no more than a faint sigh. 'Forgive me.'

Fifteen

Edwin, her husband, was dead. Tears flooding, Ruth sat with both arms on the kitchen table, her head buried in them. She had not loved him the way she had loved David, but now she felt a deep emptiness and regret; sorrow that Edwin had been taken so soon, that their life together had ended so suddenly and pointlessly. And had been so bitter.

She was conscious of Olive sitting at the table with her in silence. Perhaps her mother was filled with regret, too, for the way she had failed to understand or help her.

She heard footfalls on the back stairs leading down to the kitchen. She did not need to look up to know that her father and the others had entered the room.

'The Lord gathers those he loves to him,' Jacob said in a sombre voice.

Ruth sat up with a jerk, rising anger helping her to swallow back her tears. 'I don't need your platitudes at a time like this, Father,' she said loudly. 'Save them for the chapel.'

Olive gave a gasp and Jacob looked shocked, glancing askance at the doctor and Tom Bevan in embarrassment, but Ruth did not care what they thought.

'I forgive you for those words and so will the Lord,' he said gravely. 'He knows you're in grief.'

'I don't need your forgiveness,' Ruth said. 'And the Lord knows how badly I've been treated by my family.' She looked at the other two men. 'And by those who should know better.'

The doctor shuffled his feet, his face reddening. 'I'll be going now, Mr Williams,' he said directly to Jacob, still ignoring her. 'There's nothing more I can do here.'

With a sideways glance at Ruth he moved to the back door, followed quickly by Tom Bevan.

'Thank you both for your help,' Jacob said as they left.

'You might've given your thanks, too, Ruth,' Olive said complainingly. 'After all, the men risked the snow looking for the pastor.'

'They did it for Edwin not for me,' Ruth retorted. 'I was shunned, remember?'

'But that's past now,' Olive said complacently. 'It can all be forgotten.'

Ruth shook her head. 'Oh no, it can't,' she said quickly getting up from the table. 'I'll never forget the injustice or forgive it either. My family, my so-called friends and this village have treated me contemptibly.'

'Those are harsh sentiments,' Jacob said. 'We're your parents. You should respect us.'

'Harsh!' Ruth exclaimed. 'After you turned your backs on me? I think not.'

'Ruth, things have changed now,' Jacob said. 'Edwin released you from the shunning on his deathbed. You are vindicated, and I'm glad. It's hard to turn one's back on one's own child.'

Ruth stared at him. He obviously had no idea what he and her mother had done to her.

'But I had to, didn't I? If both of you had had more faith in me when I came to you for help in protecting my child Andrew would still be here now.' She wrung her hands in distress. 'I've lost everything, my child, my husband and my home.'

A knock sounded at the back door. Jacob went to answer. It was the man who had gone for the lawyer. He snatched off his cap and stepped over the threshold, snow still clinging to his boots.

'Mr Bromage wouldn't come out in the snow for fear of getting stuck,' he announced. 'He'll be writing to the pastor as soon as possible.'

'He's too late,' Ruth said. 'My husband died not long after you left.'

The man tipped his head. 'I'm sorry,' he mumbled.

'Do you want a hot drink?' Ruth asked.

He shuffled his feet. 'I best be getting back home. I've

been gone all night. My wife will be worrying.'

'Thank you for your efforts,' Ruth said to him as he left.

Olive rose from the table. 'We must be getting back to our cottage, too,' she said tentatively. 'You're welcome to come with us, Ruth. There's no need for you to stay here.'

Ruth shook her head. 'I'll not leave Edwin alone in an empty house,' she said quietly. 'It wouldn't be right.'

Olive nodded agreement. 'I'll go along to Madge McGinn to arrange for her to come and do the laying out.'

Ruth nodded silently, thoroughly weary.

'We must discuss arrangements for the funeral later today,' Jacob said importantly. 'There's a lot to do. There must be an emergency meeting of the chapel deacons to discuss what to do next. A new pastor must be appointed.'

'It can all wait until tomorrow as far as I'm concerned. I want to be alone for the rest of the day,' Ruth said bitterly. 'I have no interest in the deacons' deliberation and as for the chapel I'll never set foot in there again.'

'Ruth!'

Ruth shook her head firmly. 'Please leave me to my loss,' she said. 'I grieve for my lost son as well as my husband.'

Ruth turned and hurried from the kitchen leaving them to find their own way out. She went upstairs, walking slowly past the bedroom she had shared with Edwin, the door now closed on the room's occupant now past all of life's cares.

She went to the second bedroom. Weak winter sunlight flooded the room. She felt exhausted and had almost forgotten it was almost mid-morning. Without bothering to undress, she climbed on to the bed and pulled the covers over her. She did not know if she could find relief or solace in sleep at this strange hour, but she must try.

It was early evening and dark when Ruth woke feeling a stab of guilt that she had slept when Edwin lay dead in the other room.

She got off the bed and lit a candle to make her way downstairs, but paused outside the bedroom door where he lay.

Quietly she opened it to peer in at the silent form under the sheet and stood gazing a few moments more, still unable to believe what had happened. And there was probably more strife to come, for now her future was uncertain.

Ruth closed the door as quietly as she had opened it and went downstairs, going straight to the kitchen to make a cup of tea. She had to think and plan.

She would not be allowed to stay at the Manse now and she did not want to. She would not even stay in Gowerton. Her heart ached for Andrew, her beloved son, and she was determined to go in search of Mrs Beale to get the boy back. As soon as Edwin's funeral was over she would leave.

Ruth was up early the next day expecting her parents to call to talk about funeral arrangements. She was in the kitchen when the back door opened unexpectedly and in walked Mrs Cardew.

Ruth was momentarily stunned to see her.

'I heard about the pastor. Tsk! Tsk! What a tragedy,' Mrs Cardew said, her glance anywhere except looking Ruth straight in the eyes. 'You'll want help with the funeral tea, I expect.'

'Get out!' Ruth screeched at her.

'That's no way to behave when someone offers help,' Mrs Cardew said huffily, taking a step back.

'You're only here for what you can get your thieving hands on,' Ruth shouted. 'You poisonous old crone.'

'Oh! I'm not staying here to be insulted,' Mrs Cardew spluttered. 'I'll take the wages owing to me and be off.'

'Huh!' Ruth scoffed. 'You'll not get a penny piece out of me so you can be off as soon as you like.'

'You can't swindle me!' Mrs Cardew squeaked with fury. 'I'll have the law on you, I will.'

Ruth picked up the wooden breadboard on the table where she had been cutting slices off a loaf and raised it above her shoulder.

'Get out of my sight before I throw this at your head, you poisonous witch!' Ruth yelled. 'Go on! Get out!'

With another squeak Mrs Cardew turned and scuttled out of the door. Ruth put the breadboard down and sank on to a chair nearby, trembling and feeling a little ashamed that she had lost control of her temper so readily.

Jacob and Olive called mid-morning. She took them into the sitting room where a fire was lit.

'The thaw has set in,' Olive said, sitting with her hands outstretched to the warm glow from the fireplace. 'Your father went down to the shop this morning early. He found the road itself clear of snow. Things are getting back to normal.'

Ruth gazed at her mother's complacent expression. Normal? Her life had not been normal since she had married Edwin. But now that part of her life was over and she must plan for a new beginning with her son.

'I have news from the deacons' meeting,' Jacob said. He stood before the mantelpiece, thumbs in his waistcoat pockets. 'I've prevailed upon them to let you remain at the Manse until the new pastor whoever he might be is ready to take up residence.'

'Thank you, Father,' Ruth said. 'When is that likely to happen?'

'Some weeks yet,' Jacob said. 'Invitations will be extended to several good men to take the living. In the meanwhile it would be wise for us to make plans for your future.'

'I've already made up *my* mind what I'll do,' Ruth said with determination. She could tell from her father's expression that he believed he could still dictate to her.

'I think it prudent that you return to living with your mother and me,' Jacob went on as though she had not spoken. 'A young woman recently in widowhood can't be too careful of her reputation.

'My reputation!' Ruth gave a hollow laugh. 'That's already been destroyed in Gowerton thanks to Edwin and that scurrilous old woman, Mrs Cardew.'

'But you've been vindicated now,' Olive said. 'Edwin's death-bed words have absolved you from any wrong doing.'

'Have I?' Ruth was sceptical.

She did not doubt that her parents now felt satisfied she

was innocent hearing Edwin's last words, but how many in the village would accept it? No smoke without fire; that would be the widespread feeling in the community. She did not intend to live the rest of her life under that shadow.

'Nevertheless, Ruth,' Jacob said in a serious tone. 'Returning to the safety of our cottage will help heal opinion and keep you from further temptation. In time the village will forget.'

Ruth shook her head. It was obvious her father still did not trust her despite her vindication and that made her angry.

'But I'll not forget the injustice, Father, and neither will I take your hypocritical charity.'

Jacob gave a grunt of anger.

'Don't turn your back on us, Ruth,' Olive spoke waspishly. 'Don't be an ungrateful daughter.'

'How dare you, Mam!' Ruth exploded. 'You turned your back on me and my child. You took Edwin's word over that of your own daughter. You were very quick to believe the worst of me, and for no reason.'

'There was no choice,' Jacob thundered. 'The evidence was there plain to see.'

'What evidence?' Ruth flared. 'The word of a thief and a liar?' She shook her head. 'There's no place for me here any longer. After the funeral I'll leave Gowerton for good.'

'Where will you go?' Olive's tone was uncertain.

'I'm going in search of my child,' Ruth said firmly. 'Andrew is Edwin's son, I remind you. I deeply regret giving him away, but I had to to save his life. It's broken my heart. My one hope is that I can find him again and we'll be reunited.'

Jacob shuffled his feet, looking down at the mat. Ruth had rarely, if ever, seen her father contrite.

'If this is your wish, Ruth, than we must dispute Edwin's will,' he said soberly. 'Otherwise you and the child will be penniless.'

'I'll find work in Swansea,' Ruth said. 'I'll wash my hands of all that has happened in the past. I don't want anything of Edwin's.'

'Brave words, Ruth,' Jacob said sternly. 'But you've never known want.'

'I'm strong and not afraid of work, Father. I'll take any job no matter how menial.'

'Poverty can force women alone into sinful ways,' Jacob cautioned severely, rousing Ruth's anger again. 'Especially in a town like Swansea, with its seaport, and alehouses on every corner.'

'You may not credit me with morals and principles, Father,' she said loudly. 'But I have them and mine are strong. We'll say no more on this matter, if you please. My mind is made up.'

Word had obviously got around that on his death bed Pastor Allerton had rescinded the edict to shun his wife and in the days that followed his passing a steady stream of people from the village called at the Manse to offer their condolences.

Ruth welcomed them, although many were not able to look her in the eye, she noted, but she was gracious in the name of Edwin's memory.

Louisa came with her husband Mervyn. Ruth was glad to see them in spite of the differences they had had in the past. They stayed to tea, and Ruth poured out her heart about Andrew. Louisa was supportive in her vow to get her son back, but was sorry to learn that Ruth intended to leave the village for good.

'We could've renewed our friendship,' Louisa said. 'I'll miss you, Ruth, dear.'

One afternoon two days before the funeral Ruth had an un-expected visitor. She opened the front door to find a tall big-boned woman dressed in black standing on the doorstep who looked to be in her late forties. Beside her on the step were two carpet bags.

'I'm Mrs Myra Campbell,' the woman announced im-periously in a strong Scottish accent. 'I'm Edwin's cousin, down from Scotland for the funeral and the reading of the will.'

Ruth stared at her open-mouthed.

'Well!' Myra Campbell exclaimed huffily, picking up the two carpet bags. 'Am I not to come inside?'

'I'm sorry,' Ruth said confused. She stepped aside to allow

the woman to enter the hallway. 'I had no idea you were attending the funeral.'

They stood together in the hallway.

'I take it you're Edwin's widow,' Myra Campbell said dropping the bags unceremoniously on the parquet floor.

Ruth nodded.

'Well, Bromage should have warned you,' Myra Campbell went on. 'Personally, I doubt the man's competence.' She glanced around her. 'It's very cold here. I hope the bed is aired.'

Ruth swallowed. 'You're staying here?'

Myra Campbell lifted her chin. 'Indeed, where else would I go? I am Edwin's main beneficiary, you know.'

Ruth frowned. 'How do you know that? No one knows exactly what's in the will.'

Myra Campbell sniffed. 'Bromage wrote and told me.'

Ruth was annoyed. The lawyer had not even come to see her, Edwin's widow, but was very free with information to Edwin's relative.

'The Manse doesn't belong to Edwin, you know,' Ruth said quickly. 'It's chapel property.'

Myra Campbell sniffed. 'I know that,' she snapped. 'But everything in it belongs to me or will do after the reading. I hope you're not going to dispute that.'

Ruth shook her head. 'No, I'll keep only my own personal things.'

'See that you do. Now where is the body?'

Ruth put her hand to her mouth shocked. 'At the chapel in the village,' she said after a moment. 'Why?'

'I wish to see my cousin's remains before the funeral to pay my respects,' Myra Campbell said. 'He's my benefactor. I'm a widow-woman left poorly off. This legacy will keep me from abject poverty in my old age.'

'Were you very close to my late husband?' Ruth asked.

'I never met Edwin Allerton in my life,' Myra Campbell said frankly. 'And I'm very surprised he remembered me in his will. Of course, I'm his only living blood relative.'

That was not true, Ruth thought. Andrew was Edwin's closest living relative, but she decided to say nothing about that at present.

Myra Campbell gave an impatient sigh at her silence. 'Well, come along, Mrs Allerton,' she said, picking up the bags again. 'Show me to my room. And mark me I refuse to sleep in the rumpus room. I need space.'

Ruth led the way upstairs to the main bedroom, which had been thoroughly cleaned, the bed pristine.

'Will this do?' she asked with some sarcasm. 'It's the master bedroom.'

Myra Campbell put her bags on the bed. 'It'll do very well.' She took off her gloves and unbuttoned her coat. 'I'll require a pot of tea, if you please.'

It was her tone of voice that annoyed Ruth. 'I'm Edwin's widow not a servant,' she said clearly. 'And this is not a guest house.'

'I'm a guest, nevertheless,' Myra Campbell snapped back an answer. 'And the main beneficiary, I remind you. I expect some courtesy.'

'Well, you can come down and take tea in the kitchen,' Ruth said with asperity.

'I most certainly will come down.' Myra Campbell stared around her. 'It's like an icehouse in here.' She glanced at the empty fireplace. 'I'll want a fire lit in my room this evening.'

Ruth left her and went downstairs fuming. She had never met anyone so highhanded and felt annoyed with Mr Bromage, too, for not warning her of the woman's arrival.

There was not a lot to eat in the house but Ruth did the best she could with what there was and provided her guest with a decent hot meal at supper time.

'I'll go to bed now,' Myra Campbell said after the meal. 'It was a long train journey down from Scotland to Swansea yesterday. I spent the night in a bed and breakfast house. The bed was hard and the breakfast foul. I hardly slept.'

'Goodnight, Mrs Campbell,' Ruth said. 'I hope you sleep well here.'

Myra Campbell paused. 'We're cousins by marriage,' she said. 'You may call me Myra. Your name is Ruth I understand?'

Ruth was surprised. 'Yes.'

'I doubt we'll ever meet again once the will is read,' Myra said loftily. 'And I take possession of all that is likely to be mine, but in the meantime there is no reason for us to be distant with each other.'

Ruth was flabbergasted. 'Take possession?'

'When in Swansea yesterday I arranged for a sale to be held here at the Manse the day after the will is read.'

'What?' Ruth stared.

'I suggest you use tomorrow to gather together your personal possessions. Everything else, furniture, fittings, rugs, curtains will be sold.'

'You intend to sell my bed from under me?' Ruth could not believe it.

'It's not your bed, Ruth.'

'But the chapel deacons have given me permission to stay at the Manse until a new pastor is appointed, which could be weeks yet,' Ruth said. 'How will I manage without even a bed?'

Myra sniffed. 'That's not my concern. I have to return home to Scotland by the beginning of next week, and I expect all my business to have been concluded by then.'

'You're being unreasonable,' Ruth exploded. 'And cavalier as well, not to mention mercenary. I don't think Edwin would have approved of your behaviour.'

'Huh!' Myra drew in her chin in arrogance. 'I hardly care about that. I know my rights in this matter.'

The following morning Ruth got up to find Myra already up, dressed and breakfasted and touring the house with paper and pencil making a note of all saleable articles of furniture and fittings.

'This Welsh dresser is a good one,' she remarked thoughtfully to Ruth as she entered the kitchen. 'It'll fetch a good sum I think.'

Ruth did not bother to answer, disgusted at the way Myra was examining the household goods in almost a gloating way.

When Jacob and Olive called later, Ruth introduced Edwin's cousin to them. Ruth watched as her mother and

142

Myra eyed one another, both making assessments.

'Mrs Campbell will be selling up the household after the funeral,' Ruth told her parents. 'Lock, stock and barrel.'

'Dear me!'

'I won't be able to stay on here after all,' she went on.

'Then you must come to us.'

'No, Mam, I'll leave Gowerton the day after the funeral,' Ruth declared. 'Well before the sale starts. Luckily, the motor coach to Swansea passes through the village that day. But I'll wait at your cottage until it's due, if you don't mind.'

'I wish you wouldn't go,' Jacob said, speaking for the first time. He gave Myra a glaring glance. 'It's monstrous that you must be evicted at such short notice.'

Myra tossed her head, giving him an arrogant look. 'I must be getting home soon, and I'll not go without my inheritance.'

Fearing an argument would ensue, Ruth lifted her hands for silence. 'Perhaps it is just as well,' she said calmly. 'The sooner I go to Swansea the sooner I'll be reunited with my son.'

'Edwin has a son?' Myra looked astonished, glancing from one to another. 'Why didn't he inherit? I don't understand.'

'Vicious gossip turned my husband against his own child,' Ruth said, feeling a lump rising in her throat. 'He turned his back on both of us until it was too late. He died before he could make amends.'

'He wanted to change his will again,' Jacob stated. 'But the Lord took him before he could do so. There were witnesses to his dying wishes.'

'Now look here!' Myra exclaimed hotly. 'Ruth promised she would not contest my cousin's will. The legacy is mine, fair and square. Bromage assured me of that.'

'I don't intend to dispute your claim,' Ruth said wearily.

'Well, I intend to have it out with that lawyer,' Jacob said gruffly. 'The man's a charlatan.'

'Father, Mr Bromage is doing his job.' Ruth intervened. 'I hold no grudge against him. He's not responsible for poisoning Edwin's mind against me.' She lifted her chin and looked him directly in the eye. 'Even my own parents had no faith in me. You were very ready to believe the worst.'

Jacob made a grunting sound and turned away and Ruth wondered if she would ever be able to forgive them.

The day of Edwin's funeral was sharp and cold. The snow had gone, and seemed gone for good, but there was a heavy frost during the night. Ruth had been to the village the day before accompanied by Myra Campbell to buy provisions. Ruth expected a large gathering at the Manse after the funeral and was determined no one should sneer at the repast she would provide for the mourners.

Ruth sensed that Myra was with her to check on her expenditure, so convinced was she that Ruth was spending her inheritance.

'So much ham,' Myra remarked as they emerged from the grocer's. 'So much bread.'

'Edwin was well-respected,' Ruth said. 'Mourners will come long distances from surrounding villages and hamlets. I'll not see him shamed for want for an extra ounce of ham.'

In all fairness to Myra, Ruth thought, the woman pitched in to help prepare the food. She was glad attending the funeral was not expected of her, that being a male prerogative, so she and Myra remained behind with Olive at the Manse while the men of the village went about their solemn business.

The mourners gathered in the sitting room later, drinking port or sherry and eating the ham sandwiches. The room seemed very crowded with most of the prominent men from Gowerton and the surrounding villages present.

Ruth was glad to see that Mr Bromage, Edwin's lawyer, had condescended to attend the funeral, even though he had made no attempt to contact her beforehand.

The lawyer was talking earnestly with some of the more important men. Ruth could see her father was trying to join the selective group, and was apprehensive at what he intended to do. She hoped he would not tackle the lawyer about the will so publicly.

'So that's Bromage,' Myra said, standing at her elbow. 'He looks in his dotage as I suspected.'

'I suggest we get about the washing-up,' Ruth said shortly. Disparagement of anyone, no matter how mild, made her very angry. 'Some of the mourners have already left.'

Eventually the sitting room was empty except for family members and the lawyer. Mr Bromage was now sitting in front of the fire, a glass of port in his hand. His head was nodding slightly and his glass tipping dangerously.

Sharp-eyed Myra noticed and tutted impatiently. 'Time for the reading of the will, I think, Mr Bromage,' she said loudly, startling him awake. She settled herself in a chair opposite him.

'Before that,' Jacob spoke up. 'I must raise an objection.'

'What?' Myra glared at him in fury. 'You and your wife have no business to be here,' she declared. 'You're not beneficiaries.'

'Ah! But Mr Williams is a beneficiary,' Mr Bromage said. 'A small bequest, which must be discussed.'

'Oh!' She stared at him for a moment as though she would challenge his word, but said no more.

'I'm deeply touched,' Jacob said. 'I had no idea.'

Myra fidgeted impatiently. 'Please get on with the reading, Mr Bromage,' she said testily. 'Otherwise we'll be here for hours.'

The lawyer cleared his throat, putting his unfinished glass of port on a table nearby.

'The will is straightforward,' he began. 'The small bequest to Mr Jacob Williams is Mr Allerton's horse and gig.' He cleared his throat again. 'Since the horse has now been destroyed and the gig too, it is deemed right that the value of same shall be handed to Mr Williams as a sum of money.'

'Huh!' Myra tossed her head. 'That comes out of my inheritance, I suppose,' she said crossly.

'You shouldn't be inheriting anything,' Jacob snapped. He glanced at the lawyer. 'Mr Bromage, my son-in-law, on his deathbed, made a new will.'

'What?' Myra was on her feet in a flash. 'This is outrageous!'

Mr Bromage looked at Jacob enquiringly. 'And where is this new document, pray?'

'There is no document,' Jacob blustered, going red in the face. 'It was his spoken wish, his dying wish, that his wife and child inherit all his money and possessions.'

'Oh, you would say that, wouldn't you?' Myra shouted. 'Hoping for a share yourself, no doubt.'

Ruth felt dreadful wishing the floor would open up and swallow her. Had everyone forgotten she was in mourning? She wished her father would leave the matter alone, but she could tell from his furious expression he would not.

'How dare you, woman?' Jacob glared at Myra and then turned to the lawyer. 'My intentions are honourable, sir. I am a man of strong Christian conviction.'

Mr Bromage shook his head, and Jacob rushed on. 'There were witnesses to his words,' he said hurriedly. 'The doctor who attended him and Tom Bevan, farm labourer; both men of integrity.'

'That's as maybe,' Mr Bromage said. 'But word of mouth cannot be taken as evidence of a change of heart by Mr Allerton.' He waved the document in his hand. 'Here we have a legal document duly signed and witnessed. This will must stand.'

'I should hope so, too,' Myra said and sat down again.

'But I protest . . .' Jacob exclaimed loudly.

Unable to bear the altercation any longer Ruth rose to her feet. 'I, Edwin's widow, do not contest the will,' she said firmly. 'I want no further argument. Please get on with the reading. I wish to be done with it all.'

'But Ruth, you'll be penniless. How will you live?' Olive said. 'It's not right.'

'It wasn't right when Edwin denounced me from the pulpit,' Ruth cried. 'It was cruel and appalling, but no one rushed to my defence then. I don't want your help now.'

She was conscious of Myra's expression, full of shock and curiosity. Well, her husband's cousin could think what she liked.

Suddenly Ruth felt her spirits rise. She was determined to shake the dust of Gowerton from her shoes tomorrow. Somewhere in Swansea was her son, Andrew. She would find him and claim him and go forward to a new life, forgetting all the unhappiness of the past. She deserved some happiness and she would fight for it.

Sixteen

It was fortunate that the weekly motor coach to Swansea ran through Gowerton on the very day that she had to leave the village. Ruth left the Manse early without bothering to say goodbye to Myra, and made her way to her parents' cottage knowing they would be up early.

Olive opened the door to her. 'Ruth, we've been waiting for you,' she said anxiously, glancing at the two carpet bags on the step at Ruth's feet. 'I can't believe you really mean to leave us.'

'My mind is made up, Mam,' Ruth answered firmly.

'Your father wants a word with you.'

Ruth stepped over the threshold as Olive stood aside.

'Nothing he can say will change my plans,' she said. She had been through too much and her heart ached now to put all her misery behind her.

'He's in the parlour waiting for you.'

Ruth pulled out a chair at the kitchen table and sat down.

'Let him come to me here if he wishes to speak,' she said lifting her chin. 'I'm no longer beholden to him, Mam.'

'He's still your father,' Olive said, an edge of disapproval in her tone.

'Yes, a father who believes me weak and without moral character. He let me walk a lone path when I was shunned, and didn't lift a finger to help me.'

Olive wrung her hands. 'Oh, can't that bad time be put behind us?'

'That just what I'm doing in leaving Gowerton,' Ruth said sharply. 'I learned to survive when I stood alone. I can do it again elsewhere. Tell Father that I'm here.'

Olive left the kitchen and returned within a few minutes with her father. He came into the kitchen looking angry.

147

'Ruth, have you no respect for your parents?'

'I used to respect you both,' Ruth said without rising from her seat. 'But when you abandoned me I lost faith in you.'

'Those are bitter words,' Jacob said heavily.

'I received bitter treatment, Father,' Ruth reminded him. 'And it was not deserved.'

He pulled up a chair and sat. 'I don't want you to leave Gowerton,' he said soberly. 'Your place is here. You're a widow and should abide with us. That is the respectable thing to do. You should heed your parents' wishes.'

'You want to keep me here so that you can continue to dictate to me the way I should live?' she said, keeping her gaze averted.

'No,' Jacob said. 'So that I can provide for you as a responsible father should.'

At his softened tone, Ruth looked at him. Perhaps he regretted his lack of faith in her. If he did it must be a sharp lesson for him. Her heart softened a little too. Her father was what he was and would never change, but she should not condemn him for it. He was a good man who lived a clean life. But it was too late. Things could never be as they once were.

'That's good of you, Father, and I appreciate your concern,' Ruth said softly. 'But I must now make my own way in the world, and make a life for my son.'

'But you are penniless, girl,' Jacob said strongly. 'How will you live?'

'I have a little money saved from my yearly dress allowance,' Ruth said. She looked down at her left hand. 'When I get to Swansea I'll pawn my wedding ring and also the string of pearls that Edwin gave me. He told me they were valuable. I'll find work of some kind. I'll manage, Father.'

'I'm afraid for your soul, girl.'

'I'm my father's daughter,' Ruth said stalwartly. 'My faith and my moral courage are strong. No harm will come to me.' She paused. 'However, I would be grateful for your blessing.'

Olive burst into tears. 'Oh, Ruth, I'll miss you so much and the baby too.' She sobbed. 'I was at his birth and I love him, you know. I was proud of him even though pride may be sinful. He's a bonny boy.'

'I can't change your mind then, my daughter?' Jacob said.

'No, Father. I have to do this. There's no life possible for me here.'

'Then go with my blessing, my daughter. Let us say a prayer together,' Jacob said quietly. 'We'll ask the Lord to bless and protect you and the child.'

Later, as she was about to leave, Olive clutched at her arm.

'Write to us, Ruth,' she begged. 'Let us know what's happening to you. Don't cut us off.'

Ruth promised solemnly that she would and left the cottage then, waving a last goodbye at her parents standing on the door step. Her glance lingered on them and a lump came into her throat at the sight of their sorrowful faces. She had resented them for their treatment of her, but now they were parting she felt a great sadness.

She turned the bend in the road and the cottage was lost to sight. Ruth quickened her steps forward, feeling as though she was now hurrying towards that new life that she longed for.

She reached the Star Inn where the coach usually stopped and sitting on a stone seat outside she waited. It was no more than a few minutes before the vehicle came along and stopped.

The only passenger waiting, Ruth boarded the bus and bought a ticket for Swansea from the driver. She took a seat and stared though the window. The bus moved off retracing her own steps. Within a few moments it passed her parents' cottage. They were no longer on the step and the door was closed. Ruth felt a stab of pain, as though a knife had cut through a vital vessel in her heart and she had to get control of herself to stop tears from welling up.

The coach rolled on through the village. She watched the little shops and cottages slide past, and then they were in open countryside.

As soon as the last of the village was behind her, Ruth felt her spirits lift again. Her excitement grew. She was going to find her beloved son. They would be together again. A new life was opening out for her and she felt revitalized. It was going to be a good life, she was sure of it.

*   *   *

149

It was midday when the coach, now quite full of passengers, reached Swansea. Ruth peered through the window as the vehicle made its way to the bustling centre of the town: the streets teemed with wagons and drays, people swarmed the pavements all seeming to be in a hurry to get somewhere. Obviously it was market day.

'Market!' the driver sang out.

Almost all of the passengers stood up, ready to descend. Ruth followed suit, stepping down on to the pavement. As the coach moved away she found herself outside the big middle gates of Swansea Market, a red-brick, glass-roofed building, and watched, fascinated, the cockle women in their white aprons clustered around the entrance, their baskets of sea produce spread invitingly before them.

The sight made her feel hungry, but before she could eat there was business to see to. The little money she had would not last long. She was determined to pawn her wedding ring and the string of pearls as soon as possible and so set off down Oxford Street to find a pawnbroker's shop.

She had gone some distance along the crowded street being bumped and buffeted by fellow pedestrians, feeling nervous. Gowerton had never been like this. Stopping at a corner to allow a brewer's dray to pass, she noticed the traditional sign of the pawnbroker down a side street, and immediately made her way towards it.

She paused outside the shop nervously, staring in the window at the items on offer. There were quite a few wedding rings and other jewellery on display. Would the proprietor be fair with her, she wondered anxiously.

Taking courage, knowing she had little choice she opened the door, startled as a bell rang loudly, and stepped inside. A counter stretched across the room at the far end, screened off by iron bars. A man stood at the opening between the bars.

He nodded at her. 'What can I do for you, madam?'

'I want to sell my wedding ring,' she began hesitantly.

'I see.' He sounded bored.

She took off her glove and removed the ring from her finger and held it out to him. 'How much can I expect to get for it?'

He examined the ring, placed it on a small weighing machine and peered at the dial.

He pursed his lips doubtfully. 'I'll give you a guinea for it.'

Ruth was very disappointed, and dismayed too. 'But it's twenty-two carat gold,' she said.

He shrugged. 'Missus, I have too many similar wedding rings in stock I hardly need another,' he answered. He put the ring on the counter before her as though no longer interested.

'Are you sure you can't offer more . . .?' Ruth began hopefully, but he shook his head. 'Very well then,' she went on dispirited. 'I have no choice but to accept.'

He took up the ring and going to the cash register returned with the money and handed it to her. Ruth took it and then hesitated.

'Have you something more to offer?' he asked.

Ruth delved into her handbag and brought out the blue velvet box that contained the pearls. He took them and held them up to the light, peering at each pearl though an eyeglass.

Ruth caught a fleeting expression of eagerness on his face which he immediately corrected as he turned to her.

'Where did you get these pearls?'

'They were a gift from my deceased husband. Circumstances are forcing me to sell. I understand they're valuable,' she said.

He shrugged again. 'They're quite good but nothing out of the ordinary,' he said too casually. 'I'll give you five guineas for them.'

'No!' Ruth was angry. 'They are worth much more than that.'

'Ten then,' he said.

Ruth snatched the pearls from his fingers and put them back into the box. 'I think not!'

'How do I know they're not stolen?' he asked nastily.

Ruth paused, scowling at him. 'Because my husband kept the receipt, and I have it. Good day to you.'

Fuming, Ruth left the shop slamming the door behind her as she went, sending the bell tinkling madly. She walked smartly back along Oxford Street, passing the red-brick walls of the market again, and then saw the sign for the Market Café. It reminded her that she was hungry and so she went through the gates and into the busy market where the café occupied one corner of the building.

Ruth looked for a vacant seat at one of the long tables covered in oil cloth which stretched across the width of the room, which was very crowded and noisy. She found an empty space at the very end of one table and sat down thankfully. Quite soon a young girl came and asked for her order.

'A cup of tea, please,' Ruth said. 'And something to eat. What have you got?'

'What about a nice ham bakestone?' the girl suggested helpfully. 'They're fresh today.'

Ruth smiled. 'Thank you. That would be lovely.'

The food and drink were brought to her within minutes.

'That'll be sixpence altogether,' the girl said.

Ruth handed her the money. 'Oh, by the way, miss,' she said quickly. 'Are there any good lodging houses around here?'

The girl put her finger to her lips thoughtfully. 'It's best to go just outside the town centre to find lodgings. They'll be cheaper than in town. Go along St Helens Road, I would.'

'Where's that,' asked Ruth.

'Go back out through the middle market gate and then go up Portland Street to St Helens Road. You'll probably see rooms to let at the lower end.'

With a nod of thanks Ruth finished off her meal and then made her way. She stood on the pavement at the top of Portland Street and gazed around trying to get her bearings. A little way up on the opposite side stood an imposing chapel with iron railings around it. There was no chapel so splendid in Gowerton.

Intrigued, Ruth crossed the road for a closer look. The board outside said Mount Pleasant Chapel. Although she had vowed never to set foot in the chapel back home, she had missed her regular services of worship. This chapel looked as though it might have a good congregation. She could attend there and be lost in the crowd.

As she turned away something caught her attention in the narrow street that ran along the side of the chapel. Dynevor Place was lined with many-storied gabled houses. What caught her eye was a sign in the window of one house advertizing a room to let.

On impulse Ruth walked along the street to examine it, but the house looked dingy; lace curtains yellowed with grime and lack of soap and water and Ruth turned away disappointed. Walking further along, she came to another house with a sign advertising a vacancy for a live-in maid.

Ruth stopped and looked the house over. Here was a chance to find work and lodgings together. The place looked respectable, clean and well-cared for, and after a moment's hesitation she walked up the three steps from the pavement to the front door and knocked.

There was a long delay and Ruth was about to turn away when the door opened and she faced a tall, gaunt-looking woman probably in her mid-fifties. Her prominent nose pointed aggressively at Ruth and her dark eyes flashed suspicion.

'Yes? What do you want?'

Ruth swallowed. 'I've come about the notice for a live-in maid,' she began.

The woman opened the door wider and looked her up and down shrewdly. Ruth felt confident that she would pass inspection in her wool coat of Prince of Wales check which was only a year old, and her black felt cloche hat.

The woman sniffed. 'You'd better come inside.'

Ruth edged past her and the woman closed the door securely.

'I don't normally answer the door,' the woman said in an imperious tone. 'But my maid has run off without so much as a by-your-leave.'

She moved off down a wide hallway. 'This way.'

Ruth followed in her footsteps, wondering why the previous maid had left so abruptly.

Several doors let off the hallway and the woman opened the first one. 'In here, if you please.'

Ruth obediently followed her inside. The room was a typical Victorian sitting room. The heavy furniture was of excellent quality, but dated. Obviously nothing had been changed for decades.

'Well, now,' the woman said in a cultured voice. 'What qualifications do you have?'

Ruth didn't hesitate. 'I kept house and cooked for a pastor of the chapel back home,' she said, which was very true.

The woman raised her eyebrows. 'From cook to maid? A bit of a come-down?'

'The minister died,' Ruth said. 'I have no family,' she fibbed. 'So decided to look for work elsewhere.'

'Yes, well . . .' She looked Ruth up and down again. 'You can't expect to get the same wages as a cook. Maids are two a penny here in Swansea, you know.'

'I can be cook, too,' Ruth said helpfully.

'That won't be necessary. We have a cook.' She paused. 'How old are you?'

'Twenty-one.'

'I don't allow followers for my servants,' the woman said sharply. 'This is a respectable Christian house.'

'And I don't encourage followers,' Ruth responded quickly. 'I too am respectable.'

The woman blinked and then pointed her nose again in response to Ruth's retort. 'I won't tolerate disrespectful servants,' she said curtly. 'It's not your place to answer back.' Her tongue clicked with displeasure. 'It seems to me that servants have got above themselves since the war.'

'I'm sorry,' Ruth said humbly.

She knew she wanted this position. Despite the woman's lofty attitude Ruth sensed the atmosphere of the house was good. It would suit her nicely to live and work at the centre of the town, making it easier to search for the Beales' shop in her spare time.

'Very well,' the woman said, acknowledging the apology. 'What is your name?'

'Ruth Allerton,' Ruth said.

'Are you married?' the woman asked, her eyes narrowing suspiciously.

'What makes you ask?' Ruth countered, her voice faltering.

'There's a pale mark on the ring finger of your left hand.'

154

Ruth covered her hand self-consciously. 'I'm a widow,' she said.

'Are there dependant children?' The woman's gaze was penetrating now. 'I can't have a maid who's always running off to see to sick children.'

'I have no children,' Ruth said thickly.

'Well, I'll have to take your word for it I suppose, but I warn you, the slightest neglect of your duties will mean instant dismissal.'

'I understand.'

'Very well, then,' the woman said. 'I am Miss Hamilton but you may address me as Miss Lydia. I'll call you by your first name if you decide to take the work.'

'What is the wage, ma'am?' Ruth asked carefully conscious that her prospective employer had a prickly nature.

Miss Lydia tilted her head craftily. 'Five shillings a week, all found; every Wednesday afternoon off. It's half day closing on Thursdays in Swansea, so you see I'm being very generous.'

'Thank you,' Ruth said, still striving to sound humble. She had hoped for more, but at least there would be no rent to pay.

'When can you start?'

'Right away,' Ruth said eagerly. 'I arrived in Swansea only a few hours ago. I have nowhere to stay.'

'Very enterprising of you to find work and a place to sleep so soon,' Miss Lydia said. 'I hope you'll be as diligent in your work.' She glanced at Ruth's carpet bags. 'Is that all your luggage?'

'Yes, Miss Lydia.'

'Your room is in the attic, up the last flight of stairs,' Miss Lydia said. 'There is a paraffin heater provided for your use. You see I am a generous employer.'

Ruth dipped her head and smiled her gratitude. Lydia Hamilton would require careful handling, but Ruth was used to watching her every word and look with her mother, Olive.

'Take your bags up to your room,' Miss Lydia instructed. 'You'll find a maid's uniform in the wardrobe.' She glanced at Ruth's figure. 'It should fit you. If not you can alter it on your own time.'

'Yes, Miss Lydia.'

'Now go and change and then come down to the base-ment kitchen and I'll introduce you to our cook, Mrs Withers.' Miss Lydia paused. 'Oh and yes, in future use the basement entrance if you please.'

'Yes, Miss Lydia.'

Without another word the older woman walked out smartly and Ruth went into the hallway.

The house was a tall one and Ruth found the attic bedroom on the fourth floor under the eves. It was quite a large room with a single bed, a wardrobe and chest-of-drawers of the same heavy furniture as downstairs. There was an oak wash-stand on which stood a white china bowl and jug. The round paraffin heater stood in the centre of the room looking for all the world like a black mushroom, but Ruth was glad to see it because the room felt cold.

She put her bag on the bed and then opened the wardrobe. A maid's uniform – dark blue dress and white cotton apron – hung there. On a shelf in the wardrobe was a stiff cotton cap. Ruth took the uniform out and inspected it, wondering again about the previous wearer. It looked clean so she put it on, hanging her dress in the wardrobe. It took her a while to fix the cotton cap safely, but she finally managed it with a hairpin.

The wardrobe mirror showed her that the uniform was a little slack on her neat figure, but she would soon put that right. She felt pleased with the day's progress so far.

She glanced out of the small rather grimy window before she left the room. The attic was so high up it overlooked the chapel roof opposite where a family of pigeons strutted about. She wished it overlooked the town itself, but she could not expect everything.

After one last glance around the room that would be her home for the foreseeable future, Ruth went downstairs to begin her duties.

The kitchen was large; it was clean and smelled delicious from whatever was cooking on the big range at the far end. Mrs Withers, the cook, proved to be a short stout woman with a pleasant friendly expression and Ruth took a liking to her straight away. Miss Lydia introduced them in a stiff fashion as though she thought the task was beneath her.

'Ruth will be living in, of course, Mrs Withers,' Miss Lydia said. 'She'll take her meals here in the kitchen with you. She may help you in preparing meals if it doesn't interfere with her own duties.'

'Yes, ma'am.' Mrs Withers gave a little bobbing curtsey.

'Is lunch ready?' asked Miss Lydia. 'Mr Timothy will want his in the study. Prepare a tray and Ruth can take it up to him. I'll have mine in the dining room as usual.' She gave Ruth an all-enveloping glance. 'I trust you'll soon learn our routine, Ruth.' With that she left the kitchen.

When she had gone Mrs Withers released a long sigh. 'She likes the look of you, I can tell, Ruth,' she said cheerfully. 'Her Nibs can be a tartar on times. And it's no fun getting on the sharp end of her tongue.'

'Thanks for the warning,' Ruth smiled. 'Who is Mr Timothy?'

'Miss Lydia's bachelor brother,' Mrs Withers told her. 'He's a dear old soul; not prickly like her.'

'How many in the family?'

'Just her and him,' Mrs Withers said. 'Rattling around in this great big house. Born here they were and their father before them. Richer than royalty they are, I reckon, but careful with it.'

Ruth's stomach rumbled loudly and she felt her face flush up with embarrassment.

Mrs Withers chuckled. 'Right then,' she said. 'Let's deal with their lunches then we can have ours.'

Ruth was relieved to hear that a meal was on offer. She was famished even after the ham bakestone.

'Mr Timothy first.' Mrs Withers handed Ruth a tray with a covered plate on it. 'Up the main stairs to the first landing, second door on your left.'

Ruth knocked on Mr Timothy's door and went in. Books were stacked everywhere, on shelves, heaped on chairs, tables, even piled against skirting boards. Amidst it all a small hunched figure sat at a desk.

'Your lunch, sir,' Ruth began hesitantly.

The white-haired man in his sixties turned to peer at her over half-rimmed spectacles. He had a gentle perplexed expression and kindly eyes.

'It is that time already?'

'Yes, sir.' Ruth came forward with the tray and placed it on the desk in front of him.

He looked up at her in a puzzled way. 'Who are you?'

'I'm the new maid, sir. My name is Ruth.'

He smiled. 'Ah! Good. Someone to help me with my books.'

Ruth smiled uncertainly. 'Miss Lydia didn't say anything about that, sir.'

'Call me Mr Timothy,' he said cheerfully. 'Sit down, sit down young woman and tell me your life story.'

Ruth removed the dish covering his plate. 'You'd best eat your lunch, Mr Timothy,' she said. 'Before it gets cold.'

Ruth left him and went back down to the kitchen. Mrs Withers had Miss Lydia's tray ready.

'The dining room is the last door along the passage,' she told Ruth. 'Hurry back so we can have ours.'

Later that night Ruth took a tray of tea up to her own bedroom, lit the paraffin lamp, undressed and got into bed. She sat propped up by pillows, sipping her tea, marvelling at her lucky chance in finding this house. Good fortune was on her side at last.

She thought of her parents. They would be anxious. She had brought writing paper and ink with her, and so she set about writing her first letter home, telling them of the good place she had found and of her hopes of soon finding Andrew.

Later, she lay in the darkness, feeling the strangeness of her new surroundings up in the eves, but cheered herself with thoughts of her first half day off which she would spend searching the streets for a sign of the Beales. Perhaps she would find Andrew next week or the week after. But she would surely find him again; she felt that in her heart with certainty.

Seventeen

'Jacob! Jacob!' Olive hurried into the kitchen where her husband was having his breakfast. 'Here's a letter from Ruth.'

He glanced up as she came in and she could see he was annoyed at being disturbed at his meal. She sat down at the table opposite him.

'I'll read it to you,' she offered, trying to suppress her excitement before him for she knew he did not approve of excessive cheerfulness, which was sometimes trying.

'Make it short,' he said. 'I have to get off to the shop.'

'Ruth says she's found work and lodgings together.' She glanced up at him. 'Isn't that fortunate?'

'I pray that it's in a God-fearing household,' Jacob murmured gloomily. 'I fear she'll be tempted into great wickedness away from our protection.'

Olive glanced up from the page she was reading, suddenly impatient with him. 'We should've had more faith in her when she was here, Jacob,' she said. 'I feel we've driven her away by being over zealous. Ruth is a good girl.'

Jacob frowned. 'Is that a rebuke, woman?'

Olive said nothing. Much doubt had taken over her thoughts since Ruth had left, and she had been fearful that they might never hear from her again. But now this letter had come. Perhaps Ruth had forgiven them after all.

'She's found a new chapel to attend already,' she told her husband with alacrity. 'It's right across the road from where she lodges.' She looked at her husband. 'You see, Jacob, she's not falling into wicked ways for all your gloomy predictions.'

'Huh! She's only been gone a few days.'

159

Olive stood up abruptly. 'I bitterly miss our daughter,' she said. 'I'd have thought you missed her too. After all, she's our only child.'

She folded the letter and put it in the pocket of her apron to mull over again later.

'She's a wayward girl in many ways,' Jacob said.

'No!' Olive exclaimed, and he looked shocked at her vehement tone. 'No, she's a good Christian, and we let her down, Jacob,' she went on strongly. 'I believe now that we were wrong to act as we did. We should never have insisted that she marry Edwin Allerton.'

'Woman, you're beside yourself!' Jacob exclaimed loudly, getting to his feet. 'You'll be suggesting next that she should have married that backslider, Beale.'

Olive held back a sob of regret. 'If she had she'd be here in the village with us, and we'd have the pleasure of grandchildren about us.'

He looked exasperated, and knowing him well she knew he was struggling to remember a scripture which would censure her natural feelings.

'You'll be late for the shop,' she said, forestalling him. 'Ruth says she's searching for Andrew. I just pray she finds him and that she allows us to see him again.'

Miss Lydia insisted Ruth should work a week in hand before receiving any wages and it was two weeks before she was allowed a half day off. On her first half day at the beginning of April she toured Oxford Street and the many little side streets round about to no avail. It was disappointing but she wasn't too downcast knowing she could resume her search again the following Wednesday.

Mrs Withers was looking rather flustered as Ruth let herself into the basement kitchen.

'Oh, thank goodness you're back,' she exclaimed to Ruth. 'You're just in time to take up the tea tray to the sitting room. Mr Richard has turned up.'

'Who's Mr Richard?' Ruth hurriedly put on her white apron and fixed her cap.

'Richard Hamilton. He's the nephew,' Mrs Withers said.

160

'He has an invalid wife – very sad.' Mrs Withers handed Ruth the tray of tea things. 'Her Nibs doesn't like to keep Mr Richard waiting. He's her pet. Very protective of him she is.'

Ruth took the tray up to the sitting room and was surprised to see that Mr Timothy had emerged from his den for once and was sitting before the fireplace with Miss Lydia.

A tall young man stood before the mantelpiece wearing a very well-cut three piece suit of fine pinstripe cloth. Even if she hadn't been told she would have known him for a Hamilton; his resemblance to his aunt and uncle, strong nose and firm mouth, was unmistakable although his features were a little finer; his expression pleasant.

'Pour the tea please, Ruth,' Miss Lydia commanded.

Ruth proceeded to do as asked.

'How's the boy?' Mr Timothy asked his nephew as Ruth handed him his tea cup and offered a plate of biscuits. He smiled up at her as he accepted it. 'Thank you, Ruth, my dear.'

Miss Lydia grunted disapproval at this pleasantry to a servant.

'Very well, thank you, Uncle Tim,' Mr Richard answered cheerfully. 'He's an exceedingly healthy child; a perfect child in fact. Annette has taken him to her heart; we both have. She seems to be in much better spirits since he arrived. And I'm so thankful for that.'

Miss Lydia gave a disdainful sniff. 'But it's not like one of your own, is it?' she said disparagingly as Ruth passed her a cup and saucer and offered the biscuits. 'I always said Annette was too sickly to produce healthy children.' She took two biscuits. 'And I was proved right,' she went on. 'But your father wouldn't listen to me.'

Ruth looked up into Mr Richard's face as she offered him his tea. He smiled tentatively and nodded briefly as he took the cup from her.

'It's water under the bridge now, Aunt Lydia,' Richard said.

Ruth detected weariness in his voice as though this was a frequent topic of conversation between them.

'But it's such a tragedy that you'll never have a child of your own flesh and blood,' his aunt persisted.

'You're wrong, Aunt Lydia,' Richard said resolutely. 'As far as I'm concerned James *is* my flesh and blood. I love him so dearly already and so does Annette. James is everything to us, and we couldn't be without him.'

'Oh, so you are naming him after your father then?' Mr Timothy said. 'I think that an excellent idea, my boy.'

'I thought it appropriate and Annette approved,' Richard said.

He drank his tea as though thirsty and then strolled across to Ruth as she stood at the small side table, awaiting Miss Lydia's further instructions.

'Is there another cup of Mrs Withers' excellent tea in the pot?' he asked.

'Yes, sir.' Ruth took his cup from him and refilled it. 'And it's still hot,' she remarked with a smile.

'You're new,' he observed as he watched her add a dash of milk. 'What's your name?'

'Ruth, sir. Ruth Allerton.'

'I'm Mr Richard,' he said simply with a ghost of a smile as he took the filled cup from her, his glance lingering on her face.

'That will be all, Ruth!' Miss Lydia exclaimed loudly. 'You're dismissed. Get back to the kitchen.'

Mr Richard frowned at the interruption but said nothing and walked back to stand before the fireplace again. Ruth quickly gathered up the empty cups and saucers and left the room.

'Mr Richard seems a nice man,' Ruth observed to Mrs Withers as she washed up.

She was impressed with him; his features somehow imprinted on her mind. He had kindly eyes and had his uncle's affability. He obviously wasn't a snob like his aunt.

'It's no fun having a sickly wife,' Mrs Withers observed. 'An arranged marriage, you know,' she went on. 'His father was adamant he marry into the wealthy Kreppel family of Cardiff. They own more coalmines than you could shake a stick at; not only in Wales but up North, too.'

Ruth felt immediate sympathy for Mr Richard. She knew only too well what misery there could be in an arranged marriage.

162

'Has he lost a child recently?' Ruth asked, remembering his words in the sitting room.

'Yes, an ailing mite like its mother, apparently,' Mrs Withers said. 'They've adopted a baby boy, as I understand it, to ease the poor young mother's grief.'

Ruth felt a lump in her throat. She had lost Andrew so she had a good idea of the mother's pain. She prayed her own son was alive and well and that they would soon be reunited.

'Miss Lydia was always against the marriage, you know,' Mrs Withers went on. 'And she's bitter about the fact that a child, not of Hamilton blood, will inherit the family business and fortune.'

'Perhaps they'll have another child,' Ruth suggested.

Mrs Withers shook her head. 'This one nearly killed her,' she said gravely.

Ruth was sad to hear it. 'Mr Richard is a young man,' she observed. 'It's so unfair.'

At that moment the sitting-room bell rang and Ruth went immediately to answer.

Miss Lydia was alone in the sitting room standing at the window gazing out.

'You rang, Miss Lydia. What can I get you?'

Her employer turned from the window and stared at her, there was a hard glint in her eyes.

'Do you value your position here, Ruth?'

'Why, yes, Miss Lydia, of course I do,' Ruth answered, puzzled by the hostility of her tone.

'Well, if you do,' Miss Lydia went on sternly. 'You'll desist from flaunting yourself before my nephew. I have never seen such blatant coquettish behaviour in my life.'

Ruth was stunned and stared open-mouthed, unable to find a reply.

'Young widows ought not to behave so outrageously, especially before married men.' Miss Lydia said emphatically. 'Since the war morality in young women has sunk to disgraceful depths. I dread to think where it will all lead.'

Ruth found her tongue at last. 'I assure you, Miss Lydia I did not flaunt myself as you put it. I did nothing outrageous.'

'You had the impertinence to smile at my nephew in a most brazen way. I saw you!' Miss Lydia snapped. 'It's not your place to smile or draw attention to yourself in any way when he is visiting.'

'But . . .'

'Don't answer me back!' Miss Lydia exclaimed, a touch of hysteria in her voice. 'I'll not tolerate defiance in my servants.'

Ruth waited silently for a moment while her employer regained her composure.

'That will be all, Ruth,' Miss Lydia said.

'I'm sorry you think I've acted wrongly, Miss Lydia,' Ruth ventured quietly, although her blood was boiling with anger. She did not want to lose this position. She felt comfortable and safe in this house.

'I have nothing more to say on the subject at present,' Miss Lydia said. 'But bear my warning in mind in future.'

Miss Lydia swept past her and left the room. After a moment Ruth followed and returned to the kitchen. Mrs Withers had already left. Ruth sat at the kitchen table for a while trying to understand why she had given offence. Had Mr Richard complained about her? Had she misjudged the kind of man he was?

A few days later the front door bell rang about four o'clock in the afternoon. She was taken aback to see Mr Richard.

'Hello, Ruth,' he said affably. 'Is my aunt at home?'

'Yes, sir,' Ruth kept her gaze lowered and her tone neutral in case she offended again.

He was about to take off his hat and coat to hang them on the hallstand, but paused looking at her. 'Is something wrong, Ruth?'

'No, sir.' Ruth ventured to lift her gaze. 'Well, yes, sir,' she went on quickly, bracing herself to speak out. 'I understand you've complained about my . . . forward behaviour to your aunt.'

'What?' There was a look of consternation on his face.

'Miss Lydia has reprimanded me for being familiar,' Ruth said stiffly. She bit her lip in consternation at being obliged

164

to apologize for something she had not done. 'I'm sorry if I've offended you, sir.'

He frowned. 'I haven't complained, Ruth, and I'm not offended, quite the reverse . . .' He paused. 'I mean, I like . . .' He stopped again. 'Where is my aunt?' he went on in a different tone.

'She's in the sitting room, sir.' Ruth was relieved that the subject was changed.

He took off his coat and hat and hung them on the coat stand.

'Any chance of a pot of tea?' he asked, his glance now averted.

Ruth was about to answer when she heard steps behind her as Miss Lydia came into the hallway.

'That will be all, Ruth, if you please.'

Ruth turned away immediately and went to the far end of the hallway where stairs led down to the kitchen.

Mrs Withers was rolling out pastry. 'Who was that?' she asked.

'Mr Richard,' Ruth told her.

The cook stopped what she was doing and looked up surprised.

'What, twice in one week?' She sniffed. 'There must be something up. Once a month is his limit to visit his aunt. Perhaps his wife has taken a turn for the worse.'

Ruth shrugged. 'He didn't look or sound perturbed,' she said. 'He wants a pot of tea. I'll put the kettle on.'

As Ruth was making the tea Miss Lydia came down to the kitchen. 'I was just coming up with the tea tray, Miss Lydia,' Ruth said hastily.

'That will not be necessary. Mrs Withers will serve the tea this afternoon,' Miss Lydia said imperiously.

Ruth was taken aback and Mrs Withers looked astonished. 'Yes, ma'am,' she said.

Miss Lydia left the kitchen and Mrs Withers turned to Ruth, with a puzzled expression.

'What's going on, Ruth?' she asked. 'What've you done to get her back up?'

Ruth shook her head. 'I did nothing wrong, Mrs Withers, I assure you.'

Reluctantly she told Mrs Withers about the warning she had been given regarding her behaviour with Mr Richard and how she had challenged him about it.

'I was annoyed that he'd complained. It seemed so petty,' Ruth said. She paused uncertain. 'Do you think I made things worse for myself by speaking to him?'

Mrs Withers chuckled. 'You've got backbone, Ruth. I'll say that for you.'

'It's so unfair,' Ruth said. 'I did nothing.' Why was it that people, even her own family, were willing to think the worst of her?

'I believe you, my girl,' Mrs Withers assured her. 'Her Nibs has got a bee in her bonnet and I'm beginning to think Mr Richard put it there. He's shown too much interest in you, that's the problem. With a sickly wife Her Nibs is afraid he'll stray, given the chance.'

'But he's a married man. He doesn't look that sort.'

'All men are that sort,' Mrs Withers said with a sniff. She clicked her tongue in sympathy. 'Mind you, I don't blame him really. He can't have much of a life with a wife who's always so poorly. It's unnatural for any man.'

Feeling embarrassed and uncomfortable at Mrs Withers' remarks, Ruth said nothing.

'Him visiting his aunt twice in one week.' Mrs Withers shook her head. 'There's something behind that.' She looked at Ruth with amusement in her eyes. 'He's never done it before, not while I've been working here anyway, which is years.'

'We'd better get this tray upstairs,' Ruth said quickly, not wanting Mrs Withers to speculate further. 'Or she'll be ringing that bell.'

Ruth carried the tray of tea things up to the hallway and put them on the table there.

'Leave it here when you're finished with it,' Ruth said. 'I'll take it down to the kitchen later.'

Mrs Withers was some time upstairs. Ruth made a pot of tea for them both while she waited and drank hers, wondering what on earth was going on.

The cook returned at last and sank on to a chair at the table.

'Standing around waiting on Her Nibs doesn't do my poor old legs any good at all,' she said in an aggrieved voice. 'I hope this won't become a habit.' She glanced at Ruth mischievously. 'Mr Richard looked quite put out to see me with the tray instead of you. I really think you've caught his eye.'

'Mrs Withers!'

Ruth set about her search for Andrew the following Wednesday. She went first to the Market Café and bought a cup of tea. The same young girl came along to rub the tables over with a damp cloth.

'Do you know of any new bakeries opening anywhere in town?' Ruth asked.

'Now you come to mention it,' the girl said. 'I noticed a new shop in Nelson Street, back of the market.' She pursed her lips thoughtfully. 'You know, I believe it is a bakery. All right, love?'

Ruth was filled with new optimism and offered a three-penny piece as a tip.

'Oh!' The girl looked delighted. 'Thanks, miss.'

Ruth hurried through the market to Nelson Street. She took her time to inspect each individual shop as she passed along the pavement.

Eventually she noticed one shop with a new looking red and white striped canopy and sparkling fresh paint. Sure enough the sign above the door proclaimed George Beale and son, Baker.

It struck her that David might be there behind the counter. She wasn't sure she wanted to set eyes on him again. The feelings she once had for him were buried beneath all the misery she'd known these last few years. Seeing him would rake it all up again. The past was best left undisturbed.

As she looked through the window, Ruth could make out the stout figure of David's father, George Beale, behind the counter.

Were the rest of the family there too? Perhaps they lived on the premises. Her beloved son could be just yards away from her. She might see him at any moment.

Excited by the thought Ruth stepped into the shop. Several women were clustered around the counter trying to attract the baker's attention. Ruth hung back waiting for them to be served. She did not want an audience when she made herself known to him.

The number of customers thinned at last.

'Who's next?' George Beale called.

'I am, Mr Beale,' Ruth said stepping forward.

'Yes, what is it you want, missus?' Clearly he did not recognize her.

'I want my son, Andrew,' Ruth said clearly. 'Where is he, Mr Beale?'

He stared at her open-mouthed, and his face went pale.

'Ruth!' Confusion and panic raced across his face, and Ruth was alarmed.

'What is it, Mr Beale?' she asked breathlessly. 'Has something happened to Andrew? For God's sake! Tell me!'

'Ruth, what're you doing here in Swansea?'

'Where's my child, Mr Beale?' Ruth demanded, her voice rising as an unnamed fear gripped her heart.

'Now don't get excited,' George Beale blustered. 'Andrew is well; he's fine.'

'I want to see him.'

'Look!' George Beale said somewhat tetchily. 'You've caught me on the hop. I don't think I should be talking to you, Ruth.'

'Why not? What's happened?'

'Well, you did give your child away, didn't you?' he said sternly. 'You can't just waltz in here and demand to see him.'

'I'm his mother!' Ruth cried out. 'I've every right to see him. Where is he?' she demanded. 'Upstairs?'

'No!' George Beale said. He glanced at waiting customers. 'You're holding up business, Ruth,' he said. 'Please go.'

'No, I won't go,' Ruth said belligerently. 'Not until I've seen Andrew. I demand . . .'

'If you don't leave, Ruth,' George Beale said heavily, 'I'll call a constable to you. You're causing a disturbance on business premises. You'll get arrested.'

'What?'

'I mean it, Ruth,' George Beale said vehemently. 'Leave my shop now!'

Feeling helpless and deeply disappointed, Ruth backed away, his threat to have her arrested frightening her. Her hopes had been so high and now they were crushed again.

Distraught she walked up and down Nelson Street for a while, wondering at George Beale's open hostility. Her sudden appearance had certainly knocked him for six. It was obvious he was concealing something from her.

She felt sick with fear for Andrew's well-being. How could she go on living with this terrible dread hanging over her? All she could do was pray that her beloved son had come to no harm.

Eighteen

With worried thoughts of Andrew crowding her mind, Ruth went down the area steps from the pavement to the basement kitchen and let herself in through the back door.

Mrs Withers swung away from the range, a saucepan in her hand as Ruth came in.

'Oh, there you are, Ruth,' the cook said in an agitated tone. 'Her Nibs wants to see you in the sitting room as soon as you come in. She's in a right old temper.'

Upset as she was by George Beale ordering her out of his shop in such a hostile way, Miss Lydia's bad mood seemed trivial. Hastily donning cap and apron, Ruth went up to the sitting room.

Lydia Hamilton was standing before the mantelpiece, her straight bony back turned. She swung round as Ruth entered.

'Well!' she exclaimed loudly. 'At last!'

'It is my afternoon off, ma'am,' Ruth reminded her. 'And I'm not late back.'

'Never mind that,' Miss Lydia said in a heavy tone. 'Something very serious has come to my attention.'

Ruth waited, wondering what stupid house rule she had broken.

Miss Lydia turned to the mantelpiece again and lifted something off and held it out. Ruth took in a sharp breath to recognize the blue velvet box in which she kept her string of pearls.

'Yes,' Miss Lydia exclaimed. 'You might look guilty. Now! I demand to know from where you stole these pearls. Was it your last employer?'

'Give me that!' Ruth rushed forward and attempted to

170

snatch the box from her employer's hand. 'You've been rummaging in my room!' she flared. 'How dare you!'

Miss Lydia whipped the box out of Ruth's reach. 'Just as well that I did,' she said archly. 'I've uncovered a thief.'

'Hand over that box,' Ruth demanded, thoroughly angry. 'That's my property. You've no right to search my belongings.'

'These pearls yours? Huh! As if I'd believe such nonsense.' Miss Lydia lifted her chin imperially. 'Now, you'd better confess and tell me who these really belong to, otherwise I'll have to call the law to deal with you.'

Ruth stared. That was the second time today that she had been threatened with the law.

'The pearls are mine; a gift from my late husband,' Ruth said more calmly. 'And I can prove it. I have the receipt.'

Miss Lydia's eyebrows rose sceptically. 'Oh, really!'

'I'll fetch the receipt,' Ruth said gratingly. 'And then I'll expect an apology from you, Miss Lydia.'

Ruth turned and hurried from the room. The receipt was always kept safely in her handbag. Returning with the document she handed it to Miss Lydia.

'You can see it's from well-known jewellers in my home town, and dated more than two years ago,' she said in a hard tone, furious that the appellation of thief had been attached to her.

Miss Lydia took a sharp intake of breath as she looked at the receipt, obviously surprised at the sum the pearls had cost. It had always astonished Ruth, too.

'My husband's name, Edwin Allerton, is also on the receipt,' Ruth went on. Feeling vindicated she took the receipt back and gave her employer a defiant stare, holding out her hand for the velvet box. 'Return my property, please, and I'm waiting for an apology, Miss Lydia.'

Miss Lydia looked haughty.

'I do not apologize to servants,' she said. She handed the box to Ruth. 'But I'll say this. I think it most inconsiderate and careless of you to keep such expensive jewellery in the house. It will attract burglars.' Miss Lydia put her hand to her throat. 'As long as those pearls are in this house I'll have no rest,' she said. 'I suggest you sell them.'

171

'Easier said than done,' Ruth retorted sharply. 'I'll not take less than their worth.'

Miss Lydia looked thoughtful. 'I'll speak to my nephew about it. He might be able to help,' she said. 'Leave them with me.'

'No,' Ruth said hastily. 'The pearls are none of your concern or Mr Richard's. I'll dispose of them when I find the right buyer.'

'But . . .'

'You branded me a thief without cause,' Ruth said angrily. 'And now you refuse to apologize. So much for Christian charity.'

'Well, really! The impertinence!'

Ruth returned to the kitchen. Mrs Withers' expression showed she was anxious. 'Are you sacked?'

'No,' Ruth said grimly.

'What happened?'

'Miss Lydia called me a thief to my face.'

'What!' Mrs Withers drew back looking astounded. 'What was it you were supposed to have stolen?'

'My own jewellery,' Ruth said. 'According to our employer servants are not allowed valuables, and so must have thieved them.'

She shook her head despairingly. She had been wrongly branded a thief as if she did not have enough misery in her life.

Sarah Beale had just risen from her afternoon nap and was sitting at the dressing table brushing her hair when the bedroom door burst open and her husband rushed in.

'Oh, hello, dear,' she said. 'You're home early. Is David with you?'

'David is up in Neath again at the coalmine,' he said bitterly. 'He spends more time up there now than he does at the bakery.'

'George, you know full well that Esther wants him to enter the business with Sydney,' Sarah said impatiently. 'And you can't deny it would be the best thing for him. Much more profitable than the bakery.'

'But he's a baker,' George snapped. 'That's his trade. What

172

does he know about coalmines? He should follow in my footsteps like any proper son.'

'You mustn't stand in his way, George,' Sarah said severely. 'He'll never make a fortune as a baker.' She sniffed. 'Did you shut the shop early?'

'I've left the young lad in charge,' he said with a gulp as though suddenly unable to catch his breath. 'Sarah, something's happened. Ruth Allerton is in Swansea and she wants her boy.'

The tortoiseshell hairbrush dropped from Sarah's fingers and fell with a clatter. 'What did you say?'

'She came into the shop,' George said. 'And demanded to know where Andrew was.' He threw up his hands. 'What could I say? I asked her to leave and even threatened her with calling a constable when she wouldn't go.'

'Oh, George!'

He looked exasperated. 'Well, what else could I do? I couldn't face the woman.' George shook his head. 'Sarah this is very serious. She's going to find out what we did, and I suspect it's illegal.' He sat down on the bed with a flop. 'I'll be ruined in this town before I even start!'

'We must tell David straight away,' Sarah said, hastily pinning up her hair. 'He'll know what to do.'

'I don't know about that,' he muttered bitterly. 'It's Esther who wears the trousers around here!'

'George!' Sarah frowned angrily at her husband. 'What a disloyal thing to say.'

She had come to that conclusion herself, but would never give voice to the thought. After all, David had been pressed into the marriage and he had been through so much in the war. She suspected his spirit had been broken, especially after losing Ruth.

'Ruth just walked in out of the blue,' George said. 'But I'll tell you this she'll be back asking the same question, and I've got no answer for her.' He shrugged helplessly. 'She'll make trouble for us all.'

Sarah bit her lip pensively. She had made Ruth promise never to have anything to do with Andrew again, but in her heart she had known a mother's love for her child is impossible to bury. And when a friend at Gowerton had written to her with the news of Pastor Allerton's untimely death, she knew it was just a matter of time before Ruth came into their lives again.

'You're right. She won't rest until she has him back,' she murmured in agreement.

'We had no right to give her child away to strangers,' George said. 'Damn Esther's interference!'

'Richard Hamilton isn't a stranger,' Sarah protested.

'Our daughter-in-law has a lot to answer for,' he said furiously. 'Sometimes I'm heartily sorry that . . .'

'George, keep your voice down,' Sarah hissed. 'We're guests in their home.'

'We've got to tell them,' George said. 'Ruth could show up here any time. It's Esther's mess by right and she must sort it out.'

They made their way down to the sitting room and some minutes later David and Esther arrived. Sarah felt anxious. What would Esther do when she knew the child's mother had turned up?

David went to the chiffonier and poured Esther a glass of sherry. 'Can I get you a drink, Dad?'

'No thanks.' George cleared his throat. 'David, something has happened,' he began. 'Ruth Allerton is in town and she's looking for Andrew.'

David turned from pouring the drink and stared at his father.

'Ruth is here?' he said, an eagerness unmistakable in his voice.

'That hardly concerns us,' Esther said loudly, sending David a meaningful glance.

'Of course it concerns us,' George blurted. 'She made a scene in the shop today,' he went on. 'She wants her son back and mark my words, she won't be stopped.'

Esther rose abruptly from her place on the sofa.

'Well, she can't have him back,' she said forcefully. 'It's unthinkable. Annette Hamilton is enchanted with the child, so Richard tells me. I won't allow this person, Ruth Allerton, to disturb the new-found happiness of Richard and his wife.'

'Why are you so concerned for them?' David asked with an edge of anger in his voice.

'They're my dear friends,' Esther said resolutely. 'I won't have them upset by a woman who can lightly give her child away one moment and calmly ask for him back the next.'

'I doubt she did it lightly,' Sarah said sharply. She felt she must defend Ruth. There had been fear and desperation in the girl's eyes that day she had handed over her child. 'I firmly believe she was driven to it.'

'Well, you've changed your tune, Sarah,' Esther said nastily. 'You maintained she was an unfit mother, and you'd never let Andrew go back to her.'

Sarah was cross at this reminder. 'I've had time to think since then,' she said. 'It was very wrong what we did.'

Esther gave her mother-in-law a disdainful glance. 'The point is,' she said dismissively, 'Mrs Allerton has no way of finding us. We're quite safe.'

'I'm not so sure,' George said. 'Ruth looked determined to me.'

Esther sat down again. 'We must make Ruth Allerton believe her search for her child is hopeless,' she said firmly. She looked at Sarah. 'If she comes here she must be told that the child was put up for adoption in January.'

'That won't work,' George said irritably. 'She'll want the name of the adoption agency.'

'Not if we say the child was adopted straight away.' She paused thinking again. 'Yes, that's it! He was adopted by a couple who were emigrating to Australia immediately,' she went on quickly. 'So the child is in Australia, out of her reach. There's nothing she can do.'

'Oh, that's so cruel!' Sarah exclaimed, upset by the thought of the pain and anguish it would cause Ruth. 'There must be some other way.'

'There is no other way, Sarah,' Esther said emphatically, a warning tone in her voice. 'We must protect Richard.'

'Protect Richard! I'm sick of this!' David strode from the chiffonier and stood over Esther. 'I say we tell Richard the truth, take the child back and restore him to his mother.'

'And how will she live?' Esther asked belligerently. 'She's

probably working somewhere in the town. No employer will accept a baby. Ruth Allerton is better off on her own, even if she doesn't know it.'

Sarah put her handkerchief to her mouth overcome with remorse. She could not forgive herself for what she had allowed Esther to do.

'I want you all to promise,' Esther said, 'that if Ruth Allerton ever comes to this house, this is the story she'll be told.'

'What am I to do when she comes back to the shop?' George asked. 'It's all very well for you, but I'm the one who has to face her.'

Esther shrugged. 'If she makes a disturbance then have her arrested,' she said in a hard voice. 'It's no more than she deserves in my opinion.'

'How can you say that,' Sarah cried. 'It's understandable that the girl wants her child.'

'*Does* she want him back though?' Esther asked sceptically. 'I think she's after money. Blackmail, that's her game.'

'Your assertion is outrageous!' David exclaimed angrily. 'Ruth has principles. Her only thought is for her child.'

Esther smiled mockingly. 'Haven't you learned your lesson yet, David?' she said. 'You told me yourself that she dropped you without a second thought when a better prospect for a husband came on the scene.'

David looked confounded and was silent.

'Don't be Ruth's fool again, David,' Esther said disdainfully. She rose from the sofa and walked to the door. 'I'm going up to dress for dinner.'

On Monday Richard Hamilton visited Dynevor Place again and Ruth was summoned upstairs. She entered the room in trepidation. Richard Hamilton stood up immediately on her entrance, confusing her.

'My aunt tells me you have a valuable pearl necklace which you want to dispose of,' he began straight away.

Ruth lifted her chin. 'Did she also tell you that she accused me of stealing it?'

Richard looked disconcerted. 'I'm sure you misunderstood her,' he said tightly.

'It was a natural assumption,' Miss Lydia put in strongly. 'One does not expect one's servants to possess such luxuries.'

Ruth held her tongue. Arguing against such arrogant opinions was futile.

'Perhaps you'll allow me to be of some service to you, Ruth,' Mr Richard said soothingly. 'I could have pearls assessed by a reputable jeweller who could probably arrange a fair sale. What do you say?'

Ruth ran her tongue over her lips. Anger still rankled in her breast, but his suggestion did seem an ideal solution, and there was no point in cutting off her nose to spite her face.

'I'll require a receipt from you,' she said archly.

Miss Lydia made a sound indicating her outrage, but Mr Richard smiled widely at her.

'Very sensible,' he said genially. 'And of course I'll comply. Perhaps you'll fetch the pearls now and the jeweller's receipt.'

Ruth did so, handing the blue velvet box and receipt to him. If he could secure only half the pearls' value, it would make her financial situation reasonably secure for the time being so that she could pick and choose her employment and continue her search for Andrew.

'You can go now, Ruth,' Miss Lydia said severely, as though to remind Ruth of her place.

'I'll go when I have Mr Richard's receipt,' Ruth said smartly.

Mr Richard went to a small scroll top desk in the corner of the room and sat down before it. Ruth watched surreptitiously as he took a sheet of writing paper and his fountain pen and wrote something. He stood and came towards her holding out the sheet.

'There you are, Ruth,' he said. 'Duly noted and signed. Give me a few days to see to it and I'm sure I'll have some good news for you shortly.'

He smiled down at her and Ruth looked up into his eyes suddenly disturbed to see real kindness and concern in his gaze.

'Thank you,' she said, taking the sheet from his fingers.

'I said that will be all, Ruth,' Miss Lydia said loudly.

Ruth was glad to escape from the room, but she carried the image of Mr Richard's smiling eyes with her.

Nineteen

'Miss Lydia isn't up yet,' Ruth told Richard Hamilton when he called on the last Friday of May. 'It's quite early.'

'It's you I've come to see, Ruth,' he said, removing his hat and gloves, and leaving his cane in the umbrella stand. 'Come to the sitting room. I've some good news for you.'

Ruth hesitated.

'Come along!' he encouraged affably on seeing her expression of doubt, and strode off toward the sitting room.

Ruth followed. His good news must be that he had managed to dispose of the pearls, and she would be very glad of that.

'Come and sit down,' Mr Richard said as she entered the room. 'While I explain what I've achieved.'

'I'll stand, thank you,' Ruth said quietly.

He looked at her puzzled for a moment and then frowned. 'Are you afraid of me, Ruth?'

'No, sir.'

'Well, come in and sit then,' he said firmly.

'Miss Lydia wouldn't like it,' Ruth said. 'She'd think I was taking liberties.'

'If you're worried about the sack,' he said, his eyes dancing. 'That need never bother you again. You're a woman of means now, well, in a modest way, of course.'

'What?' Ruth moved a few steps forward.

'I've secured a purchaser for the pearls with the aid of the jeweller,' Mr Richard told her, taking something out of his pocket to hand to her. 'Here's the cheque. A handsome amount, even if I say so myself.'

With trembling fingers Ruth took the cheque from him and glanced at it, drawing in a sharp breath of astonishment.

She could not help flopping down on to a nearby chair at the surprise of it.

'But this is more than the original cost,' she said, looking up at him in awe. 'I can hardly believe it.'

'The jeweller and I drove a hard bargain,' Mr Richard told her. 'And the purchaser was very eager to get them, I may add. They are handsome pearls; worth every penny and a good investment. Your late husband was an astute man.'

Ruth lowered her gaze. 'Yes, I suppose he was.'

'Well, what do you propose to do with your new found capital?'

Ruth glanced up at him. 'I haven't really had time to think about it.'

Mr Richard indicated the cheque. 'Wisely invested that sum will accrue a good monthly return; enough for you to live in a modest way. That is to say, you need not worry about finding work.'

'Thank you so much, Mr Richard,' she said earnestly. 'You don't know what this means to me.'

He touched his tie self-consciously. 'Glad to be of service.'

Still unable to believe her good fortune, Ruth stared down at the cheque expecting to see the purchaser's name because she was curious as to who now owned the pearls, but it gave nothing away. It was the jeweller's own cheque.

'Would you like me to set up a bank account for you?' Mr Richard asked, interrupting her thoughts. 'It would be no trouble. And I can also find the best investment for you.'

Ruth rose to her feet. 'It's very good of you to offer your help, Mr Richard,' she said. 'But I believe I can do that for myself.' She wondered if that had sounded churlish to him. 'I'm very grateful,' she went on hastily. 'But I've been used to doing things for myself since my husband died. I like the feeling of independence it gives me.'

'Quite so.' He touched his tie again. 'I suppose you intend to leave my aunt's employ now?' he asked.

She thought there was a touch of regret in his voice.

'I haven't decided yet,' she said.

'Well. If you do leave, I . . . I hope you'll keep in touch, Ruth.' He cleared his thought as though embarrassed. 'What

I mean is, I hope you might consider me a friend in future, no matter what you decide.'

Ruth felt her cheeks burn with embarrassment. 'You're very kind, Mr Richard, I'm sure,' she said awkwardly.

There was a long pause as she remembered Mrs Withers' words. Did his interest in her amount to more than kindness and friendship? Ruth's disturbed thoughts stilled her tongue and all at once she was wary of him and his motive in helping her.

'Well,' Mr Richard said at last. 'I must be getting on about my business. Congratulations again on your good fortune.'

Ruth saw him out, glad to close the door on his retreating back. This sudden change in her circumstances was bewildering and yet very exciting. So many new avenues had opened up for her, but her main concern was finding Andrew, and surely this new financial security would help her achieve that.

After supper was served to the family that evening, she and Mrs Withers were sitting down to their meal and a cup of tea, when Ruth broached the subject on her mind.

'If I were trying to find someone, Mrs Withers,' she began hesitantly, not wishing to give anything away. 'Say an old friend, how do you think I might go about it?'

Mrs Withers smiled, giving Ruth an old-fashioned look. 'A long lost sweetheart, is it?'

Ruth flushed. 'No, nothing like that. A relative, say.'

Mrs Withers sat back in her chair looking thoughtful, holding her cup and saucer against her chest.

'Well, I suppose an inquiry agent would be the thing.'

'What's an inquiry agent?'

Mrs Withers sniffed. 'Someone who goes around asking questions. Does it for a living, like.' She put her cup and saucer on the table. 'My friend Mrs Gibbons employed one of these inquiry agents last year,' she went on. 'Her husband went out for a packet of cigarettes one day and never came back.'

'Good gracious! Was he found?'

'Oh yes.' Mrs Withers nodded. 'The inquiry agent discovered he was living over the brush with the landlady of the Bell and Bucket pub just up by the fire brigade station.'

Ruth's eyes widened. 'Oh dear!'

'Yes, such a shock to my friend,' Mrs Withers said earnestly. 'She was hoping he'd kicked the bucket so she could claim on his insurance.'

Ruth put her hand over her mouth for a moment to cover her smile.

'How would I get in touch with one of these inquiry agents, do you think,' she asked at last.

'Mrs Gibbons had his name out of the advertisements in the *Cambrian Leader*,' Mrs Withers told her. 'Mind you, he wasn't cheap. A guinea a day he charged her, plus his expenses.'

'That's steep, isn't it?' Ruth agreed guardedly. 'Might be worth it in the end though.'

Mrs Withers shrugged. 'Mrs Gibbons didn't think so, under the circumstances,' she said. 'But she's keeping up with the insurance policy premiums just in case.'

'Mr Timothy takes the *Cambrian Leader* every evening, doesn't he?' Ruth asked. 'I'll check the advertisements over before I use the papers to light the fires.'

'Well, good luck to you,' Mrs Withers said, rising from the table and reaching for her coat and hat behind the back door. 'Hope you get better luck than Mrs Gibbons.'

'I'll be very happy to find my relative alive,' Ruth said in a heartfelt tone, thinking of her beloved son Andrew. 'He's very dear to me.'

Over the following few evenings, Ruth closely read the advertisement page of Mr Timothy's discarded evening papers and at last in the Saturday evening edition she found what she was looking for. It was an address in Alexandra Road opposite the railway station at the top of the High Street.

On her next half day, Ruth opened an account in a bank in Wind Street and then went to Alexandra Road. The address was above a gentleman's barber shop, the entrance to one side. Ruth climbed some steep dusty stairs to a small landing and, knocking, went in.

181

A thin middle-aged woman sat behind a desk; bespectacled, with mousy coloured hair drawn back in a bun. She looked up as Ruth came in.

'Yes?'

'I'd like to see the inquiry agent, please.'

'I'm the inquiry agent,' the woman said defensively. 'My name is Miss Stebbings, Maud Stebbings.' She gave Ruth a hard stare. 'And I'm as good at the work as any man,' she added.

'I don't doubt it for a moment,' Ruth said.

'What can I do for you?' Maud Stebbings asked in a bored voice. 'I suppose you want your husband followed? You suspect he's up to no good.'

Ruth shook her head. 'No,' she said. 'I'm trying to find my baby son, Andrew. I'm a widow.'

Maud Stebbings jerked upright, sudden interest sparking behind her spectacles. 'Well, that's more like it,' she said with enthusiasm, drawing a sheet of paper towards her and taking up a pen. 'Sit down, Mrs . . .'

'Allerton, Ruth Allerton,' Ruth said, taking a chair, and gave her the address in Dynevor Place. 'I work there as maid at present.'

Maud Stebbings wrote that down and then glanced up. 'And when did you last see your son and under what circumstances?'

Ruth ran her tongue over her lips. 'Last January,' she said quietly. 'When I gave him away.'

Maud Stebbings sat back in her chair. 'What? You gave him away?' She looked at Ruth suspiciously. 'You gave him up for adoption, you mean?'

'No,' Ruth said with great sadness, remembering that awful day. 'No, I gave him to a neighbour who was leaving my village. I had to!' she cried out at Maud Stebbings's shocked gaze. 'His life was being threatened.'

Miss Stebbings put her pen down. 'Are you wasting my time?' she asked brusquely. 'This sounds like a matter for the police.'

'No, no!' Ruth shook her head, realizing she would have to explain further, and told her companion of Edwin's erroneous belief that Andrew was another man's son and his terrible threats against the child.

'I thought I'd never be able to see my son again,' she went on. 'But my husband met with an accident and I was free. I *must* find my child, but the people I gave him to refuse to talk to me or even see me. I'm desperate, Miss Stebbings. Can you help me?' Ruth asked hopefully.

Miss Stebbings nodded slowly. 'I believe I can. I've had a lot of experience at these things.'

Ruth remained silent, praying that help might be at hand after all.

'Now, tell me all you know about the family who has your son,' Maud Stebbings said, and then got to writing furiously as Ruth poured out all she knew about the Beales.

'The baker's shop in Nelson Street is a good starting place,' Miss Stebbings said thoughtfully. 'I'll need a full description of this man George Beale.'

Ruth described him as best she could. 'You'll follow him home, I suppose? But what if he travels by motorcar?'

Miss Stebbings smiled knowingly. 'I have a motorbike,' she said. 'My one little luxury in life.'

Ruth stared, open-mouthed, astounded.

Miss Stebbings seemed to read her thoughts. 'I may be thin, but I'm wiry,' she said rather defensively.

Ruth was in admiration of the woman's resourcefulness and enterprise. 'We haven't talked about your fee,' she said quickly. She opened her handbag. 'I'm ready to make a down payment, if it's not too much.'

Miss Stebbings waved her hand. 'You'll get my invoice when I've finished the investigation,' she said. 'I charge seventeen and six a day, plus expenses; like petrol for instance and food, if I have to eat out as I work.' She looked keenly at Ruth. 'Do these terms suit your pocket?'

'I'd give all I have to get my son back,' Ruth said earnestly. 'And if you can really help me you'll have my undying gratitude, Miss Stebbings.'

The other woman gave her a vague smile and then glanced at the clock standing on the mantelpiece above a cold grate.

'There's time to catch this George Beale before he closes

the shop today,' she said enthusiastically. 'I haven't had a real case for such a long time,' she confided to Ruth. 'You'd be surprised how many husbands are deceiving their wives in this town. That work is so boring.'

Ruth rose to leave. 'You'll keep me informed, Miss Stebbings? I want to know everything as soon as you do.'

'I'll be in touch, don't worry.' Miss Stebbings rose too. 'Now I must get to work. Good day to you, Mrs Allerton.'

Her employer looked as haughty as ever as Ruth served her supper that evening.

'I understand my nephew has found a buyer for those pearls of yours, at a good price,' she began.

'Yes, ma'am,' Ruth answered reluctantly.

'I'm relieved to hear it,' Miss Lydia said sharply and then paused. 'I suppose now you're a woman of some small independence you'll be leaving my employ?'

Ruth ran her tongue on her lips nervously. 'Well, Miss Lydia, I thought to stay on, with your permission, of course.'

Miss Lydia looked surprised. 'Really? Why?' She frowned. 'Your decision has nothing to do with my nephew, I hope,' she said sharply.

'Certainly not!' Ruth exclaimed hotly. 'The truth is the position suits me very well for the time being,' she went on quickly. 'I don't wish to live alone at present.'

'Yes, well, but just remember, I have my eye on you, Ruth,' Miss Lydia said. 'I'll not tolerate liberties, especially where my nephew is concerned. Now you may go.'

Ruth was livid as she went back to the kitchen. Perhaps she should think again about her position here. There were many comfortable boarding houses about. She need not remain under this roof to be insulted and spied upon.

'There's a woman asking for you,' Mrs Withers came to tell her quite early one morning as she was laying the fire in the sitting room. 'She wouldn't give her name. She's waiting in the kitchen.'

Ruth hurried down. Miss Stebbings was seated on a chair near the range. She wore a close-fitting leather helmet, fastened under her chin. A pair of driving goggles rested on her forehead, while her hands were encased in a pair of brown leather gauntlets.

'Good gracious!' Ruth exclaimed. 'You're an early bird, Miss Stebbings.'

'I thought you'd want to know straight away,' Miss Stebbings began and then stopped, eyeing Mrs Withers suspiciously.

'It's all right, Miss Stebbings,' Ruth said after an awkward moment. 'Mrs Withers is trustworthy.'

Miss Stebbings sniffed. 'It's up to you,' she said. 'I wanted you to know that I've found out where the man George Beale is living.'

'Oh, excellent!' Ruth came forward very excited. 'And what of Andrew? Have you learned anything about him?'

'Would you like a cup of tea,' Mrs Withers offered quickly, going at once to fill the kettle.

'That would be welcome,' Miss Stebbings said removing the gauntlets and laying them on the table top. 'I didn't stop for breakfast this morning.'

Ruth sat down too. 'Well? What've you discovered, Miss Stebbings.'

'I traced the gentleman in question to an address in Sketty,' Miss Stebbings began. 'Later in the week I managed to get into conversation with the cook there, a Mrs Cooper.' She tapped the side of her nose and winked. 'Servants are a mine of information.'

Mrs Withers coughed.

Miss Stebbings threw her a brief glance and then turned her attention back to Ruth.

'The house is owned by one Sydney Beale, coal merchant, and brother of George Beale,' she went on. 'Pretty well off, too. His daughter and her husband live there also, and George and Sarah Beale are staying with him at present.

'And Andrew . . .?' Ruth asked urgently. 'What of my son?'

Ruth heard Mrs Withers take in an astonished gasp, but was too concerned about her child's welfare to care.

Miss Stebbings compressed her lips. 'There's no child

living in the house at present, Mrs Allerton,' she said sombrely. 'According to the cook, a baby was brought there in January, but was gone before the month was out.'

'Oh! God! No!' Ruth rose to her feet, her hands flying to cover her face.

'Not dead!' Miss Stebbings exclaimed. 'Just there one day and gone the next. She doesn't know where.'

Ruth flopped on to a chair, relief making her legs too weak to bear her weight. 'What have they done with my son? I trusted Sarah Beale. She's betrayed me.'

'I could make further enquiries,' Miss Stebbings said quickly.

'No,' Ruth said firmly. 'I must confront her myself and have it out with her.'

'It's not my place to butt in,' Mrs Withers interposed. 'But isn't it likely that the woman's given the child to someone else?'

'She had no right to do that!' Ruth cried out, clasping her hands tightly together. 'Andrew, where are you? Oh God! This is a punishment on me for giving my child away in the first place.'

'You had no choice,' Miss Stebbings said kindly.

Ruth shook her head. 'I should've had the courage to leave my husband and take the child with me. At least we would've been together.'

'And starving most like,' Miss Stebbings remarked flatly. 'Or in the workhouse. They'd have taken him from you anyway.'

'Give me the address, Miss Stebbings,' Ruth said quickly, making up her mind firmly. 'I must go there today and see Sarah Beale.'

'Her Nibs won't let you have time off,' Mrs Wither warned. 'And if she gets to know about the child, you'll be sacked straight away.'

'I don't care!' Ruth cried. 'I'm going and I'm going now.'

'I'll take you,' Miss Stebbings offered, getting to her feet. 'If you don't mind riding pillion.'

'I'd ride on the Devil's tail to find my boy,' Ruth said with heartfelt emotion.

'What'll I tell Her Nibs?' Mrs Withers blurted. 'She'll expect you to bring up her morning tea and then there're the fires; they haven't been lit yet.'

'Tell her anything you like,' Ruth said resolutely. 'No one will keep me from my son any longer.'

Ruth had tied a scarf around her hat as she rode behind Miss Stebbings on the motorbike, an alarming experience, and now felt windswept, as the machine came to a halt in a leafy cul-de-sac in Sketty.

'This is it,' Miss Stebbings said indicating one large house.

Ruth approached the front door down a long driveway. She had no doubt the servants would be up at this hour, but wondered about the family members.

The door was opened by a maid who looked at her in surprise.

'Yes. What do you want?'

'I want to see Mrs Beale,' Ruth requested nervously. 'It's a personal matter.'

'Which Mrs Beale?'

Ruth had temporarily forgotten David's wife.

'Mrs Sarah Beale,' she said. 'Tell her Ruth Allerton wishes to see her.'

'Wait here,' the girl said and started to close the door.

'I'll wait inside, if you please,' Ruth said firmly, putting her hand against the closing door.

'Well, all right,' the maid replied stiffly. 'But wait in the hall. I'll see whether Mrs Beale is at home for you. She may not have risen yet.' She gave Ruth a haughty stare. 'It's still very early you know.' Then she disappeared up the wide staircase.

The wait seemed endless. There was activity in a room one side of the hall, where the rattle of cutlery and crockery could be heard, and Ruth guessed the breakfast table was being laid for the family.

She turned swiftly towards the staircase when she heard quick footsteps, expecting to see the maid, but instead a tall young woman came down the stairs. She was pretty, fashionably dressed with her hair cut in the current bobbed style.

She stared at Ruth in puzzlement. 'Who are you?' she asked in an authoritative tone. 'What are you doing here?'

'I'm waiting to see Mrs Sarah Beale,' Ruth answered, lifting her chin. She guessed immediately that this must be David's wife. 'It's a private matter.'

'I'm Esther Beale,' the girl said haughtily. 'Sarah's daughter-in-law. And you are?'

'Ruth Allerton.'

Esther Beale started visibly and then pursed her lips. 'I should've guessed,' she said dryly.

Ruth paused, staring at her, puzzled by her tone. 'You were expecting me?'

'In a way. It stands to reason you'd find your way here some time or other,' Esther said. She gave a narrow smile. 'But sooner than I anticipated.'

'My business isn't with you,' Ruth countered. 'Only Sarah can answer my questions.'

'It was *my* husband who was accused . . .' Esther stopped abruptly as another maid came out of the breakfast room. 'You'd better come into the sitting room,' she said. 'We can't talk here in the hall.'

She opened a door on the opposite side and Ruth followed her in. Esther turned to face her.

'As I was saying,' she went on. 'It was my husband who was accused of fathering your child, so your reason for coming here today is certainly my business.'

'David was falsely accused . . .' Ruth began.

'I know that,' Esther sneered. 'And that is precisely why something had to be done about the child.'

'What have you done?' Ruth cried out an interruption. 'Where is my son? Tell me!' Ruth took a step towards the other woman. 'Tell me at once.'

'I'll thank you not to raise your voice,' Esther said arrogantly. 'You'll disturb the servants, not to mention my father.'

'I gave my child to Sarah,' Ruth gasped. 'She promised to protect my boy.'

'Only after you lied to her,' Esther snapped. 'She believed David was the child's father.'

188

'That may be so,' Ruth said defensively. 'But she betrayed me just the same.'

'No I didn't,' a breathless voice interposed. 'I had no choice myself.'

Ruth swung around to see Sarah Beale in the doorway, her stout frame wrapped in an old woollen dressing gown. She looked out of place against the finery of the room.

'Sarah! Where's my child.'

'Leave this to me, Sarah,' Esther interrupted in a warning tone. 'I'll explain to Mrs Allerton.'

Sarah hurried forward. 'I'm sorry, Ruth. But it seemed the best thing to do.'

'Sarah, please!' Esther commanded. 'Go back to bed.'

'Someone explain!' Ruth cried out. 'Tell me where my son is. I want him back. I demand to have him back. You can't keep me from him.'

Sarah Beale put her fingers to her lips and whimpered. She collapsed on a chair nearby and taking a handkerchief out of the pocket of the dressing gown, wiped her moist eyes, but remained silent. Ruth stared at her distressed face in growing dread.

'It's really your own fault, Mrs Allerton,' Esther said in a hard voice. 'Lying as you did.'

Ruth was silent. Whatever had happened to Andrew it was her fault. She could not deny that.

'Sarah was certain you'd washed your hands of the boy,' Esther went on resolutely. 'David and I, naturally, refused to have anything to do with him.'

'Where is he?' Ruth asked in a small voice. 'Please, please tell me!'

'He was placed with an adoption society in late January.' Esther paused for a moment, and then continued. 'And as I understand it, early in February he was chosen by a suitable couple who were to emigrate. They adopted him and he went with them to their new home in Australia in the last week of March.'

'No!' Ruth shook her head vehemently, unwilling to believe it. 'You're lying!'

'It's the truth. Your son Andrew is now with his adoptive

parents in Australia, Mrs Allerton,' Esther said in a tone of finality. 'So, you see, he is out of your reach, now and for ever.'

'Esther, don't . . .' Sarah cried out.

'She had to be told,' Esther said firmly. 'It's for her good. She has to know searching further will be fruitless.'

Sarah burst into tears. Ruth stared from one to the other feeling cold and numb inside. So cold and numb it felt like being dead.

Without another word to either of them, Ruth turned and walked slowly out of the room and out of the house. She had lost her child, really lost him for ever, and it was all her own doing. There seemed no point in being alive without Andrew; without hope there was no reason to live any longer.

Twenty

When they returned to Dynevor Place, Maud Stebbings brought the motorbike to a standstill at the curb outside the house. Ruth dismounted and then stood helplessly not knowing what to do next.

She was stunned; her mind without thought, except for the last words Esther Beale had spoken. Andrew, her beloved son, was lost to her. All her cherished hopes and dreams of being united with him were crushed.

Maud pushed her motorbike on to the pavement and leant it against the railings. 'Are you all right, Ruth?'

'Maud, what am I going to do?' she asked. 'I've lost my child, really lost him this time and I can't bear it!'

Maud lifted up her goggles and then took her arm. 'Steady on,' she said encouragingly. 'We must talk about this indoors. I'm sure Mrs Withers can rustle up a cup of tea for us.'

Maud held on to her arm as they went down the front area steps to the kitchen door, and Ruth was glad of her steadying hand as her legs felt weak and shaky.

Mrs Withers looked agitated as they came in to the kitchen. 'Thank goodness you're back,' she said. 'I told Her Nibs you're poorly with a migraine, but I didn't know how much longer I could fool her.'

Ruth sank down on to a chair at the table and putting her arms on it, laid down her head. 'I just don't care any longer,' she said wretchedly. 'My life is over.'

'What?'

'Ruth's had a terrible shock,' Maud explained. 'She needs hot sweet tea.'

Mrs Withers bustled with the iron kettle. 'What happened, for heaven's sake?'

Ruth lifted her head. 'My son has been adopted, Mrs Withers, and he's been taken out of the country to Australia. It's the other side of the world!'

'Oh, my goodness! What a terrible thing? What can you do?'

'Nothing,' Ruth said miserably. 'Everything is finished. I'm finished. There's no future for me without Andrew.'

'Don't talk like that,' Maud said. 'You're young. You can have more children.'

'I want Andrew!' Ruth cried piteously. 'This is a punishment on me.'

'I don't understand,' Mrs Withers said bemusedly. 'Punishment for what?'

Ruth looked up. Mrs Withers had been her only friend since coming to Swansea. She was beginning to think of Maud as a friend now, too, but Mrs Withers deserved an explanation. So with a lump in her throat, Ruth related to Mrs Withers all the misfortune that had befallen her in Gowerton and how she had been so desperate with fear that she had given her child away.

'Oh, you poor girl,' Mrs Withers said with feeling. 'You've been though the mill and now this. Life isn't fair, is it?'

'I've been thinking,' Maud said as they sat around the table drinking the hot tea. 'There's something fishy about this adoption business.'

Ruth could hardly lift up her head to look at her. 'What do you mean, Maud?'

Taking off her leather helmet Maud shook her head doubtfully.

'Well,' she said. 'I've had dealings with adoption societies in the course of my work. They're not easy organizations to deal with; very secretive.'

'That's right, and they take adoptions very seriously,' Mrs Withers volunteered. 'My brother-in-law and his wife wanted to adopt a child, but they were turned down after six months of negotiations. Very disappointed, they were.'

'That's just it,' Maud said. 'They check and recheck prospective parents for months. Nothing is hurried. And it makes me suspicious that the adoption of Ruth's son was so quick, unless . . .'

'Unless what?'

Maud tightened her lips. 'Unless he was sold on.'

'Sold!' Ruth cried out. 'Oh, no!'

'It happens, Ruth,' Maud said. 'And if this *is* the case then it's illegal.'

Ruth shook her head. 'Sarah Beale wouldn't do a thing like that,' she said emphatically. 'I've known her for years. She's a Christian woman.'

'Maybe she had no choice,' Maud said. 'After all, as you told me, it was her daughter-in-law who did all the talking this morning.'

'Still, I can't believe that David would have any part in something illegal,' Ruth went on. 'I know he was bitter because I married someone else, but he couldn't be that cruel, surely.'

'Umm! I think I'll make some further enquiries,' Maud said thoughtfully. 'I'll bet anything the child was given or sold to a family member or a close friend. They wouldn't risk strangers. I should be able to uncover something.'

'Oh, Maud!' Ruth exclaimed guiltily. 'I haven't yet given you your fee for the work you've already done for me.'

Maud patted her hand. 'You'll pay me,' she said with confidence. 'I know people; I can read them like a book and you're a really decent sort, Ruth. I want to help you.'

Ruth smiled at her new found friend through tears. 'Thank you, Maud,' she said gratefully and with little spirit.

Maud meant well, but Ruth had the sinking feeling that her quest to be reunited with her child was still at an end.

'Look, Ruth, my dear,' Maud went on. 'If I'm right about your son being passed on to family or friends, then chances are Andrew is still in Swansea, or at least still in Wales.'

'Oh, Maud!' Ruth grasped at her friend's hand on the table. 'Do you really think so?' Despite her distress and helplessness a small spark of hope rekindled.

'Now, wait a minute,' Mrs Withers said cautiously. 'Don't go getting the girl's hopes up. Maybe the Beales were telling the truth. Maybe the boy was sold to people emigrating. He could well be in Australia by now.'

Ruth could not quell a sob erupting in her throat at the thought. 'God help me if that's true,' she murmured miserably.

Maud shook her head. 'Don't upset yourself, Ruth,' she said. 'My nose tells me something isn't right in their story. It can do no harm to ask more questions, can it?'

The bell for the sitting room rang at that moment which made Ruth jump. 'I'd better answer that.'

'Her Nibs will see at once that you've been crying, Ruth,' Mrs Withers remarked anxiously.

'I'll use my headache as an excuse,' Ruth said dully.

'I'd better be on my way,' Maud said, rising to her feet. 'I'll begin my inquiries as soon as possible.'

'Where will you start?' Ruth asked quietly. It seemed a hopeless task to her.

'With the Beale family,' Maud said confidently. 'Don't worry. I can ferret out anything once I put my mind to it.'

'Thank you, Maud,' Ruth said, her heart full. 'I'll come around to Alexandra Road on Wednesday to settle your fee.'

'No, don't do that,' Maud warned. 'If I'm out on inquiries the office will be closed up.' She paused to think. 'I tell you what, I'll call here of an evening if Mrs Withers doesn't mind. Keep you up to date on what I've discovered.'

'Oh, come to tea,' Mrs Withers invited. 'We'll be glad of the company, won't we, Ruth?'

'Very much so,' Ruth said with enthusiasm. She had been so fortunate in meeting Maud.

Several evenings later, Ruth, having finished serving tea in the sitting room to Miss Lydia and Mr Timothy, went down to the kitchen to find Maud sitting at the table with Mrs Withers, a cup of tea and a slice of fruit cake before her.

'Maud! I'm glad to see you,' Ruth said delighted. 'Do you have any news?'

Maud nodded, but didn't speak. Her usually sallow complexion was flushed and there was suppressed excitement in her gaze.

'What is it?' Ruth asked, anxious for news.

Maud took a deep breath before speaking. 'Ruth, I believe I've found your son.'

'What?' Ruth almost dropped the tray she was carrying as her step faltered, and she felt as though her heart would stop. 'Where? Where is he?'

Mrs Withers jumped up and took the tray from her. 'Steady on, Ruth, girl,' she said, concern in her voice. 'You've gone as white as a sheet. Sit down.'

Ruth flopped on to the chair at the table. She looked imploringly at Maud. 'Where is Andrew, Maud? Tell me, please.'

Maud reached across and patted her hand. 'I'm certain the child I've traced is yours,' she said. 'He's quite safe and being well looked after.'

'Please, Maud!'

Maud hesitated a moment more. 'I think you know a man called Richard Hamilton, don't you?' she asked at last.

Ruth was astonished by the unexpected question. 'Yes, of course.' She glanced at Mrs Withers feeling confused. 'He's the nephew of my employer. But what has he to do with Andrew?'

'He has your boy, Ruth.'

It was the last thing she expected to hear and Ruth stared at her friend open-mouthed.

'What?' she said at last. She shook her head doubtfully. 'Maud, I can't believe this. It's not possible.'

'There's no mistake,' Maud said emphatically. 'And I can prove it, too.'

'How?'

Maud grinned. 'Yesterday, I followed the Beales' parlour maid on her half day, and managed to get talking to her in the Market Café. We got quite chummy. She was grumbling that she'd been made to act as nursemaid at the beginning of the year to a baby boy. As parlour maid of long standing she thought the position was beneath her.'

'That was *my* Andrew?' Ruth asked, putting her hand to her throat in agitation.

Maud nodded. 'The maid told me that Esther Beale kicked

up a big rumpus over the baby and demanded he had to go, much to the maid's relief.'

Ruth felt a cold shiver go through her. She remembered the unfeeling look in Esther Beale's eyes when she had told Ruth that she'd never see her child again. She had been deliberately cruel.

'What happened?' Ruth asked, unable to keep a quiver from her voice.

'Well, one day towards the end of January, Esther Beale instructed the maid to pack up the child's things and get him ready to leave,' Maud said. 'Later that morning, Esther and the maid carrying the baby were driven to Richard Hamilton's house. The baby was handed over to another nursemaid and she never saw him again. She was instructed on pain of dismissal not to breathe a word of it.'

Ruth remembered a conversation between Miss Lydia and Richard Hamilton the first time she had met him. They had discussed a child, but Richard had called the boy James. That child was Andrew, her son!

'This coincidence is incredible!' Ruth said. 'But Andrew might as well be in Australia. How will I ever get to him? I'll never be able to see him.'

'Another interesting coincidence is that the Beales' cook and Richard Hamilton's housekeeper are sisters.' Maud tapped the side of her nose. 'What happens in one household is common knowledge to the servants in the other.'

'And there are no bigger gossips than live-in servants,' Mrs Withers stated, and then threw a glance at Ruth. 'Present company excluded, of course.'

'According to servants' tittle-tattle,' Maud went on. 'The health of Richard's wife, Annette had gone downhill since the death of her first child at the end of last year. But she has been revived somewhat and is totally enthralled with their adopted son, dotes on him.'

Ruth put both hands over her face, unable to speak. The thought that others would tend her son, would watch him grow, would know his child-like love that belonged to her caused such a pain in her heart, like a knife being thrust through it.

'What am I to do?' she murmured at last.

'Well, you mustn't give up hope,' Maud said firmly. 'Now we know where he is I can keep an eye on things. Something will turn up, Ruth.'

Ruth felt the sympathy of her friends, but she could not share their optimism. She had given her child away, and fate would continue to punish her for that transgression.

Ruth dreaded meeting Richard Hamilton again for fear of giving herself away. Knowing he had her child, how could she stop herself bursting out with the truth? Instinct told her it would be a big mistake to reveal what she knew.

When she did answer the front door one afternoon the following week, her heart in her mouth at the prospect of confronting him, she was astonished to find Sarah Beale on the door step instead.

'Sarah! What are you doing here?'

'Ruth, my dear, don't send me away,' the older woman burst out. 'I must speak to you.'

Ruth stepped aside. 'You'd better come in.'

Sarah Beale came into the hall at a trot. 'I had to see you,' she told her in an agitated voice. 'I must confess something to you. It's playing on my mind. I can't sleep.'

Sarah looked unhappy, but there was sheepishness about her too, as though she felt guilty, and Ruth could guess why she had come.

At that moment Miss Lydia appeared in the hallway. 'Who is it, Ruth?'

'It's . . . a friend of mine,' she stammered. 'From my home village.'

'At the front door!' Miss Lydia exclaimed in high dudgeon. 'Well, really!' She lifted her nose arrogantly. 'Take her downstairs, if you please.' She tutted crossly. 'I don't know what servants have come to since that dreadful war.'

'Yes, ma'am.'

Ruth hastily hustled her visitor down the back stairs. Sarah was out of breath by the time she entered the kitchen.

'What a dreadful woman,' she said to Ruth. 'I pity you working for her.'

'Her bark is worse than her bite,' Ruth said. 'I'm quite content here, at least for the time being.'

Mrs Withers was standing by, her expression curious. Ruth introduced them.

'So you're the one who's responsible for Ruth's misery,' Mrs Withers challenged. 'You've got a lot to answer for, I must say.'

Sarah stared. 'What? I couldn't help it.'

'No, that's not fair, Mrs Withers,' Ruth cut in quickly. 'Sarah helped me by taking Andrew to safety and I'll always be grateful for that.'

'Huh!' Mrs Withers gave Sarah a frosty look, but said no more.

'Would you like a cup, Sarah?' Ruth asked.

'I wouldn't say no,' said Sarah.

'Sit down and tell me why you're here,' Ruth said.

Sarah sat at the table while Mrs Withers put the iron kettle over the range fire to boil.

'I'm ashamed to tell you,' Sarah began breathlessly. 'I let Esther do a dreadful thing, lying to you about Andrew.'

She put her hand over her mouth and bent her head while Ruth waited. She knew what Sarah was about to say, but was unwilling to make things easy for her. After all, she had been wounded by Esther's lies.

'Andrew is not in Australia,' Sarah blurted out, looking up shamefacedly at Ruth. 'He's still here in Swansea, but he's in safe hands.'

'I know,' Ruth said sharply unable to contain her anger any longer. 'I know exactly what Esther did. Andrew was given to Richard Hamilton like someone would give away an unwanted puppy.'

Sarah's mouth dropped open and she looked astonished. 'It wasn't as thoughtless as that,' she said at last.

'Yes it was!' Ruth said. 'And what is so hurtful is that you and David allowed it to happen.'

Sarah appeared to rally. 'You gave him away, Ruth,' she reminded her. 'I should've refused to help you. If I had none of this would have happened. I only took him because you said he was David's child.'

Ruth's shoulders dropped. Yes, she was partly to blame for the mess she was in.

'I had to do that, Sarah,' Ruth said quietly. 'Edwin threatened Andrew's life. I knew you wouldn't take him otherwise.'

There was silence for a moment.

'How did you find out about Richard?' Sarah asked.

'Ruth has friends, you know,' Mrs Withers said fiercely placing a cup of tea on the table before Sarah. 'People who know about adoption procedures.'

Ruth glanced up gratefully at the cook and then at Sarah. 'My friend was suspicious of what Esther had told me and inquiries were made.'

'You sent someone to spy on us?' Sarah looked startled.

'I was searching for my son,' Ruth said emphatically. 'I was desperate.'

'So what are you going to do about it, Ruth?' Sarah's voice quivered. 'If Esther ever finds out I came here and told you I don't know what she'll do.'

'You've told me nothing I didn't know already,' Ruth reminded her. 'But tell me about Andrew, please. I've had no real news of him. Is he well?'

Sarah took a sip of tea. 'Annette Hamilton dotes on him utterly, even though she's a very sick woman,' she said. She looked at Ruth imploringly. 'He couldn't have a better life, you know, Ruth.'

'Except with his real mother,' Mrs Withers cut in waspishly. 'There's no substitute for a mother's love.'

'Was Richard Hamilton told about Andrew's parents?'

Sarah ran her tongue over her lips. 'Only that he's unwanted by his mother and that his father is dead.'

'Oh!' Ruth turned away, cut to the quick. But she was thankful that Richard Hamilton did not know the truth. He would think her very callous if he discovered she had given her child away.

'Annette suffers from tuberculosis, you know,' Sarah volunteered. 'But she's taken a turn for the worse recently. She's frustrated at not being able to look after the boy herself and has been at odds with their nursemaid for weeks over the baby's needs. There have been arguments.'

Ruth was fearful. 'Oh, Sarah! Is my child being neglected?'

'No, nothing like that.' Sarah shook her head. 'I'm sure it's nothing more than a difference of opinion,' she added hastily. 'But Richard blames this tension for her worsening condition. He's not left her side.'

Ruth understood then why he had not been near Dynevor Place recently. She wanted to learn all she could about her son's life with Richard Hamilton, and yet hearing the details made her feel helpless and very unhappy.

'From what Esther tells me,' Sarah went on. 'Richard is thinking seriously of sacking the nursemaid, but he needs to find a replacement first.'

Ruth's heart turned over in her breast. If only she could secure that position; anything to be near her child at last. But it seemed impossible. She could not ask Richard Hamilton outright for the post. He would realize immediately that she knew more of his household than she ought, and would suspect her motives.

Sarah was staring at her. 'I know what you're thinking, Ruth,' she said. 'But I daren't put a word in for you and even if you did manage to get the post, I'm sure Esther would make trouble for you.'

'I'll not let Esther stand between me and my child,' Ruth said forcefully.

Sarah was ready to leave.

'Sarah, please keep me informed about what's happening around Andrew,' Ruth pleaded. 'If you're afraid to call here again, you could write to me.'

Ruth was glad to see Maud at tea time, and told her about Sarah Beale's news.

Maud nodded. 'I've heard the same story from the Beales' maid, Doris.' She shook her head. 'The outlook for Annette Hamilton is not good, apparently.'

Ruth was upset. 'If anything happens to her what will become of my son?' she said, feeling a lump rise in her throat.

More than once the urge to go and demand the return of her son was almost overwhelming, but she knew she must act with caution. She had no real proof that the child Richard had taken was Andrew. And the other reason which stayed her hand was the thought of Annette Hamilton. The child's presence gave her a reason to go on fighting to live. Ruth would not be the one to take that away from her and bring her more grief.

'Perhaps we can do something about getting you into the household,' Maud said quickly. 'When I learned about the friction between Mrs Hamilton and the nursemaid I made it my business to find out which employment agency Richard Hamilton uses to recruit staff. This is a chance for you, Ruth.'

'If only that were possible,' Ruth said.

'I suggest you go along there as soon as possible,' Maud said. 'And register as a nursemaid.'

'But I've no experience.'

Maud laughed. 'Good gracious, Ruth, you're a mother. What better experience can anyone have than that?'

Ruth smiled. 'You're right.'

If she registered with the agency beforehand it might seem merely a strange coincidence to Richard Hamilton when she applied for the post.

Maud passed a slip of paper to her. 'Here's the address in Carlton Terrace.'

'Try and get away for an hour after luncheon tomorrow,' Mrs Withers suggested helpfully. 'Her Nibs will probably be resting then. I'll hold the fort here.'

Ruth's spirits lifted as hope filled her heart. It seemed unlikely now that she would get Andrew back for herself, at least not while Annette Hamilton lived, but if she was given the chance to be near her child and take care of him, watch him grow, she would give heartfelt thanks for that blessing.

Twenty-One

June, 1920

There were two other women sitting in the waiting room at the agency, and Ruth sat too, feeling rather self-conscious as though she were there under false pretences.

Eventually her turn came to be seen. The woman behind the desk examined Ruth's appearance in a professional way.

'I'm Mrs Mountford,' the woman began pleasantly. 'What can I do for you?'

Ruth wetted her lips nervously. 'I'm looking for a post as live-in nursemaid,' she said. 'In the Swansea area,' she added hastily.

'I've nothing like that on my books at the moment,' Mrs Mountford told her. 'I have several positions vacant for parlour maids.' She looked enquiringly at Ruth.

Ruth smiled faintly and shook her head. 'I hold such a position at present,' she said. 'But I want a change.'

'Well, you can register with me,' Mrs Mountford offered. 'But I'm afraid I won't be able to let you know when and if a suitable position arises, but you can pop in as often as you like to check what's on the books.'

Ruth nodded eagerly and gave her name.

'I'll need some references, of course,' Mrs Mountford said.

Ruth hesitated, unsure.

'Your present employer, for instance,' the woman suggested helpfully. 'And I would certainly accept a word on your behalf from any doctor or clergyman of your acquaintance.'

'I'll arrange references,' Ruth promised.

She was unsure who to ask to provide a reference, apart from Miss Lydia. She could hardly approach Richard Hamilton to speak for her.

Of course, she could speak to the minister at Mount Pleasant Chapel. She had been attending Sunday services regularly since she had come to Dynevor Place, always sitting at the back of the chapel, well away from Miss Lydia's pew.

She had not gone out of her way to make herself known to him previously, but he might oblige if he knew she was in the employ of Miss Hamilton who was a staunch member of the chapel.

Ruth came away from the employment agency feeling very much elated. Things were now going her way she was sure of it, and not before time, either.

Asking Miss Lydia for a written reference was a ticklish business she discovered the following morning. Miss Lydia stared up at her from her seat at the breakfast table without speaking for a moment.

'And why pray do you want to leave my employ all of a sudden?' she asked at last, her tone offended.

'I wish to try other work,' Ruth answered frankly, which was true. 'A lady's companion for instance,' she went on, plucking the idea out of the blue. 'Or even a . . . nursemaid.'

'Tish-tosh! What nonsense!' Miss Lydia scoffed. 'I doubt you have the aptitude.'

'All I require is a character reference,' Ruth said, feeling offended herself. 'I hope, Miss Lydia, that you have no doubt about my good character?'

Miss Lydia sniffed. 'I can't say that I do.' She frowned as though with annoyance that she could not pick fault. 'But it's most inconsiderate of you to be leaving now that I've become . . .' She paused and tried to look stern. 'Now that I've become used to you, not to mention my brother, Timothy.'

'But you said yourself, Miss Lydia, that after coming into that money I would most likely move on,' Ruth reminded her.

'Yes.' She sniffed again. 'My nephew has a lot to answer

for.' She sighed heavily. 'Oh, very well. You'll have the wretched reference later on today.'

Ruth waited until Sunday morning after the service to approach the minister, Mr Owen ap Davies. He was a tall thin man with twinkling eyes, so very different from Edwin's serious demeanour.

'Ah! You work for Miss Lydia Hamilton.' He beamed at her. 'My stalwart, you know. Of course I'll provide a reference for you, Mrs Allerton. It's my pleasure. See me after this evening's service. I'll have it ready for you.'

It was the following morning that she received a letter from Sarah Beale. The Hamiltons' nursemaid was under notice, and Richard was already looking for a replacement and had applied to an employment agency.

Ruth did not hesitate. As soon as breakfast was served and Miss Lydia had settled in the sitting room to read the papers as usual, Ruth made her request.

'Miss Lydia, do I have your permission to slip out to the employment agency to see if they have anything for me?'

Miss Lydia looked up startled, putting down the newspaper.

'So soon? Well, really!'

'I'll be less than an hour, I assure you,' Ruth continued hastily.

'Why can't you wait until your half day?'

'That may be too late,' Ruth pointed out anxiously. 'The best posts are snapped up immediately, you know.'

'I see.' Miss Lydia sighed as though very much hurt. 'Then I suppose you must.' She sat forward suddenly as though struck with an idea. 'Ask them if they have someone to replace you, will you?'

Ruth was taken aback. 'Yes, Miss Lydia.'

Ruth wasted no more time. She was out of breath as she entered the waiting room, disconcerted to find several women and girls already there. She was on pins as each woman was seen and left, wondering if they were walking away with her prize.

When her time came to be seen she decided to be bold. She sat down in front of the desk and watched Mrs Mountford eagerly as she sorted through boxes of cards.

'Nursemaid, you say, well . . .'

'I've heard, on the grapevine,' Ruth rushed on to say, 'that a suitable position for nursemaid has become vacant with Mr Richard Hamilton of Gower Road. I'd like to apply for that. I'm known to Mr Hamilton.' She handed over her references. 'I work for his aunt at present as you can see.'

Mrs Mountford raised her eyebrows. 'You're quick off the mark I must say!' she said. 'Notice of that vacancy has only just come in.'

'It's just the post I'm looking for,' Ruth blurted out.

'Yes, but are you qualified as a nursemaid?' Mrs Mountford asked doubtfully. 'It's not just about pushing prams in the park, you know.'

Ruth felt a quiver of alarm. She must not fail to get this post, but she decided to be truthful. 'I've not worked as a nursemaid previously, but I have been a mother, so I do know about young children's needs.'

Mrs Mountford raised her brows again. 'Really? You didn't mention that you had dependant children.' She shook her head. 'That makes it awkward. Employers don't like that.'

'No, you don't understand,' Ruth hurried to explain. 'I had a child, but I . . . lost him.' She felt a stab of anguish. 'I have no such responsibility now,' she went on.

'Oh, I see. I'm sorry.'

'I was a good mother,' Ruth said defensively. 'I lost my child through no fault of my own.'

Mrs Mountford was silent, drumming a pencil on the desk as she considered.

'I deserve a trial period, surely,' Ruth blurted. 'I'm sure Mr Hamilton will dismiss me quickly enough if I prove inadequate.'

Mrs Mountford sniffed. 'That's easy to say, but I have the reputation of the agency to consider. Mr Hamilton is a client of long standing.'

'Obviously, he's not very happy with the last nursemaid

you sent him,' Ruth said in a forthright tone. 'But he's still given you the business again.'

'My word! You're a fit one, aren't you?' observed Mrs Mountford in surprise. 'Very well, then,' she continued. 'We'll do it on a trial basis, and I'll make that clear to Mr Hamilton.'

'Oh, thank you!' Ruth was overjoyed.

Mrs Mountford took a form from a box on the desk and wrote Richard's address on it together with Ruth's details, and some further observations. She handed it to Ruth.

'Take this along to Mr Hamilton at his house in Gower Road at your earliest convenience,' Mrs Mountford instructed.

Ruth swallowed. 'Are there other applicants?'

Mrs Mountford sighed. 'Not at present. I'm a fair woman. I'll give you a chance as you're so keen, but remember, my client must be fully satisfied otherwise I'll have to take you off my books.'

Ruth left Carlton Terrace and walked up Walter Road where she felt certain she could get a bus to Gower Road, probably half an hour's journey west of Swansea.

She had promised Miss Lydia to return promptly, but felt in her bones that she should strike while the iron was hot. Mrs Mountford might change her mind and send another applicant. She could not chance that, even if it meant that Miss Lydia was put out to the point of sacking her. Being without work was no longer a nightmare, thanks to Richard Hamilton's effort with the sale of the pearls, and she felt a rush of gratitude towards him.

The June day was warm and promised to get warmer, and the bus ride was pleasant. She showed the bus conductor Richard's address and asked to be alerted to the nearest stop.

Later he touched her on the shoulder. 'This is it, miss.'

Ruth walked probably a hundred yards before she was certain she had found the right address. She walked down the drive feeling nerves flutter unpleasantly in her stomach.

A young maid answered her knock. 'Yes?'

'I'm here to see Mr Hamilton,' Ruth began. 'I've been sent by Mrs Mountford's agency for the position of nurse-maid.'

The maid looked her up and down. 'You'd better come in then,' she said letting Ruth pass her into the hall. 'Stay by here, please. I'll see if Mr Hamilton can see you.'

She returned in a moment. 'Mr Hamilton will see you. This way please.'

Ruth followed the girl to an oak-panelled door lower down the hall. The maid ushered her inside and then left, closing the door noiselessly behind her.

Ruth could see straight away it was the study and Richard Hamilton sat at the desk facing the windows, his back to her.

'Now then, you're from the employment agency,' he said in a business-like tone and then turned to look at her. His mouth dropped open with astonishment at the sight of her, and he stood up abruptly.

'Ruth! What are you doing here?' he asked. 'I was expecting someone from an employment agency.'

Ruth was all of a quiver with nerves at coming face to face with him, but she struggled not to show it. She must remain calm and in control of her emotions if she was to convince him she was the right one for the post.

'Yes, sir,' she said, trying to steady her voice. 'I've been sent by Mrs Mountford. I wish to apply for the position of nursemaid.'

'You're the last person I expected.' There was a puzzled look on his face. 'How did you know the post was vacant?' he went on. 'I've only just put it on the agency's books.'

Ruth wetted her lips nervously, realizing she would have to lie. 'A coincidence, really,' she said. 'I'd decided to become a nursemaid and I registered at the agency last week.' She smiled trying to hide her own disquiet. 'This morning Mrs Mountford said she had something suitable for me.' She lifted a hand to her breast as a gesture of her own surprise. 'And here I am.'

'I had thought you'd want to live off your income from selling the pearls,' he said and smiled. 'Become a lady of leisure instead of working for someone else.'

'The idle life would never suit me,' Ruth said, which was true. 'And I'm very fond of children.'

'Yes, I see.' He looked around. 'Please, do sit down, Ruth.'

Ruth perched on the edge of an upright chair at the side of his desk feeling awkward, willing her hands not to tremble. Richard sat at the desk, pulling his chair around to face her.

'I have to ask you some questions, you understand,' he began almost apologetically. 'I know of course that you are of good character or you wouldn't still be in my aunt's employ.'

Ruth smiled and said nothing. She was dreading the question he might ask about her experience at looking after children. She had made up her mind that she would tell him the truth, or at least a partial truth.

'I must ask,' he said. 'And my wife will certainly want to know, what experience do you have for this post?'

Although she was expecting it and was well prepared, the question touched a nerve. This was the tricky part; a danger of saying too much and giving herself away, exposing her ulterior motive.

Ruth clasped her hands together in her lap, and looked down at them and saw her knuckles were white and tried to relax to relieve the tension she was under.

'I've not been altogether frank with Miss Lydia,' she began tremulously despite herself, wondering if she was doing the right thing in revealing so much. It had been a small deception but now she was ashamed of it.

He raised his brows, and frowned. 'In what way?'

'Miss Lydia asked if I had children. I said no, but in fact, I did have a child once, but I . . . lost him at the beginning of this year.'

'My dear Ruth!' Suddenly his pleasant face was full of concern, and he stretched out a hand as though to touch hers but drew back at the last moment. 'I'm so sorry. I share your grief,' he said solemnly. 'My wife and I suffered the same loss last year.'

Instinct warned her to appear to be in ignorance. 'I had no idea,' she said, but her dissembling caused a bitter taste in her mouth. She hated being underhand with him. 'Your present child . . .?'

He hesitated, his expression momentarily guarded. 'James

is our adopted son,' he explained, but she noticed his gaze, usually so direct, was turned away.

'James, yes, I see,' Ruth said, feeling an ache in her heart. 'Well, Mr Hamilton, to answer your question, having been a mother I'm well versed in the needs of young children. How old is your son, James,' she asked artfully.

'A year old,' he said. 'A very healthy, happy child, he is, too.' He smiled with obvious pleasure.

Ruth's heart swelled with gladness that her child was thriving, even though he was parted from his true mother.

She bit her lip. 'Is there anything further you wish to know about me, Mr Hamilton?'

'Forgive me for asking such a painful question, Ruth,' he said gravely. 'But how did your child die?'

Ruth's breath caught in her throat, and she lifted a hand to her breast. She should have been prepared for this, but wasn't. She must again tell a partial truth.

'My son didn't die,' she said swallowing hard. She caught an expression of astonishment on his face and hurried to explain. 'His father, my late husband, was responsible for my parting from my child.' She hesitated again. 'There was a . . . dispute, and my husband took strong measures . . .'

She stopped, not wanting to say anything further, hoping it would be enough to satisfy him. In fact, she suspected she might have already said too much. Richard Hamilton was an astute and shrewd man.

'I see,' he said slowly. He stared at her seriously for a moment. 'And where is your child now.'

She had no way of knowing what Esther Beale and David had told Richard of Andrew's past. Panic almost overtook her, but she steeled herself to remain calm. She *must* secure this post, she thought, her heart pounding in her breast. It was her one chance to be with her child again and that was all that mattered. She could not look beyond that aching longing.

To think that her long cherished hope might be snatched from her all too soon was more than she could bear. If she had to weave a web of lies she would do it. She would do anything for Andrew; make any sacrifice, even sacrifice her own happiness.

'I've no idea,' she said as steadfastly as she could, steeling herself to look him directly in the eye. 'I . . . I suspect my husband took him abroad before he himself died. I've not heard one word of him since.'

His expression was sombre. 'I'm sorry for your misfortune, Ruth, and your pain,' he said. 'Your child is as good as dead to you. And I understand your desire to look after children to fill the void. It's very natural.'

'Thank you for your understanding, sir,' Ruth said. She fidgeted in her chair. 'Have you come to a decision? Will you consider me for the post?'

He rose to his feet. 'Before I do that, my wife must meet you,' he said carefully. 'Annette is a sensitive woman, who goes by instinct when it comes to employing people. I trust her judgement implicitly. This way.'

Richard led her to a room downstairs and Ruth saw at once that it had been turned into a pleasant bedroom where open French windows looked out over gardens in full bloom.

Her gaze went to the figure reclining on pillows on the bed, and was taken aback. Annette Hamilton's face was pale, almost colourless, and the skin around her mouth and nose appeared stretched across her bones. Her abundant dark hair seemed to make her skin look transparent by comparison and she was painfully thin.

Ruth's heart was filled with pity. Although she longed for Andrew, she could never knowingly hurt this woman who was suffering so much; a grieving mother like herself.

'Annette, my dear,' Richard began. 'This is Ruth Allerton, who's applying for the post of nursemaid,' Richard said. 'I've checked her references. I'm satisfied, but you must make the final decision.'

Ruth noticed he did not mention that she was currently employed by his aunt.

Annette made a feeble effort to push herself into a better sitting position and immediately Richard went to her aid.

'Sit down, Miss Allerton,' Annette invited, her voice underlying her physical weakness. 'Let's chat a moment.'

210

Ruth wetted her lips. 'It's Mrs Allerton, ma'am,' she said. 'I'm a widow.'

'I'm sorry,' Annette said quickly. 'Do you have children of your own?'

Ruth hesitated to answer for a split second and before she could speak Richard chimed in.

'Mrs Allerton did have a child, Annette,' he said quickly. 'But sadly she lost him at the beginning of this year.'

A dark shadow passed across Annette's features and she sank back against the pillows. Richard went to her side immediately.

'I'm sorry, my dear,' he said anxiously bending over her. 'Mentioning that was thoughtless of me.'

Annette smiled up at him weakly, and took his hand. 'It's all right, Richard. It just brought back memories . . .'

'Please forgive me,' he said tenderly, and watching his solicitousness, Ruth felt a little stab of envy.

Annette looked at her and smiled sadly. 'We have tragedy in common, Mrs Allerton,' she said. 'You understand what a mother feels. I can think of no better qualification than that.' She glanced up at her husband with a smile. 'If Richard is satisfied that you answer all our needs, then I too am satisfied. When can you start?'

Ruth's breath caught in her throat. 'Well, in a week's time,' she said.

She was sure Miss Lydia would grant her that. And of course she would have to tell her of her new post. She would certainly be surprised and probably suspicious.

'Then it's settled,' Richard said cheerfully. 'Ruth . . . that is Mrs Allerton, will live-in, of course.'

'Ruth,' Annette repeated thoughtfully. 'That's a pretty name. Yes, you'll be known in the household as Ruth; much better I think than Nurse.'

Ruth gave a little nod. 'Thank you, ma'am.'

'My husband will introduce you to the servants; Cook and two parlour maids. Now, I expect you'd like to meet your charge, our son James.'

Ruth felt almost overpowered with emotion at the thought of seeing Andrew, here and now! And she prayed that the depth of her feelings would not give her away. She must stay in control. There would be plenty of time for her and Andrew to be together now.

Ruth rose shakily from her chair. 'Yes, I'd like to meet James,' she said carefully. 'But I don't want to upset the present nursemaid.'

'She's gone,' Richard said. 'One of the maids is standing in temporarily. I'll ring for her, and she'll take you up to the nursery.'

The nursery was on the top floor of the house, and consisted of a suite of rooms; the nursery itself, a small kitchen, a sluice room and the nursemaid's bedroom and small sitting room.

As she climbed the narrow staircase to the top behind Elsie, the parlour maid, Ruth trembled with anticipation. At last, after six long months of pain and yearning she would be with Andrew again; she would hold him, nurse him; tend to his every need. She could shower him with love and no one would think it strange.

'Here we are, Nurse,' the maid said opening the nursery door. 'Master James is in his playpen. I expect he'll be glad of a bit of company. He's been on his own a lot since the last nurse left.'

Ruth stepped over the threshold on shaking legs. The playpen stood in the centre of the room. A child, about a year old, stood on wobbly legs, clutching the bars of the pen, grinning at the newcomers hopefully, and immediately made an attempt at conversation.

Ruth's heart swelled in her breast at the sight of him. She would have known her own child anywhere. It took a massive grip of will power to stop her dashing forward to snatch the child into her arms. There would be time enough for that when she and Andrew were alone.

Ruth walked forward and stood by the pen, looking down on her son trying to stay controlled.

'Here's James, Nurse,' Elsie said. 'I'll be glad to hand him over to you; the sooner the better, too.'

'Don't you like children, then?' Ruth said vaguely. Andrew

was all she wanted to concentrate on. She longed to be alone with him.

Elsie made a grimace. 'A lot of hard work they are if you ask me. I wouldn't be a full time nursemaid for anything.'

'Well, if you're busy elsewhere, Elsie,' Ruth said quickly. 'You needn't wait here with me. I'll find my own way down later. I want to get to know my new charge.'

'Right you are!' Elsie said and hurried off, obviously relieved.

As soon as the maid was gone, Ruth scooped the child up into her arms, and held him tightly against her breast. 'Oh, Andrew, my little darling son. How I've ached to hold you in my arms once again.'

Andrew burbled at her in delight and made a grab for her hat brim. Ruth laughed in great happiness.

Ruth wondered fancifully whether he recognized her as his mother but knew sensibly that it was unlikely after all these months. Tears were streaming down her face now, but she didn't care.

She walked to a chair nearby and sat him on her lap to examine him properly, while he stared up at her, his eyes bright. She was amazed how much he had grown in the last six months. Whatever disagreements the previous nursemaid had had with Annette Hamilton, she had taken good care of the child. He was plump and healthy looking, and there was a sparkle in his eyes as though everything was right in his world.

Ruth kissed his apple cheek. 'Oh Andrew, my lovely boy. I love you so much. We'll never be parted again, I promise you.'

Ruth paused suddenly, cautious. She must learn to use the name the Hamiltons had given him. He must always be James. She must never use his real name, not even to herself.

Perhaps Ruth had spent too long upstairs for after a while Elsie reappeared. 'Mr Hamilton suggests you come down to the kitchen and be introduced to the rest of the staff,' the maid said.

Glancing at the clock on the mantelpiece Ruth saw she had been almost an hour in the nursery. The moments with her son had flown by.

213

'Of course,' Ruth said carefully, placing Andrew back in the playpen. She gave him one last lingering look and then walked toward the door. The child gave a little whimper and stared at her through the bars, tears beginning to glisten in his eyes.

'Oh, he's taken to you, all right,' Elsie said lightly. 'I hope you can start soon,' she went on chattily. 'I want to get back to my own work.'

Ruth met Mrs Roderick, the housekeeper, and the other older parlour maid, Florence. They were all friendly and knew she would fit in with them very well.

Elsie finally took her back upstairs to see the master of the house. Ruth entered the study and felt as though she were walking on air.

'Well, Ruth,' Richard Hamilton said. 'You met James and the staff. When can you begin duty, do you think?'

'It depends on when Miss Lydia will let me go,' Ruth said 'But I'd like to start as soon as possible. James is such a little darling . . .' She paused, confused.

He was smiling at her eagerly. 'Leave Aunt Lydia to me,' he said confidently. 'When my aunt knows how much James needs you, I'm sure she'll be reasonable.'

'Thank you, sir,' Ruth said, almost overcome with happiness at the thought of being with her son all day and every day from now on.

'Call me Mr Richard. All the staff does,' he said. He held out his hand, and Ruth grasped it, and they shook hands firmly. 'Welcome to my household, Ruth,' he said, sincerity in his voice. 'I hope you'll be very happy with us.'

Twenty-Two

In the hallway at Dynevor Place, Evans, the Hamiltons' chauffeur, picked up Ruth's few bags. 'I'll take these out to the motor, miss,' he said.

'Thank you,' Ruth said.

She had said her goodbyes to Mr Timothy, and to Mrs Withers, although she intended to call and see the woman who had befriended her as often as she could.

Miss Lydia was standing halfway up the staircase watching; her disapproval almost tangible.

'I'll say goodbye, then, Miss Lydia,' Ruth ventured. 'Though I'm sure I'll see you again when I bring James to visit you and Mr Timothy.'

Miss Lydia took another step down, her figure stiff and forbidding. Her eyes were narrowed as she looked at Ruth.

'It wouldn't surprise me if you hadn't arranged this whole situation for your own ends,' she said suspiciously. 'To worm your way into Richard's house.'

'It was pure coincidence,' Ruth said quickly, although the lie tasted bitter on her tongue.

'Huh! An extraordinary coincidence to me.'

Evans came back into the hall. 'If that's all, miss, I think we should be going,' he said. 'Mr Hamilton will want the car later this morning.'

'Yes, of course. I'm ready,' Ruth said. She gave one last look at her former employer. 'Goodbye for now, Miss Lydia.'

'Huh!' The older woman turned her back and climbed the stairs; a bitter dismissal indeed.

Ruth turned eagerly to the open front door where Evans was waiting impatiently. There was so much to look forward to now. At last her long-cherished wish had come true. She would be with Andrew once again. The thought filled her with joy.

Ruth's introduction into life in the Hamiltons' household went smoothly and pleasantly. She devoted herself entirely to her son, and revelled in tending to his every need; spending every waking moment she could with him.

Every morning after he was bathed and dressed Ruth took Andrew into Annette's room. Her pale face and sunken eyes lit up feverishly at the sight of the bonny child.

But Annette tired very easily, and when she fell back against her pillows, Ruth knew it was time to leave her to rest.

In bed at night, in the room next to the nursery where Andrew slept, Ruth would lie awake for a while, giving thanks for her good fortune that at last she had charge of her child. But deep down in her heart she knew in time it would not be enough. Her happiness would only be complete if she could acknowledge Andrew as hers alone.

She wished she had the courage to tell Richard Hamilton the truth about his son. But would he believe her? She had no proof. The only other person who knew the whole truth was Sarah Beale. But would she speak? Would she be *allowed* to speak? Ruth doubted it. It was clear David's wife Esther was an enemy and Sarah was afraid of her.

Then there was Annette Hamilton's devotion to the child. It was sadly obvious that Annette's life was precarious. She could never cause the woman any anguish. Ruth knew that for the moment she must be content with her lot.

His mother was waiting in the hallway for him when he returned from business and David could see from her expression she was disturbed about something.

He wondered with a sigh whether Esther had been laying the law down again. It would be a good thing for his parents; for him, too, if they found a house of their own soon.

'David, I must talk to you,' Sarah said in an agitated tone that was becoming more and more noticeable these days.

'Mam, I'm tired. I need a drink,' he said, taking off his

hat and shrugging out of his overcoat. 'Can't it wait until after dinner?'

'No. It's about Ruth.'

That stopped him in his tracks. 'What about her?'

'Cook had it from her sister, Mrs Roderick,' Sarah said. 'Of course the woman doesn't understand the significance . . .'

'Mam, what about Ruth?'

'Richard Hamilton has taken her on as nursemaid,' Sarah blurted. 'She's managed to worm her way into his household.'

'What? The devil she has!' He was astonished. 'How on earth did she find out where her child was, I wonder?'

Sarah put her fingers to her mouth, and stared at him in alarm.

'I told her,' she said in a small voice.

'Good God, Mam!' He was flabbergasted. 'Whatever possessed you to do such a thing?'

'I had to,' Sarah said, wringing her hands. 'I couldn't bear the thought that she believed her child was on the other side of the world where she'd never see him again,' Sarah gabbled. 'It wasn't right, David, telling her that cruel lie.'

David took a deep breath. He had to agree with her. Esther's ruthless behaviour was unforgivable. But even so, his mother's meddling had brought them to a pretty mess.

'You shouldn't have interfered, Mam.'

'But Ruth knew about Richard Hamilton before I told her anything,' Sarah said defensively. 'She'd already hired one of those inquiry agents to find the child.'

David could only admire Ruth's ingenuity. He hadn't realized she possessed such spirit and determination.

'Oh, David, I'm so worried. Esther is bound to find out what I did. There'll be trouble.' Sarah wrung her hands again. 'What do you think Esther will do?'

David rubbed his thumb against his jaw. More to the point – what should he do about it? Despite his mother's fears, Esther would have to be told. He cringed at the thought of her reaction.

'Are you going to tell Esther?' His mother always seemed to be able to read his thoughts.

He did not answer.

'Do you think Ruth means to steal the child away?' Sarah asked in a querulous voice.

'Mam, don't be so melodramatic!' David was angry with her. 'Ruth's not irresponsible. She can't prove the child is hers. It would be kidnapping.'

Sarah looked relieved. 'No, that's true.'

'Perhaps we should do nothing,' he suggested hopefully. 'Perhaps Ruth just wants to be with her son, and doesn't mean to do anything else. We shouldn't jump to conclusions.'

Sarah bit her lip. 'But even if you don't tell her Esther is bound to find out. She's back and forth Richard's house all the time.' She gave him a sidelong glance. 'You know that.'

David turned his gaze away. He knew his mother was hinting at Esther's inordinate interest in Richard Hamilton. It was hard for him to take, especially knowing he had no control over her.

'She'd better be told, I suppose,' Sarah said meekly with the air of submission of one who knows she must face the consequences.

David looked keenly at his mother. 'You know what'll happen to Ruth, don't you?' he said. 'She'll lose her position. She'll be thrown out; parted from her child again and this time for good.'

Sarah clamped her hand over her mouth and turning, hurried up the staircase.

David followed at a more leisurely pace. Esther was probably dressing for dinner, a tiresome ritual as far as he was concerned. Sometimes he longed for the old days and the modest family bakery in Gowerton. And Ruth.

Esther was at the dressing table putting final touches to her hair. She glanced at him through the mirror.

'What's wrong with you? she asked sharply. 'Why are you scowling like that?'

'Have you seen Richard this week?'

She raised her brows in surprise. 'Haven't had time, really.' She grimaced. 'That beastly disturbance at the lower pit; rumours of a strike had to be dealt with, you know that full well.'

'You should leave those things to me and your father,' David said gratingly. 'The men don't take kindly to be told what to do by a woman.'

She gave him a sardonic smile, raising her eyebrows. 'So I've noticed.'

He ground his teeth, wanting to shake that arrogance of hers.

'If you'd been to Gower Road lately,' he said brusquely. 'You'd know that Ruth Allerton has ensconced herself there as nursemaid to the child.'

It was rare to see Esther's features etched with such marked consternation. Her face went white and then red. She jumped up from the dressing table stool and whirled to face him.

'Did you have something to do with this, David?' she shouted at him furiously.

'Don't be absurd!'

'I wouldn't put it past you. I know you still have feelings for her.'

'Talking of feelings,' he retorted heatedly. 'What about you and Richard? Is there something I should know?'

Esther took in a deep breath as though to calm herself.

'Richard is a friend, that's all.'

'If only Annette were out of the way, eh?'

Esther sprang forward and slapped him across the face. 'How dare you?'

He stepped back, astonished and speechless.

'Who told Ruth where to find the child?' Esther demanded to know. 'Was it Sarah?'

David shook his head. He must protect his mother. 'No, as a matter of fact,' he said. 'I have it on good authority that Ruth employed an inquiry agent to trace Andrew. She's not as stupid as you suppose.'

Esther, her hands twisting together, whirled away. 'Well, it won't do her any good,' she said triumphantly. 'I'll call on Annette soon. She needs to know what a viper she's taken to her bosom.'

'Why can't you leave things alone,' David demanded wretchedly. 'What harm can it do that Ruth is with her son?'

Esther turned to face him, a malicious gleam in her eyes.

'Still protecting your lost love, are you, even though she threw you over for a man with social position and money? More fool you!'

'You don't know what you're talking about,' he answered.

'Do you think Ruth will be content to just go on acting as nursemaid to her own son indefinitely?' Esther asked scornfully. 'Of course not! She's up to something, and I'll not stand by and let her destroy Richard's happiness.'

'Richard! Richard! It's always Richard!' David stormed. 'I'm sick of it Esther; sick of our empty life together.'

She stared at him stonily for a moment before she turned away and walked out of the door.

Esther marched into the hall at Richard's house in Gower Road, pulling off her gloves.

'Where's the nursemaid?' she demanded to know of the maid who had answered the door.

The maid closed the door behind her. 'The chauffeur has taken Master James and Mrs Allerton to Singleton Park,' the girl said. 'Is anything wrong, ma'am?'

'Let me know the second they get back,' Esther ordered haughtily. 'Now tell Mrs Hamilton that Mrs Beale is here to see her.'

'But it's early, ma'am. I mean . . . the mistress isn't properly awake yet,' the maid answered, a look of uncertainty on her face. 'She hasn't bathed or had breakfast.'

'Don't be a fool, girl,' Esther snapped impatiently. 'I must see her immediately. It's a matter of urgency. Now, tell her I'm here or must I do it myself?'

The girl dipped a nervous curtsy. 'Yes, ma'am. If you'll just wait . . .'

'Nonsense! Lead the way.'

Esther waved a hand in an authoritative fashion, and the maid hurried along the hallway to Annette's ground-floor bedroom. Esther followed and as she approached the open door she heard the maid speaking. Not waiting to be invited, she marched straight in.

The maid was just helping her mistress into a sitting position, plumping up the pillows to support her. Her face pale and drawn Annette looked up startled and a little embarrassed as Esther entered.

'Esther, this is a surprise and so early, too,' Annette said in a faint voice. 'You've missed Richard. He often leaves for business almost at the crack of dawn.'

'I haven't come to see Richard, not yet anyway,' Esther said. She moved closer to the bed. 'Annette, I've come to warn you.'

'Warn me?' Annette's hands clutched at the counterpane. 'Esther, whatever do you mean?'

The maid was hovering and Esther glowered at her. 'That will be all thank you,' she said firmly. 'Mrs Hamilton will ring when she needs you again.'

The maid left, closing the door behind her. Annette's eyes were large and worried as she looked at her visitor.

'Esther, you're frightening me. Whatever is the matter?'

'I've come to warn you that James may be in danger.'

'Oh no!'

'The woman you've taken on as nursemaid, Ruth Allerton,' Esther went on. 'She's not what she appears. She's here under false pretences and she's out to do mischief.'

'Ruth?' Annette looked fearfully at her and Esther was satisfied that her words were having the right effect. 'If you know something against Ruth you must tell me at once,' Annette said. 'What has she done?'

'It's what she intends to do,' Esther said emphatically. 'The truth is Ruth Allerton is James' natural mother, and I believe she's just waiting for an opportunity to make off with the child.'

'What?' Annette clutched at her throat. 'Oh my God! She's supposed to be taking him to the park this morning, but she could be anywhere.' Annette pushed the counterpane back and tried to get out of bed. 'We must do something; call the police,' she said in breathless agitation. 'Richard must be sent for.'

Esther moved forward. 'There's nothing you can do for the moment,' she said, placing a restraining hand on Annette's thin shoulder to push her back into the bed.

'But she could be abducting my son this very minute,' Annette cried out desperately.

221

Her son? Esther looked at the other woman with concealed disdain. To think that Richard had been forced to marry this weakling, who never could be a proper wife to him or bear him an heir.

'You can do nothing,' Esther repeated ruthlessly. 'You're far too weakened to be of any use to James.'

Annette fell back on the pillows and Esther saw she could hardly speak for breathlessness.

'Please Esther, ring for the maid,' she gasped. 'She must send for my husband.'

Esther viewed the other woman's pale sickness-ravaged face with cold contempt, knowing that if Richard's father hadn't interfered she would probably be his wife now instead of this feeble creature.

'I doubt even he can do anything. From what I know of Ruth Allerton she'll have made plans,' Esther went on brutally. 'It may be too late already.' She hesitated. 'It's not inconceivable that she's taken him abroad. You may never see James again,' she went on.

'Dear God!' As Annette uttered the words she gave a little choking sigh; her eyes closed and her head lolled on her chest.

Esther sprang to her feet. Had she gone too far?

'Annette?' She reached for the woman's wrist and felt for a pulse. It was there, barely.

Esther pulled the bell rope that was within arm's reach of the bed. Within a few minutes the maid appeared.

'Your mistress has fainted,' she said, imperious. 'Find the smelling salts and then you'd better send for her doctor.'

The maid rushed to Annette's side, lifting up her head to look into her face, and then turned her frightened gaze on Esther. 'What have you said to set her off like this? You've upset her.'

Esther was furious. 'How dare you speak to me like that,' she rasped. 'I'll have you dismissed.'

The maid looked scared and then scrabbled in the drawer of the bedside table, bringing out a small brown flat bottle, and taking out the cork put the bottle under her mistress' nose.

Annette moved her head sluggishly to avoid the acrid smell, and then moaned softly, but her eyes remained closed.

'I'll have to get the doctor,' the maid said sullenly. 'He'll have questions, I expect.'

'Send for Mr Hamilton as well,' Esther commanded. 'We have a serious situation to discuss. Well! Immediately girl!'

Richard stared at his own reflection in the mirror above the mantelpiece, seething with anger at what Esther had just revealed to him. He had totally trusted Ruth Allerton and the revelation that she had lied to him was hard to bear. All the time she'd been scheming to get her child back. He would never have believed such dissembling of her.

'The police ought to be told,' Esther said from a chair nearby. 'Look at the time. She should've been back with the boy before this. I tell you Richard, the woman is dangerous.'

Richard did not answer. He was bitterly angry with Esther, too, for upsetting Annette to the point where she collapsed.

'What will you do when she returns?' she asked.

'I'm considering,' he said evasively.

Dr Moore entered the sitting room at that point and Richard whirled from the mantelpiece.

'How is my wife, doctor?' he asked anxiously.

'She's had some kind of a shock which hasn't done her any good at all,' Dr Moore said, putting his bag on a table. He shook his head. 'I must say I don't like her condition. It's very serious.'

Richard glanced meaningfully at Esther who was sitting nearby. She shrugged her shoulders.

'All I did was tell her who Ruth Allerton really is.'

'I wish you'd told me first,' Richard said testily. 'I could've dealt with it without Annette knowing anything about it.' He glanced at the doctor again. 'Can you give her anything to ease her?'

'She's very agitated about something,' the doctor answered. 'And quite incoherent. I've given her an injection and I've left a prescription with her maid.' The doctor shook his head again. 'Your wife must have complete rest, Mr Hamilton, and constant attention. I've advised that previously.'

223

'I had urgent business to take me from the house today and Annette seemed all right. But I'll not leave her alone again, believe me,' Richard said grimly.

'I'll arrange for a night nurse, I think, to be on the safe side,' Dr Moore said. 'I'll call in to see her again tomorrow morning, but if you're worried at all, call me.' He picked up his bag. 'I'll see myself out.'

When the doctor had left, closing the door behind him, Richard sat down. The news of Annette's collapse had shaken him and then on top of that he had learned of Ruth's deceit. He prayed that she had taken no action yet, and that she would bring his son home.

He rubbed his hands together uneasily. If James had been taken by Ruth, Annette would never get over it. It would finish her.

He would not be able to resort to the law. He was unsure of the legal implications of taking in the child without official sanction. If it was true that Ruth was James' natural mother would the law be on her side? In his heart he knew it was true, and he felt a sense of guilt in having caused her pain by accepting the child. But he had been misled by Esther, too.

He looked up as Flo the parlour maid came into the room.

'Mrs Beale wanted to be informed when Mrs Allerton returned,' the girl said stiffly. 'Evans is just parking the motor now, sir.'

Esther jumped up. 'Bring her here straight away,' she commanded.

'Wait, Flo!' Richard said, also rising to his feet. 'I'll see Mrs Allerton in the study. Ask her to wait there. I'll be along directly.'

'But Richard, dear . . .' Esther began, but he held up a hand as the maid left the room.

'I'll deal with this,' he said firmly. 'It hardly concerns you, Esther.'

'But it does concern me!' she burst out. 'I know all about Ruth Allerton, what she's capable of. I should be present when you confront her. After all, it was I who—'

Richard's lips tightened. 'I'm well aware of the part you played, Esther.'

'Richard, the woman's clever!' Esther exclaimed. 'She could easily bamboozle you like she did David.'

'David? What has your husband to do with Ruth?'

Esther bit her lip. 'It was a long time ago . . .' She paused. 'You need me, Richard. She might attempt to compromise you. The woman is desperate.'

Perhaps it would be better to have a third person present at the interview, if only to prevent him making a fool of himself. He was angry with Ruth for her deception, but could not ignore the growing feelings he had for her even though he had no right.

'Very well,' he said resignedly. 'We'll see her together in the study. But allow me to do the talking, please Esther. I'm Ruth's employer after all.'

'You must be resolute, Richard,' Esther told him. 'The woman is a trickster. She'll try to talk her way out of it.'

Ruth felt happy and even carefree as she carried Andrew into the house, leaving Evans to bring in the heavy perambulator. It was enough for the moment that she was with Andrew.

As she walked into the hall, Flo came to meet her.

'I'll take Master James, Mrs Allerton,' she said. 'Mr Hamilton wants to see you right away in the study. He'll be along shortly.'

Ruth reluctantly handed the child over to the maid and then pulling off her gloves and removing her hat, went to the study.

The room was empty and Ruth waited obediently near the desk. She wondered why she had been summoned. Had she inadvertently upset Annette Hamilton in her care of Andrew?

Within a moment of her arrival in the room, Richard Hamilton walked in, a grim expression on his usually pleasant face. She was about to ask what was wrong but then saw who had walked in right behind him; Esther Beale.

Ruth was immediately filled with consternation, realizing at once that she had been found out. They had discovered her secret.

Richard went and stood behind his desk; Esther Beale

following to stand at his side. With her mouth dry Ruth waited for him to speak first.

'Mrs Allerton – Ruth,' Richard began. 'I believe you have something to confess to me.'

'Oh for heaven's sake, Richard!' Esther exclaimed irritably. 'This woman has obviously been plotting to snatch your son away from you. She should be dismissed at once.' She glowered at Ruth. 'Did you imagine you could get away with this contemptible behaviour; that you wouldn't be found out?'

'You've no right to accuse me of anything,' Ruth blurted. 'I've done nothing wrong.'

'You lied when you applied for the post of nursemaid,' Richard said heavily. 'And that's hard to forgive. Why didn't you tell me you are the child's mother?'

'Because I'd have been shown the door, that's why,' Ruth answered angrily. 'James . . . Andrew is my son, and Mrs Beale here had no right to give him away like an unwanted pet.'

'You did that very thing yourself,' Esther accused heatedly. 'You foisted the child off on my mother-in-law. You didn't give a damn what became of him.'

'Ruth!' Richard stared at her in dismay. 'Is this true? You gave your child away? You told me your husband had abducted him and I felt very sorry for you.'

'I had no choice but to get him to a place of safety,' Ruth cried out. 'His very life was in danger. His father repeatedly threatened him.'

'So you say!' Esther was smiling nastily and Ruth knew she was enjoying every moment of her distress. 'And now the child is suited with a wealthy family,' Esther went on remorselessly. 'You suddenly want him back again.' She looked triumphantly at Ruth, her eyebrows raised scornfully. 'Or perhaps it's not really the child you want. Perhaps it's money instead. You're hoping Mr Hamilton will pay you to go away?'

'How dare you!' Ruth spluttered in fury, clenching her fists at her sides. 'That's an outrageous accusation, totally untrue. I wanted only to care for my child as any mother would.'

'You're lying,' Esther said raising her voice. 'You've shown how much you care by giving him away.'

'Please!' Richard's tone was grave. 'Be silent, both of you. Have you forgotten my wife is very ill just a few rooms away?'

'What?' Ruth was concerned. 'Mrs Hamilton was as usual when I took the boy in to see her this morning before we went out. What's happened since?'

Richard glanced at Esther.

'She had to be told about you,' Esther said with defensive belligerence. 'It's obvious to me that you intended to abduct the child. I had to warn Annette.'

'The thought never entered my head,' Ruth flared. 'I was happy just to be close to him again, tending his needs, loving him as only a mother can.'

Esther laughed lightly and shook her head. 'Do you think anyone will believe that? I certainly don't and neither does Richard. You deliberately deceived him about your kinship to the child. That dishonest behaviour speaks for itself.'

Ruth looked at Richard Hamilton. 'Since when is Mrs Beale the head of this household?' she asked angrily. She knew she was being impertinent to her employer, but what did she have to lose now? 'Have you nothing to say for yourself, sir?'

'Yes, I have. You came here under false colours, Ruth,' he said, his face reddening angrily. 'You deliberately deceived me. How can I trust anything you say after that?'

'Don't you understand? I had no choice . . .?'

'You leave me no choice, Ruth,' he interrupted brusquely. 'I discharge you from my employ as from now. I want you to leave my house tomorrow morning.'

'She must go straight away, Richard, this minute,' Esther put in spitefully. 'God knows what she might do within the next few hours.'

Ruth stepped forward. 'Please, Mr Richard, don't dismiss me. I swear I meant no harm. I just wanted to be with my son. Surely that's understandable?'

A spark of hope rose in her heart as she saw him hesitate. Esther must have seen his doubt too, for she clutched at his arm.

'Richard!' she burst out. 'Be firm. I warned you she'd try to bamboozle you; play on your sympathy. Don't be taken in. This woman is a cheat, a congenital liar. She was publicly denounced for serious misconduct in her village by her own husband. She's not to be trusted.'

'You vixen!' Ruth cried wrathfully. 'It was all untrue and you know it. This is no more than spite!'

Richard brought his clenched fist down on the desk top with a crash. 'Stop it!' he bellowed, and then swallowed hard, obviously struggling to control himself. 'There's no more to be said, Ruth. I can no longer trust you,' he grated. 'You must go from my house.'

'Oh, please, Mr Richard, don't take my boy from me again,' Ruth cried out. 'I couldn't bear it.'

'You'll pack your bags and leave immediately,' Esther said before Richard could answer. 'Evans can take you wherever you want to go.'

'But I have nowhere to go!' Ruth exclaimed.

'Well, that's your problem,' Esther snapped. 'You're lucky we're not calling the police.'

Ruth gave her a penetrating look. 'Neither of you are in a position to bring the law into the matter,' she said loudly. 'I believe it's against the law to trade in children.'

Esther's mouth dropped open and Richard looked at her with pain in his eyes.

'How could you believe I'd do anything like that, Ruth?' he asked.

Ruth lifted her chin. 'You might for your wife's sake.'

'That's insulting,' Esther spat out the words. 'No money changed hands. I found a home for a poor unwanted mother-less child, that's all.'

'No, in your case it wasn't a question of money, I'm sure.' Ruth was disdainful. 'There are other gains for you, like ingratiating yourself with the Hamiltons.' She threw Richard a sharp glance. 'Especially with Mr Richard.'

'That's enough, Ruth!' Richard said. She saw anger flare in his eyes and knew she had overstepped the mark. 'You'd better leave before more damage is done.'

'You're making a mistake,' Ruth said desperately. 'I'd

have cared for the child wholeheartedly. He'll be the poorer for my going, mark my words, Mr Richard.'

'He'll be safer,' Esther said nastily.

'Get your things now and go.' Richard's jaw jutted determinedly. 'Write and let me know where you are and I'll send any wages due to you.'

'But don't expect any references,' Esther said with spite.

Ruth looked from one to the other; from Esther's malicious smile of triumph to Richard's dark scowl. It hurt her to think he was angry with her and through no fault of her own. His good opinion of her had been most important, now he must hate her.

Lifting her head Ruth turned and left the room.

'You're not to linger in the nursery. The maid will be with you to see that you don't.' Esther's loud voice carried into the hall. 'Do you hear me, Mrs Allerton?'

Ruth did not respond to the taunt, but her steps were heavy as she went upstairs to her room next door to the nursery. She heard footsteps hurrying up behind her and knew the maid had been sent to watch her. She packed her large Gladstone bag with a few of her essentials, her heart breaking as she realized that once again she would be parted from Andrew and this time it would probably be for good. They would never let her get near her son ever again.

When she came out of her room she saw Elsie waiting by Andrew's playpen.

'I'm just taking this one bag for now, Elsie,' she said. 'Tell Mr Hamilton that I'll send for the rest of my things when I get settled.'

'Yes, Mrs Allerton.' The maid smiled sadly at her. 'I'm sorry to see you go,' she went on. 'She has a wicked tongue, that Mrs Beale. It was her that pushed poor Mrs Hamilton over the edge this morning. Criminal I call it.'

'Take care of my son, Elsie, won't you?' she asked of the maid, trying to control the sob in her voice.

She knew she wasn't telling Elsie any more than she didn't already know.

'Trust me,' Elsie said. 'Listen, pick him up. There's no harm in cuddling him one more time.'

With a smile of gratitude Ruth lifted Andrew out of his playpen and held him close to her heart. He looked up into her face, chuckling happily. She kissed him gently, tears running down her cheeks.

'Goodbye, my darling boy,' she said, as she brushed her lips against his soft scented hair. 'I'll always love you.'

With that she handed him to Elsie.

'I'd better get downstairs,' Ruth said chokingly. 'I expect Mrs Beale is waiting in the hall to see me off the premises.'

With one last tearful look at her baby son, Ruth turned and left.

Twenty-Three

Evans took her to Maud Stebbings' office in Alexandra Road. She had nowhere else to go and felt sure Maud would help her find a place.

Her friend was astonished to see her, and Ruth quickly explained what had happened.

'They have my child, Maud, and there's nothing I can do,' she murmured miserably. 'It's finished.' She burst into tears again; she just could not help herself.

'That's right, have a good cry,' Maud recommended. 'Have you eaten? No? Well, there's an Italian café opposite. We'll have a cup of tea, something to eat and discuss what to do next.'

Ruth wiped her nose on her already damp handkerchief and tried to pull herself together. 'I must find a place to lodge before this evening, Maud.'

'I have a room in a lodging house in Orchard Street not far from here,' Maud told her. 'It's clean and cheap. There might be a vacancy. We'll eat first and then go along there.'

There was a room vacant, first floor back, and Ruth gratefully paid two week's rent in advance to secure it. Breakfast and an evening meal were included in the rent, and Ruth sat down to a meal that evening in the company of Maud and a few other boarders.

Ruth felt very fortunate to have found a safe place to rest her head, and tried not to think of Andrew, for when she did the tears flowed. Her life had to go on, she supposed, miserable as it was. Money was no problem but she knew she had to find something to do with her days or go mad.

*   *   *

After telephoning Gower Road the next day, giving her new address, Evans called with all her things. After that she felt her connection to Andrew was completely severed and she moped about in her room, not wanting to face anyone, in utter despair.

'Listen, why don't you help me in the office?' Maud asked her one evening a week later. 'It would take your mind off things.'

'Me?' Surprised, Ruth looked up from the letter she was writing to her mother telling her what had happened. 'But I know nothing about your work.'

'You don't have to,' Maid said. 'The office must be closed up when I'm out on an inquiry.' She shook her head. 'I lose a lot of business that way.' She shrugged. 'I can't afford to employ a girl. It would be something to fill your hours.'

Ruth smiled gratefully. 'I'll try it,' she said. Anything was better than this wretched stupor into which she had descended.

She surprised herself on how well she took to it. While Andrew was never out of her thoughts, there were moments when dealing with Maud's clients and their problems that she lost herself in the work.

'Business is looking up,' Maud remarked at the beginning of July. 'I knew getting you to man the office was a good idea.'

'You were right, Maud,' Ruth said. 'I needed something to occupy my mind.'

'I'm keeping up my so-called friendship with the Beale's maid on her half day,' Maud told her. 'I might get news of Andrew from time to time.'

Ruth smiled gratefully, but without hope. She had given up hope of being reunited with her son. It tore her heart to pieces to know she had lost the only worthwhile thing in her life, the love of her son Andrew. He would never know she existed.

Trying not to descend into despair again, she rested her chin thoughtfully in her hand as she sat at the desk.

'What you need, Maud, is a telephone installed,' she

suggested. 'Then clients could ring us as well as calling personally.'

Maud laughed. 'I could never afford that. Profits are not that good!'

'Let me pay for it,' Ruth offered eagerly. 'You've done so much for me, Maud. I want to do something to repay you.'

'Well, now,' Maud said, her lips pursed pensively. 'If you install a telephone I'll have to make you my partner; share the profits.'

'Oh Maud!'

'I know you're financially all right for the moment,' Maud said. 'But everyone needs to work at something.'

'But . . .'

'It's not what you had in mind?' Maud looked at her, her gaze sympathetic but serious. 'I know your heart is in shreds over Andrew,' she said. 'But your life must go on, and it must be satisfying, or you'll end up a broken woman.'

Ruth knew it was true. She had to move on no matter how bitter and painful losing her child altogether was. To dwell on what might have been would lead to madness.

'You're right again, Maud, as usual,' Ruth said resignedly. 'I'll get on to the telephone company first thing tomorrow.'

At the beginning of August, Ruth was alone in the office reading the latest letter from her mother, feeling glad to receive news of her home village.

Louisa was in the family way again, and Ruth felt a little envious for a moment, but shrugged it off. The new pastor at Soar Chapel had six noisy children and a wife who painted her face, a fact which utterly scandalized Jacob.

Ruth was smiling to herself when Maud walked in, but paused abruptly when she saw by her friend's expression that she had serious news. Her heart almost stopped in her breast at the thought that something had happened to Andrew. She hurriedly put her letter to one side.

'What is it, Maud? Is it news of Andrew?'

Maud sat on the chair reserved for clients. 'Annette Hamilton passed away during the night.'

'Oh no!' Ruth was shocked. 'How did you hear?'

'I've just had tea with the Beale's maid in the Market Café,' Maud said. 'Esther Beale rushed around to the Hamilton's place in the early hours and hasn't left there since.'

Ruth was stunned and concerned for Andrew. Maud seemed to read her thoughts.

'The child is all right,' she said, 'A new nursemaid was engaged straight after you left.'

Nevertheless, Ruth was still disturbed. While Annette lived Ruth knew someone other than herself loved her son. Now there was no one but Richard. He loved Andrew too, she was sure, but Esther was always able to influence him it seemed. And he could not be with the boy constantly. He had business to attend to.

Andrew was at the mercy of servants and Esther Beale. And what plans did that scheming woman have for Richard? Whatever they were Ruth was sure they did not include Andrew. His future was in jeopardy once again. Determination consumed her. She would get Andrew back any way she could. With Annette gone nothing stood in her way.

Out of decency and consideration for Richard's feelings Ruth waited until two weeks had passed after Annette Hamilton's funeral before she went to the house. Esther Beale was still at Gower Road according to Maud's information. That did not bode well Ruth decided and knew she could not wait any longer to claim her child.

'Mrs Allerton!' Elsie looked astonished to see her at the door of Richard's house in Gower Road.

Ruth did not wait to be invited inside, but stepped quickly past the maid into the hall, walking resolutely towards the sitting room.

'I want to see Mr Hamilton,' Ruth said firmly.

'I . . . I don't know whether he's at home,' Elsie said hesitantly.

Ruth paused, pulled off her gloves, and gave the maid a direct look. 'Evans is outside washing down the motor,' she said. 'So Mr Hamilton must be at home, Elsie. Tell him I'm here.'

Elsie immediately went to the sitting room and closed the door. Listening intently, Ruth heard Esther Beale's voice raised in protest and Richard's deep tones replying.

Elsie reappeared and looked at Ruth. 'Mr Hamilton will see you, Mrs Allerton.'

With her head held high Ruth strode into the room. Both Richard and Esther instantly rose to their feet. Esther's features turned red with fury at the sight of her, but Ruth chose to ignore her. She felt nothing but disdain for David's wife.

'Ruth?' Richard began, taking a hesitant step forward. She detected a tremor in his voice. 'Why are you here?'

'You've got some nerve showing your face in this house again after what you did,' Esther flared. 'What're you after?'

'I've come for my son Andrew!' Ruth exclaimed loudly. 'I mean to have him. Hand him over to me now.'

'Ruth, I beg you . . .' Richard began, but Esther cut him short.

'This is preposterous,' she exploded. 'The child belongs to Richard. You no longer have any right to him. Get out of this house now!'

'Get out yourself!' Ruth flung the words at her furiously. 'You've no business here, and my reason for coming today has nothing to do with you.'

Esther's mouth dropped open with astonishment and high dudgeon. 'Richard! Are you going to let her, a mere one-time employee speak to me like that?'

'Esther, please!' he said. He took a few strides toward Ruth looking at her earnestly. 'I can't believe you really mean to take my son from me, Ruth.'

'He's *my* son, Mr Richard, not yours,' Ruth answered resolutely. 'And I do intend to take him back today.'

'Please, I beg you, Ruth. Don't do this.' There was anguish in his eyes.

'How can you ask that?' Ruth cried out. 'The boy belongs with me. I'm his mother! Your pain can't be greater than mine.'

'I thought we were . . . friends,' he said.

Ruth lifted her chin. 'No, Mr Richard,' she said stiffly. 'You were my employer. How could we be friends?'

'I thought we were, Ruth; perhaps closer than friends. After all we share something; our love for James.'

'My son's name is Andrew!' Ruth said, the anger clear in her voice. 'That's the name he was christened by.'

'Richard!' Esther spoke with a strident voice. 'What're you saying?'

'Ruth understands what I mean,' Richard said. There was a tone of desperation in his voice and Ruth realized he would say anything, promise anything to keep Andrew with him.

'No, I don't understand,' Ruth denied staunchly. 'And I know what you're trying to do, but it won't work, Mr Richard. Andrew belongs with me, and I can't bear to be apart from him for another day. Please give Elsie instructions to make him ready.'

'Do no such thing, Richard!' Esther cried. 'She should be shown the door.'

'Don't you understand, Ruth?' Richard said, shaking his head. 'How can I be parted with the boy so soon after Annette's . . .?'

Ruth felt sorry, but at the same time was wary. Perhaps he thought reminding her of his grief might weaken her resolve.

'Out of sympathy and consideration for Annette I couldn't take measures before, although heaven knows I yearned to,' Ruth said carefully, trying to keep her voice steady. 'I knew she genuinely loved him.'

'He was more hers than yours!' Esther said spitefully. The hatred in her eyes was undisguised. 'You abandoned him and Richard and Annette took him in; gave him a good home.'

'Andrew was no more than a bartering tool for you to curry favour with Mr Richard,' Ruth retorted hotly. 'So don't pretend concern for him now. You used him, nothing more.'

Richard was staring at her with a hurt expression and she felt she must apologize.

'I'm sorry if I've offended you, Mr Richard,' she said

quietly. 'But Mrs Beale has attempted to thwart me all along, for her own dubious reasons. I stand by what I've said to her.'

'You've no proof that the child upstairs is yours,' Esther resumed the fray, her voice quivering in wrath.

'You stay out of this!' Ruth shouted furiously. 'This mess is entirely your fault. If you had let Andrew stay with Sarah I'd have come for him as soon as I could. Instead you seized the chance to cruelly use the child knowing how much Mr Richard yearned for a son. His wife couldn't give him that, but you realized you could with Andrew.'

Esther looked momentarily shocked at Ruth's assertion.

'How dare you!' she exploded at last, her expression even more malevolent than before.

'I'll dare anything for my child,' said Ruth belligerently. 'Your scheme has failed.'

'Well, you can't have him,' Esther said vindictively, moving quickly to Richard's side to grasp his arm. 'Richard, don't listen to her. Don't let her do this to us,' she urged. 'Call the law to her.'

'Leave this to me, Esther,' Richard put in quickly shrugging her hand away. There was impatience in his tone. 'I understand Ruth's feelings only too well. I've lost a child too.'

'Don't be a fool, Richard,' Esther spat out impatiently. 'Can't you see she's bluffing? She has no proof of the child's true identity.'

'My proof lies with Sarah,' Ruth said triumphantly. 'She knows the whole story.' Ruth clenched her teeth in determination. 'I'll make her speak up.'

Ether smiled thinly. 'I wouldn't count on Sarah to support you,' she said. 'David will see that she doesn't say anything.'

'I'll make a scandal,' Ruth cried. 'I'll go to the newspapers if I have to.'

'You'll only expose yourself,' Esther said with a sneer. 'No one but an uncaring mother would give her child away.'

'And what about you, Mrs Beale?' Ruth said. 'What will your peers make of you leaving your husband to move in here straight after Annette's death, like a vulture?'

'Oh!' Esther was beside herself with fury. She glanced up

at Richard. 'You see what kind of woman she is, Richard?' she cried out. 'She won't stop at blackmail. You can't let her get away with it.'

'I'll go to any lengths to get Andrew back, Mr Richard,' Ruth said gravely, looking determinedly at him. She had been through so much heartache since the year had begun and she could not let it go on any longer. Without Andrew in her life there would be nothing worth living for. 'I intend to take Andrew with me today.'

That seemed to galvanize him. 'Ruth, I've lost my wife and I'm now to lose my son, too?' Richard burst out. 'I love the boy as my own flesh and blood.'

Ruth bit her lip, remembering he had spoken those very words to his aunt the day she had first met him. She felt pity but it did not change anything.

'I'm sorry, Mr Richard.'

He turned away and strode to the mantelpiece, leaning his elbow on it, as though in deep thought. There was silence in the room for a moment.

'Perhaps you'll ring for Elsie,' Ruth said firmly. 'Ask her to prepare Andrew to leave?'

He turned to look at her, making no attempt to ring for the maid, but stood watching her closely. 'You say you love Andrew, but how much would you sacrifice for him, Ruth?' he asked at last. 'Would you sacrifice your life?'

'Gladly,' Ruth said staunchly.

'Would you sacrifice your own happiness?'

Ruth stared at him. What was he leading up to?

'I don't understand you,' she said, her voice quivering at the strangeness of his question.

Richard moved away from the mantelpiece and sat down at his desk. He opened a drawer and took out some documents, spreading them before him on the desk top and then looked at her.

'I've told you of my deep feelings for Andrew,' he said his voice low. 'And here is proof of it. I made a new will as soon as he came to us, making him my sole beneficiary. This will still holds true even if I marry again, and have more children.'

She heard Esther gasp in astonishment.

'I don't believe you,' Ruth said stiffly. 'This is a trick to force me to give way, but I won't.'

'Come here and inspect these documents yourself,' he invited. 'They are straightforward enough to be understood by the layman.'

Ruth held back. Legal documents were meaningless to her.

'Why have you done this?'

'Because Andrew, as you call him, is as dear to me as my own son would be had he lived,' he said simply. 'I want to provide for him as a father should.'

'You're not his father!'

'I'm a very wealthy man, Ruth,' he pressed on in a serious tone. 'And since Annette's passing I've inherited the Kreppel family fortune also. A great deal of wealth, Ruth, and all of it Andrew's, if he remains my son and my son only.'

Her legs felt weak and she sat down in a chair nearby. A terrible ache was beginning in her heart, for she thought she knew the sacrifice expected of her.

'Richard, is this wise?' Esther asked coldly. 'You may have other sons. You may regret this.'

'I'll always consider Andrew as my first born son,' he said emphatically, his gaze fixed on Ruth. 'He'll want for nothing. He'll go to the best public school and have a gentleman's education. He'll *be* a gentleman, with all the Hamilton-Kreppel wealth and power at his disposal.'

Ruth stared at him bleakly and was silent.

'All this will come about if Andrew is not taken from me today or any other day.' Richard paused. 'What have you to offer him, Ruth?'

'A mother's love,' she said simply and without hesitation.

'Is that enough?' Richard asked eyebrows raised. 'When he's old enough to understand what wealth and opportunity you have deprived him of, will he resent you?'

'This is not fair!' Ruth cried.

'Fair? I'm offering Andrew a brilliant future,' he said eagerly. 'He could enter politics, take up a career in law, anything! Can you promise him such a life?'

Ruth stared at him in anguish for a long moment.

'This is a terrible thing you're asking of me,' she cried out at last, tears beginning to well. 'I lost Andrew a long time ago through no fault of my own and now you expect me to give him up completely; to spend the rest of my life without him.'

'Do it for his sake, Ruth. It's your decision,' Richard said gravely. 'You can give him love for now, but when he becomes a man I can give him the world.'

Ruth was silent in her torment. All she had ever wanted was what was best for Andrew. How could she deny him this future?

'Andrew's life is in your hands at this moment, Ruth,' Richard said. 'What is your decision?'

Ruth felt her heart would break. She recalled how, through malicious lies, Andrew had been dispossessed of the birthright that Edwin should have given him. Here was a second chance for him. It seemed like fate was making recompense, but at her expense.

'Am I never to see him again?'

Richard lowered his head for a moment and then looked up at her. 'Andrew must be my son alone. It's best you make a clean break for your own sake. You can start again.'

'You'll never be able to trust her,' Esther put in spitefully. 'Richard, I wanted you to have the child to ease your grief but making him your sole heir? I never thought you'd go this far.'

'Esther, please be quiet,' Richard said. 'This is between Ruth and me. It's not your concern.'

His tone and expression were hard, and Ruth realized she had never witnessed him act like that before. But then she barely knew him or what he was really capable of.

Esther gave a murmur of hurt.

Richard took no notice. His gaze was steady on Ruth's face. 'Well, Ruth, what have you decided?'

She held his glance bravely, knowing what she had to do. Mr Richard was right. She could not deny Andrew this opportunity, and she had no right to do so, just to save her own happiness. It would haunt her for the rest of her life if she spoilt this chance for him.

She swallowed hard before answering. 'You win, Mr Richard,' she said, her voice trembling with anguish. 'What choice do I have against that? I leave Andrew in your care.' She glanced at Esther. 'But I want you to promise me that this woman . . .' She pointed a finger at Esther. 'This woman will never have any say in his future. She's my enemy and Andrew's enemy too.'

'I promise faithfully, Ruth.'

'Richard!' Esther gave a cry of protest, but Ruth was satisfied that he meant what he said by the expression on his face.

She stood up. 'I'll leave now,' she said in a low voice. There was nothing more to be said or done, and she longed to get away to grieve alone.

Richard stood up too. 'Thank you, Ruth,' he said. 'I know you'll never regret your decision.'

She looked up at him, her heart breaking all over again.

'I'm regretting it already, Mr Richard,' she said dully. 'But I promise I'll never try to see Andrew again.'

'I want you to sign this document to that effect, please, Ruth,' he said. 'It ensures that you relinquish your claim to Andrew.'

She stared at him aghast. 'Isn't my word good enough?'

'I must insist, Ruth.'

'Very well.'

Ruth walked to the desk on weakened legs, and picking up the pen, dipped it into the ink-well and scratched her name at the bottom of the sheet of parchment Richard pushed forward.

As she watched him carefully blot her signature, Ruth felt empty and dead inside. She could hardly believe what she had just done, signed her child away. Had she done the wrong thing again? If she had, her punishment would last the rest of her life.

Without another word Ruth walked towards the door.

'Wait, Ruth,' Richard called out behind her. 'I have something here which belongs to you.'

She turned slowly to face him, wondering what he could mean. In his hand he held a familiar blue velvet box. Ruth stared at it in disbelief.

'The pearls!' she exclaimed in astonishment. 'You sold them for me. Why are they in your possession now?'

'I didn't sell them,' he said simply. 'I pretended to. You needed the money, but I felt it was too bad that you had to part with them for good; a gift from your husband.'

Richard came around the desk and walked towards her as Ruth stared dumbfounded. He put the box into her hands.

'They're yours again,' he said.

Ruth looked up into his face, her anger growing. 'That money you gave me, so much money, it was yours?'

'I never meant you to know.'

'How dare you!' Ruth burst out vehemently. 'How dare you decide that I needed your charity? I'm insulted.'

'It wasn't charity!' Richard exclaimed hastily. 'It was friendship.'

'It was pity and I despise that,' Ruth said bitterly, glaring at him. She could not believe he could be that insensitive. 'I never needed your charity or your pity, Mr Richard, and I don't need them now.'

'Ruth, you misunderstand . . .'

'Take back your property, duly paid for,' she cried, throwing down the blue velvet box at his feet. It burst open on impact and the string of pearls fell out on to the carpet.

'Ruth, please!'

'Keep them,' she said angrily. 'They're yours not mine. I never want to see them again.' She gazed up at him. 'I'll never forgive you, Mr Richard, for all that you've done today.'

Twenty-Four

Gowerton, Mid December, 1920

R uth stood at the sink, staring out of the kitchen window at the bleak winter-dead cottage garden, her hands in a bowl of quickly cooling washing-up water.

It was four long months since she had seen Andrew; it seemed like four years. Christmas would be here very soon. With a shudder she recalled the previous Christmas. She had looked forward to it so much, the first one with her child, only for it to turn into a nightmare. The festive season was here again, and her heart was breaking to be parted from her son.

How callous of Richard Hamilton to ignore the letter she had sent him in August, begging him to relent and let her see Andrew. What was he afraid of? That she'd change her mind? But she had signed that agreement relinquishing all claim. It haunted her that she might have been wrong to do so. But it was too late for regrets now.

'Ruth, haven't you finished washing up the breakfast crockery yet?' Olive's voice was sharp, and she came into the kitchen. 'We'll be late with your father's midday meal. Get a move on.'

Ruth started at the suddenness of being shaken out of her sad reverie. 'Yes, Mam.' She could not argue or fight back any more. The spirit had gone out of her.

'Have you been crying again?'

'No.'

'No, it's no good crying over spilt milk, is it? You made the decision to give your child up a second time,' she said. 'Now you must live with it.'

243

Ruth turned from the sink. 'You think I was wrong, Mam, don't you?' she asked. 'But I was thinking of Andrew. I could never give him the kind of privileged life that Richard Hamilton can.'

Olive sniffed. 'I don't blame you, my girl.' She peered at Ruth closely. 'As long as the reason for giving him up wasn't that he was Edwin's son.'

Ruth was appalled at the suggestion. 'Oh, Mam! How could you think such a thing?'

'Well, you must have grown to hate Edwin after all that he did.'

'I didn't hate him.' She had despised him for his narrowness of mind; for his lack of trust and unforgivable treatment of her. 'And I love his son more than my own life!'

'Then you did the right thing.' Olive nodded. 'Your father is not saying much, but I'm certain he feels the same. You sacrificed your happiness.' She paused. 'And ours,' she went on quietly. 'I miss my grandson so much.'

'I'm sorry, Mam.'

'You're young,' Olive said rallying. 'You'll marry again. There'll be other children, I expect.'

Ruth said nothing. Loving had done her no good; it had only brought her unhappiness.

She'd been glad to run home to the sanctuary of her parents' cottage in Gowerton, heart-sore after her difficult decision over Andrew, but after four months she was becoming restless.

Jacob had flatly refused to let her find work in the village, insisting that she remain at home, as a respectable widow should. She was beginning to feel suffocated.

Ruth quickly finished washing the dishes, dried them and then turned to her mother. 'Mam, I'm thinking of going back to Swansea in the New Year,' she said. 'I want to work.'

'Your father won't hear of it.'

'I'm over the age of consent,' Ruth reminded her quickly. 'He can't stop me doing anything I want.'

Olive's lips thinned. 'You're being ungrateful,' she said. 'Your father took you in without murmur when you came running home, didn't he?'

'He's my father,' Ruth said. 'And a Christian.'

'But why do you want to work?' Olive asked. 'You have all that money . . .'

'I won't touch a penny of it!' Ruth said quickly. She would not acknowledge Richard's charity. She had not forgiven him for that. She could hardly believe how heartless he had turned out to be. 'But my decision is not only about making my living it's also about immersing myself in something.'

Not to forget. She could never do that, but to find some kind of peace if she could.

'It's hard on us,' Olive said. 'Losing you again.'

'I'm sorry, Mam, but you've got Father and the chapel.'

Olive gave a sigh. 'Jacob will be against it, mark my words.'

Ruth came back from the village one day the following week having visited Louisa and her family to find a familiar motorcar outside her parents' cottage. She stopped and stared, dread engulfing her. This was Richard Hamilton's motor. Why had he come? Andrew!

Ruth rushed through the back door into the kitchen to find Evans, the chauffeur, sitting at the table drinking tea.

Olive was there, too, her eyes round. 'There's a gentleman to see you, Ruth. I've shown him into the parlour.'

'What's wrong?' She looked at Evans in trepidation. 'Has something happened?'

Evans was about to speak when Jacob came in at the door behind her, ready for his midday meal. He stared at the sight of the uniformed man seated in his place at his table. His face went red and his whiskers seemed to bristle.

'What's the meaning of this?' he demanded. 'Who is this stranger who sits at my table?'

'Father,' Ruth said, trying to sound calm. 'Richard Hamilton has called on us. This is Evans, his driver. I'm fearful that something has happened to Andrew.'

'Mr Hamilton is in the parlour, Jacob,' Olive volunteered.

Jacob's expression was stony. 'I'll speak to him.' Ruth made to follow him into the passage. 'Alone,' he added.

'No, Father,' Ruth said shaking her head in determination.

'This concerns Andrew, my son. Mr Hamilton has come to see me.'

'Very well,' Jacob conceded with difficulty. 'But I insist on being present.'

Ruth opened the door of the parlour and went in. Richard was standing by the aspidistra before the window, examining its dark leaves. He turned quickly at her entrance.

'Mr Richard,' Ruth began anxiously taking a few steps towards him. 'Is Andrew unwell? Please tell me what's wrong.'

'Andrew is fine, Ruth,' Richard Hamilton said calmly, but his gaze wavered. 'Although it is about him that I'm here.'

'You'd better state your business immediately,' Jacob said belligerently. 'You're causing my daughter some distress.'

'I don't mean to do that,' Richard said quickly. 'But I do need to discuss a matter with her. In private,' he added.

'I think not,' Jacob said firmly. 'Most unseemly. I'll remain and my wife also.'

'Please sit down, Mr Hamilton,' Olive said, the voice of politeness.

'Thank you.'

Richard sat on the horse-hair sofa where Edwin had once sat and Ruth could not help comparing them. They were men so different. She doubted she could ever have loved Edwin but had been drawn to Richard Hamilton from first meeting him. Yet both men had brought suffering and so much pain to her through her child.

Jacob took his usual place in his bentwood chair while Olive perched on a wooden chair nearby. There being no where else to sit except on the sofa next to Richard, Ruth continued to stand. She could not take her eyes off his face. He seemed uneasy and unsure of himself, which made her uneasy too.

'Why have you come, Mr Richard?'

He ran his tongue over his lips as though they were dry.

'I must tell you that my lawyer is looking into the possibility of my legally adopting Andrew,' he began. 'To that end he strongly advises me that I must gain consent from the child's mother first for there to be no loophole later.'

Ruth compressed her lips. 'The document I signed previously isn't enough I take it?'

Richard's jaw clenched. 'I neglected to consult him beforehand and now my lawyer tells me that the document might not be as binding as I thought. In fact, a court could easily overturn it.'

Ruth felt jubilant. 'So, you need me after all,' she said unable to keep triumph from her voice. 'You *need* my consent.'

Richard swallowed hard. 'Yes,' he said. 'Your agreement would make the adoption legal and binding. I've come today to ask you to do this.'

'You could've done that by letter,' she said angrily. 'Did you come here out of curiosity about my family? It's a bit late, isn't it?'

'No, that's not it, Ruth,' Richard said quickly. 'I thought it proper to face you squarely and openly. It would've been cowardly to do it by letter.'

'I see,' she said carefully. 'So Andrew is still mine then.' Her heart leapt at the thought.

'Don't misunderstand, Ruth,' said Richard. His jaw tightened and she saw he was angered at her words. 'Nothing else has changed. Adoption is the only option if the boy is to remain my heir,' he said tensely. 'I can still cut him from my will if you move against me.'

'Have a care, Ruth,' Jacob interposed quickly.

She was not prepared to ruin Andrew's chances of a good life, but at the same time she saw that Richard was vulnerable also. He needed her help, and because of that she might bargain for her own happiness.

'Andrew needs his mother's love,' she said stubbornly. 'He needs me in his early years, and if you had any real regard for him you'd see it too, Mr Richard.'

He raised his eyebrows. 'You mean you wish to return as his nursemaid?'

'Oh no.' Ruth shook her head vehemently. 'I'll not go back as your employee to be dismissed and banished on your whim,' she said angrily. 'My agreement is vital to make the adoption legal and is worth more than that, much more. I wish to be part of Andrew's life as his mother.'

Richard stood up abruptly. 'Are you suggesting marriage between us?' he asked, angrily.

'Heaven forbid!' she said pithily. 'No, I've endured one arranged marriage. The last thing I want is a marriage of convenience.'

'Then what do you propose instead?' He sounded wary and doubtful.

'I insist on returning to live in your house purely as Andrew's mother,' Ruth said in an adamant tone. 'Nothing more, nothing less.'

He stared at her. 'You'd willingly do that, flout convention, affront propriety?' He sounded astonished.

Ruth lifted her chin. 'I'd sacrifice anything for my son,' she said unwaveringly. 'Even my reputation.' She glanced at her father. 'I've already endured that humiliation even though I was innocent. A damaged reputation holds no more terrors for me.'

'What about my reputation?' Richard asked frowning.

Ruth's lip curled. 'I'm sure your wealth and privilege will protect you from the worst. I'm prepared to face gossip and scandal for love of Andrew. Are you, Mr Richard?'

'Just a minute, Ruth!' Jacob boomed out, rising to his feet. 'Do you mean to live in this man's house while both of you are widowed? You can't do it. I forbid it.'

Ruth turned a withering glance on him. 'You've no sovereignty over me any longer, Father. I'm of age,' she said. 'If you hadn't forced me to marry Edwin I wouldn't be here now making this decision.'

Jacob sat down. 'I forbid you to do this,' he said, but there was no power in his voice and Ruth realized that for once her father was at a loss.

'I'm sure Ruth knows what she's about, Jacob. We can trust her not to act foolishly,' Olive said surprisingly, and both Ruth and Jacob stared at her.

'Olive, please remain quiet,' Jacob commanded.

'I will not!' Olive looked appealingly at Richard. 'Mr Hamilton, my daughter has suffered greatly from being separated from the child she loves more than life,' Olive went on.

'She sacrificed her happiness, and now she's willing to sacrifice her good name. And she's right. Money is all very well, but the boy needs his mother's love and guidance to be really happy.'

Richard looked at Olive keenly but was silent.

Ruth lifted her chin determinedly. 'If you want the adoption to go through at all, Mr Richard, then you must agree to my terms. I'll live at Gower Road with my son in an independent capacity.'

'I see.'

'And,' Ruth went on resolutely. 'You must undertake never again to separate me from him and that he'll not lose the birthright which you have promised him.'

'If I agree to these terms do you swear you'll not oppose me in any way during his upbringing?'

Ruth hesitated for a brief moment. 'Yes, I do,' she said sincerely. 'Once you've adopted Andrew I won't interfere or argue against your plans for his education, but his upbringing before his school years will be in my hands alone.'

He was silent for a long moment in contemplation.

'Very well,' he said finally. 'It's agreed, and I'll get my lawyer to go into the legal matters of our arrangement in the New Year.' He paused and smiled faintly. 'For myself I'm not overly concerned with propriety.'

'That I know well,' Ruth said scathingly. 'And that brings me to Esther Beale. I'll not tolerate her interference.'

'Beale!' Jacob exclaimed pouncing on the familiar and despised name. 'What have the Beales to do with this?'

'Esther Beale, David Beale's wife, befriended me when I lost Annette, my wife,' Richard explained for the benefit of Jacob and Olive. 'I was very low and was glad of her support at the time.'

He glanced at Ruth.

'And that's all it was, friendship,' he went on. 'I swear it, Ruth. Esther left Gower Road the day after you did. I asked her to go. I've not seen her since.'

Ruth felt intense relief at the news. At last nothing stood in the way of her being reunited with her child, and she thanked heaven for it.

'When do you suggest this arrangement begins?' she asked.

Even though her heart was hammering away like a steam engine, she tried to sound calm. The prospect of Andrew being hers again made her feel heady with happiness.

'I suppose it would be appropriate for you to share Christmas with Andrew,' Richard said matter-of-factly.

'Oh!' Ruth put her hand to her throat, overcome.

'So soon!' Jacob said. 'It's less than two weeks away.'

Richard turned to him. 'After the adoption I'll be Andrew's legal father and so part of your family in a sense, Mr Williams. Therefore, I cordially invite you and your wife to my home for the festive season. You must stay through until the New Year.'

'And I must decline.' Jacob rose to his feet, his face reddening. 'I do not approve of overindulgence and frivolity during the holy season,' he said staunchly.

'I assure you, Mr Williams, the Hamiltons have always celebrated Christmas in a moderate way.' Richard's tone was laced with irony, but Ruth could not blame him for it in this instance. 'There'll be no carousing or intemperance.'

'I'll gladly accept your gracious invitation, Mr Hamilton,' Olive said firmly.

'Olive!' Jacob sounded astounded.

'I've been separated from my daughter and my grandson for too long,' Olive said firmly in the face of her husband's glaring gaze. 'I will go. You will, too, Jacob, if you have any love for your family.'

'This invitation is very good of you, Mr Richard,' Ruth said, feeling very touched at his generosity, when moments before she had practically forced his hand to accept her terms.

'Call me Richard,' he said with a smile. 'After all you're no longer in my employ, Ruth. Our mutual love and concern for Andrew makes us equals in everything.'

It was the most happy Christmas Ruth had ever known. She and Andrew were inseparable. She was filled with joy at the sight of his happy contented little face, knowing she would never tire of his excited baby chatter. And she looked forward to the years of his childhood with happiness.

She was careful not to exclude Richard from all this joy, mindful that he would probably be within the coming year Andrew's legal father. She was more than happy to share her son's love with him.

It was also the most astonishing Christmas in that Jacob and Olive shared it to a restrained degree. Her father was appreciative of Richard's good table, but in deference to his faith, did not overindulge, and Richard's motor was at his disposal to attend chapel whenever he wanted. Olive let herself enjoy Christmas for once, and made a great fuss of Andrew, much to the child's delight.

The New Year passed and her parents were returning to Gowerton that morning; Evans was driving them home. Jacob had said goodbye to her and Andrew and was outside with Richard putting their few bags in the motor.

With Andrew in her arms Ruth stood watching them from the hall, very much puzzled. She had expected her father to raise more objections to her remaining, but surprisingly he had said nothing.

'Well, goodbye, Ruth, my girl,' Olive said, giving Andrew a kiss. 'I know you'll bring Andrew to visit us in Gowerton before long.'

'Of course I will, Mam,' Ruth readily agreed, and then touched Olive's arm. 'Mam, is Father finally reconciled to my staying on here?'

'In a way,' Olive said. 'He and Richard have had a long talk about it. Your father is satisfied Richard has honourable intentions towards you.'

'What? Oh, really!' Ruth was furious. 'When will Father learn he no longer has any right to interfere in my life?'

'I'd better go,' Olive said quickly, and hurried out to the motor.

When the motor had driven off, Richard came inside.

'I believe the holiday went well, don't you?' he began as he closed the door. 'Your father melted a little, I think. Once or twice he was in real danger of enjoying himself.'

'My parents and their strong and sincere beliefs are not to be laughed at,' she said stiffly.

'Your parents are the salt of the earth,' he said smiling.

'My son Andrew comes from good stock, and I'm pleased at it.' He took Andrew from her and held him in his arms. 'I've not known such happiness for quite some time,' he went on quietly and kissed the child's cheek.

Ruth was still annoyed by Olive's remark. 'What were you and my father discussing in private?' she asked archly.

He stared at her in surprise. 'My intentions towards you,' he said flatly. 'I solemnly swore to him that I would be a gentleman at all times and not take advantage of you.'

'What?' Ruth felt silly.

Richard laughed. 'It seemed to satisfy him.'

'You'd better take our arrangement more seriously, Richard,' she said, annoyed to be made to feel foolish, and turned away.

'Ruth, wait a moment,' Richard said delaying her. 'Let's make a bargain between us. We'll always be friends, agreed?'

She paused, her annoyance melting away. Then she nodded and smiled at him. She was her own woman now, independent and free and more importantly, her son had been returned to her.

NEATH PORT TALBOT LIBRARY AND INFORMATION SERVICES							
1	11/11	25		49		73	
2		26		50		74	
3		27		51		75	
4		28		52		76	
5	10/13	29		53		77	
6		30		54		78	
7		31		55		79	
8		32		56		80	
9		33		57		81	
10		34		58		82	
11		35		59		83	
12		36		60		84	
13		37		61		85	
14		38		62		86	
15		39		63		87	
16		40		64		88	
17		41		65		89	
18		42		66		90	
19		43		67		91	
20		44		68		92	
21		45		69		COMMUNITY SERVICES	
22		46		70			
23		47		71		NPT/111	
24		48		72			